"I told you yesterday we weren't going there."

"Why not?" Jack demanded.

"It's messy and complicated, not to mention unprofessional," Kensington insisted. "We're working on a job. I'm not going to be seduced by some simple words and those come-hither eyes of yours."

Her comment left her open and he prided himself on being a man who didn't miss an opportunity. "What will you be seduced by?"

"That's not what I meant."

"But I did."

"Why do you keep pushing this?"

Why did he keep pressing the issue? And when, exactly, had that little devil planted itself on his shoulder, intent on ruffling her very smooth feathers?

Whatever the reason, it really didn't matter any longer. He was captivated by her. And he'd be damned if he wasn't going to do his level best to show her.

"Because I'm interested, Kensington." He leaned into her, the small space making it a short trip. "Very interested."

Dear Reader,

Welcome once again to the House of Steele miniseries. The Steele siblings—Liam, Campbell, Kensington and Rowan—are the founders and operators of a high-end security firm, the House of Steele.

The Rome Affair features the oldest Steele sister, Kensington, electronic forensics specialist and self-proclaimed manager of their family operation. Kensington's used to dealing with demanding, elite clients, but she never expects she'll need to partner with another firm to get a job done.

Jack Andrews has had his eye on Kensington and her family firm for quite some time. He's intrigued by the dark-haired beauty and relishes competing with her on jobs. He has deep respect for her skills, and when he lands an assignment investigating a foreign ambassador for the Italian government, he knows he can't do it alone.

I had so much fun writing *The Rome Affair*. Italy was the first foreign country I ever visited and it remains a favorite to this day. The old world charm, the incredible food and the endlessly gorgeous vistas made it a joy to revisit with an eye to some of its most romantic places.

I hope you have as much fun reading Kensington and Jack's adventures—and their deep fall into love—as much as I enjoyed writing it!

Best,

Addison Fox

THE ROME AFFAIR

—

Addison Fox

◆HARLEQUIN®ROMANTIC SUSPENSE

Recycling programs
for this product may
not exist in your area.

ISBN-13: 978-0-373-27863-3

THE ROME AFFAIR

Copyright © 2014 by Frances Karkosak

Printed in U.S.A.

HARLEQUIN®
™ www.Harlequin.com

Books by Addison Fox

Harlequin Romantic Suspense

The Paris Assignment #1762
The London Deception #1774
The Rome Affair #1793

*House of Steele

ADDISON FOX

is a Philadelphia girl transplanted to Dallas, Texas. Although her similarities to Grace Kelly stop at sharing the same place of birth, she's often dreamed of marrying a prince and living along the Mediterranean.

In the meantime, she's more than happy penning romance novels about two strong-willed and exciting people who deserve their happy ever after—after she makes them work so hard for it, of course. When she's not writing, she can be found spending time with family and friends, reading or enjoying a glass of wine.

Find out more about Addison or contact her at her website—www.addisonfox.com—or catch up with her on Facebook (addisonfoxauthor) and Twitter (@addisonfox).

To my big, wonderful, loving, crazy family. You've gifted me with the joy of holidays together and big Sunday dinners, wedding dances and summer picnics. You are my lifeblood and support system, my friends *and* my relatives. You are my heart.

And to my sister, Beth, because really, could I write a book with Rome in the title and not dedicate it to you?

Chapter 1

New York City—Today

Kensington Steele picked up the two dozen long-stemmed red roses—freshly cut and still quivering from their time in the florist's freezer—and dropped them into the trash. Although it pained her to throw away such a thing of beauty, she couldn't hold back the anger at the card that had accompanied the red blooms.

> To a most worthy opponent—
> Looking forward to next time.
> Jack

"Bastard." She muttered the word under her breath as her gaze danced from the card to the glorious beauties that winked from the top of her office garbage can. On a weary sigh, she reached in and retrieved the roses. With the exception of one slightly bent stem and a few missing petals on the flowers that edged the bouquet, her aim had been quite good.

Further proof he'd purchased excellent flowers from one of the city's top suppliers.

Kensington laid the roses back in the large white flower box and resolved to have her assistant handle the arranging. At least she could get them out of her sight.

A loud honk outside pulled her attention from the flowers, and she crossed her office to the windows that fronted the family brownstone that now served as the headquarters for the House of Steele. Their Upper East Side street was normally quiet and the racket currently taking place on the street below—two cabdrivers who'd clearly disagreed on who had the right of way on the tight street—was rare.

About as rare as losing a major contract.

The word *bastard* rose once more to her lips but she tamped it down. She wasn't a sore loser and didn't hold those who were in high regard. But damn it, her bid package had been flawless. So had the one two months ago when she'd gone up against Jack Andrews for the museum job in Memphis. And three months ago on the gallery opening in San Francisco. And five months ago for the Ming Dynasty artifact recovery in Hong Kong.

The man kept beating her out on key proposals and she had no idea how he was doing it. It clearly wasn't location based because each job was vastly different from the other. She'd had yet to find any other obvious connection, either.

So how was it every time the House of Steele went up against Andrews Holdings they lost?

The knock on her door pulled her attention from the drama on the street below. Her assistant, Molly, stood at the door, a thin tablet in hand. "You ready for our morning status?"

"Can I ask a favor first?"

"Does it involve delivering anything to your brother at home again? I'm still convinced I interrupted a rather delicate moment between him and his fiancée."

Kensington smiled at that. Molly had, in fact, interrupted Campbell and Abby in a moment *in flagrante delicto*. Of course, that's what he got for attempting a morning quickie when there was work to be done. "Not at all. Would you mind getting those roses out of my sight?"

Molly let out a long, low whistle. "These are gorgeous. When did they arrive? I've been here since eight-thirty and we haven't had any deliveries."

"Bright and early this morning. Nothing like being served up a portion of crow over your first cup of coffee."

Her assistant set her electronics down and picked up a few of the stems. "These look like flirtation and romance far more than arrogant gloating. Who's the new man?"

A light zing of awareness skimmed her spine, but Kensington banished it. Just like she banished any of the nine million other delicious thoughts she'd had about Jack Andrews over the past six months. "Trust me. They scream gloating arrogance."

"Gloating arrogance in a sexy package."

"Perhaps."

"Why are the petals all wonky on this side?" Molly turned a few of the blooms over, her concern evident in the lines that crinkled her forehead.

"They've already spent a few minutes in the trash."

Another low whistle left Molly's lips before she tossed Kensington a broad smile. "Oh, my, my. I think I read this just right. There is a romance afoot."

"There's no romance."

Molly waved a hand over her head as she walked out the door, the roses spilling from the crook of her arm.

"Save your breath, oh, straitlaced one. Thou doth protest too much."

Kensington clamped her mouth shut, her assistant's words hitting home with the force of a battering ram.

It was long moments later when she finally took a seat at her desk, the morning's drama fading so that she could concentrate on work.

But damn it if the sweet, fresh scent of roses still lingered in the air.

Jack Andrews tossed some money to the driver and slid across the backseat of his cab. The impressive Upper East Side brownstone stood five stories above him as he walked toward the front stoop of the headquarters of the House of Steele.

A small shiver of anticipation gripped him, the sensation something of a surprise after far too many years of minimal interest in anything.

It was a calculated risk to come here. Just like the roses.

Would she see it as a taunt? Or would she give him the time and hear him out?

The crisp notes of early December whipped around him and Jack huddled deeper into his wool coat as he took the front stoop two steps at a time and hit the doorbell. He'd lived in Chicago for the better part of fifteen years and he still hadn't adjusted to cold weather.

A small buzz and the sound of the front door clicking gave him entrance. As he stepped into the warmth, he wasn't surprised to see a large man hulking in the hallway, ready to greet him. Although the brownstone housed a business, no one walked in off the street. "Can I help you?"

"I'm here to see Kensington Steele."

"Ms. Steele has no appointments on her agenda. I'm afraid you're going to need to leave."

Jack took a moment to strip off his gloves. His gaze took in the large marble-floored entryway, the dark-paneled study he could see off the hall and the small camera that sat in the far corner of the elegant foyer, capturing visitors. The brownstone might have been built more than a hundred years earlier, but he had no doubt it was outfitted from top to bottom with the latest security and technological capabilities. "Please let her know Jack Andrews of Andrews Holdings is here."

"Ms. Steele isn't taking visitors."

"She'll see me."

The man stepped closer, his predatory gleam hard to miss. Jack knew his six-one wasn't small by any means, but the muscles stalking him across the hall had to have him beat by at least three inches and a hundred pounds.

The sound of heels clicking on marble pulled both their attention toward the long hallway that led to the back of the house and that shiver gripped him once more.

Tighter, this time, like a fist wrapped around the base of his spine.

"Mr. Andrews. I wasn't aware you felt it necessary to make house calls all the way from Chicago to gloat. I would have thought two dozen long-stemmed roses were more than adequate to make your point."

Kensington waved off the large man in the foyer. "Thanks, Brandon. Although I wouldn't say Mr. Andrews is a welcome visitor, I'm hardly going to kick him out."

The hulking man shot him one last dark look before taking a wary stance against the wall. "If you change your mind Ms. Steele, you know where to find me."

"Thank you."

When Jack simply stood there, taking in the long, artful waves of her dark hair and the mile-long legs that stretched from beneath her power suit, Kensington swept out a hand. "You coming, Mr. Andrews?"

And damn if he could hold back the grin that tugged the corners of his mouth at her prim tone. "Of course."

Curious, he pressed her. "You really keep security out in the hallway all day?"

"Brandon has better things to do than spend all day hanging out in my hallway. He's obviously decided to make an exception for you."

Jack filed away the interesting fact that the House of Steele felt it needed some degree of hired muscle in-house as he followed her down the long hallway. She led him into a large dining room opposite a swinging door to what had to be the kitchen. "Your home is impressive."

"It's my business now."

"Can't it be both?"

A small nod had that lush hair drifting around her shoulders. "I suppose so. It's also why we still keep a few bedrooms ready on the top floor. One of us often crashes here."

He stripped off his coat and didn't miss the scrutiny of her gaze before she moved quickly toward the sideboard and busied herself with a waiting coffee service.

Hmm…interesting.

They'd only been in each other's company a few times, but each time had captivated him more than the last. He'd thought her unaffected, but perhaps he'd been hasty—too stunned by his own attraction—to recognize a fair bit of it in return.

"Please help yourself to coffee to warm up. The wind's brutal out there."

He used the few extra minutes to take in the room. The brownstone was a classic and even as it screamed subtle opulence, it whispered something else far more powerful.

Home.

He stalled over his cream and sugar, curious to get more personal details out of her before she firmly shifted things to business. "This is your family home, yes?"

"My mother's family, actually. She grew up here and her mother and grandmother before her."

He knew of Kensington Steele's lineage—it was hardly a secret among New York's elite. Her parents, Charles and Katherine, had delighted society when a woman with some of New York's bluest blood married into one of Britain's most elite families.

Katherine Kensington Steele's lineage had given her first-born daughter her name.

And it was an accident on Charles and Katherine's twentieth anniversary trip that had left the home he now sat in—and a world of hurt and grief—to their four children.

"The Kensington family home."

"Yes."

"It's beautiful. Now it's functional, too."

"I'd like to think so." Kensington took a seat at the head of the table, the subtle power play intriguing him like nothing else could have. "What can I do for you, Mr. Andrews?"

That cultured tone did something to his insides, he admitted to himself. The tones weren't quite British, yet they were sharp with the same elocution the Brits had made their own. Her voice made him think of how he wanted to poke underneath the surface.

"First, let's get this out of the way. I have no reason to gloat and that's not why I'm here. You're a worthy opponent and I respect your business."

Her raised eyebrows let him know exactly what she thought of his statement, but she kept her voice level. "I thought the note that arrived with your flowers suggested otherwise."

"I don't know. I've always found a little spirited poking is healthy for business." He leaned forward, pleased when her crystal-blue gaze stayed level on his. "Nothing like a sense of competition to keep a person engaged."

"I have no interest in being poked."

"Oh, really?" He couldn't hold back the smile.

"Really." The light flush that was visible at the V of her blouse suggested she wasn't unaffected and he couldn't resist one more attempt at ruffling her. "Because partnership does have its benefits, Kensington."

"I've got enough partners, *Jack*." The fingers of her right hand trembled ever so slightly before she wrapped them around her coffee cup. "What I want is the opportunity to work with new business prospects."

"What if I can offer you that?"

"Excuse me?"

He'd spent the past few days thinking about the solution he was about to offer her and could only curse himself he hadn't come up with it sooner. "Business partners. It makes sense."

"I don't need a business partner. My brothers and sister and I run the House of Steele as a family. We're not selling."

"I'm not suggesting anything of the sort, especially since I've no interest in selling or merging Andrews Holdings."

The sharp set of her lips faded and the same shrewd sense—the one that had allowed Kensington to lead their family enterprise into a wildly successful business in a handful of years—took over. "What did you have in mind?"

"You and I went up against each other on the Rome job."

"As well as Memphis, San Francisco and Hong Kong." He ignored the litany of their recent skirmishes, instead focusing on the reason he'd come. "I'm talking about Rome. I met with the Italian embassy on Monday and was smugly told I nearly didn't get the assignment."

"Why not?"

"I maintain a small firm, by choice. Seems the Italians were looking for something a bit more expansive. There was a fair amount of infighting among the selection committee before I gained the nod."

"I still don't see how this involves me."

How did he explain it to her? He prided himself on reading his adversaries—and he typically put clients in that category until proven otherwise—but the meeting with the embassy's staff had caught him unawares. "They've changed the scope of the assignment."

"How so? It's a pretty straightforward protection detail with a bit of snooping on the side. Eyes and ears on the ambassador and his surroundings on his upcoming diplomatic mission."

"The Italians have begun to suspect Hubert Pryce of some unsavory practices."

Confusion stamped itself immediately on her face, but underneath he saw the flicker of interest. It was subtle, he'd give her that, but it was there all the same. She leaned forward a bit more eagerly and a small spark lit that vivid gaze. "I'm not following. A host country has to accept an ambassador from another country and can, at any point, dissolve the relationship, declaring the diplomat persona non grata. It's a basic tenant of the Vienna Convention."

"The Italians think it would be worth their while to follow Ambassador Pryce for a bit longer."

"Why? He comes from a small country in central Africa. If they're concerned, and I can't imagine why they are, they need to remove him from his post. They're within their rights to do so and no explanations are needed."

Jack briefly toyed with filtering the limited information he had but realized it was, at best, unfair and, at worst, dangerous to keep her in the dark. "Tierra Kimber may be small, but the country has seen incredible growth in the past decade as a major center for both diamonds and fashion."

Kensington took a sip of her coffee, her expression thoughtful as that interest honed to a sharp point. "They're not even a top-ten player in Italy's economy. I realize Pryce's family background is European and he's spent considerable time cultivating a reputation across the region, but the Italian government is under no obligation to allow him to remain in Italy if they have any concerns whatsoever."

"Hubert Pryce is the tip of the iceberg if what the Italians suspect him of is true."

"And what's that?"

"If they're correct, he's smuggling diamonds through the Italian wine trade."

Kensington exhaled a harsh breath, shocked at Jack's suggestion. "The man is incredibly well respected. What proof do the Italians have to even suggest something like this?"

Jack pulled a small tablet from his pocket and turned it on, flipping to a document before handing the device to her. Their fingers brushed momentarily and her gaze landed squarely on his at the contact. She swallowed hard as that intense, dark brown gaze captured hers.

Because she'd already overplayed her hand with the scrutiny, she decided to go for broke and look her fill. The hue of his eyes was a color match for his almost-black, close-cut hair. She saw some threads of gray at the temples and wondered at that. Her research indicated he was no more than thirty-six, but the lines at the corners of his eyes added to the gray, suggesting a man who worked and played hard.

"How much research did you do on Ambassador Pryce prior to the assignment?" Jack asked.

"I put together an extensive dossier. Although born in the small nation of Tierra Kimber, he's from a well-respected European family and was educated in the United States. He spent his formative years at Choate, then on to Yale. He spent another decade in the U.S., working in the New York office of his family's financial firm before returning to live in Tierra Kimber. His reputation is sterling."

"Well, the Italians don't think so. They've become increasingly convinced his interests aren't quite on the up-and-up and that he's been abusing his ambassadorship to move diamonds." Jack pointed to the tablet. "Take a look at that document."

She flipped through the various pages, immediately lost in a series of email exchanges that had obviously been intercepted and cobbled together. Although nothing about any individual email seemed off, taken as a whole it was more than obvious something was afoot. "An ambassador's communications are protected. How'd they get these?"

"They didn't share that information with me."

A strange, unwelcome panic gripped Kensington, twisting her stomach into knots. "Jack. You shouldn't have this."

"They're my client. What I probably shouldn't be doing is sharing this with you."

"No, I mean *you* shouldn't have this. Pryce has full diplomatic immunity. He's not subject to the same laws as others and possession of this communication is violating another basic tenant of the Convention."

"It's my job. Would have been your job had you won the bid."

"We'd have stepped out of it." Even as the words left her lips, she knew that wasn't entirely true. She and her siblings had built their business taking on the jobs others didn't want or weren't capable of.

And connections like the Italian government—connections who needed outside help and who would sing the House of Steele's praises for a job well-done—were always worth her time.

"You'd have really walked away?"

"I'd certainly have taken it to my family and we would have considered it as a team."

"The buck stops with me at Andrews Holdings, which is why I have team members who act as operatives, not partners. I'm not walking away from the assignment, but I'm not bullheaded enough not to realize when I need help."

"And you think I can provide that?"

"I know you can."

The curiosity that had curled in her belly the moment she realized Jack Andrews was in her home rose another several notches. "What do you want from me?"

"Join me. Two pairs of eyes are better than one."

"I'm not spying on Hubert Pryce."

"Consider it a high-level investigation."

Kensington knew full well she needed to let this go. She'd lost the bid and no matter how badly that galled her, she did not need to be brought in after the fact on a project that already had serious changes from the original brief—and international criminal implications.

And she especially needed to walk away because Jack's offer had her more than a little intrigued.

She hadn't been in the field in quite some time, deferring the majority of their business to her siblings while running things back at home. Over the past few months that lack of activity had begun to chafe.

Her brother Campbell was the hacking wiz, but she had a special skill when it came to digging up information, following threads. Campbell knew how to get into a system, but she knew how to forensically audit that system forward and backward.

Money. Leads. Connections.

Her innate tenacity, stubborn will and a strange tendency toward little sleep had ensured she was more than adept at tugging on threads until she unraveled the right mix of details.

And although she could do plenty of digging from right here, safe and sound at home, she'd begun to fear the lack of action would make her soft. "How do the Italians plan to get around Ambassador Pryce's own security detail? I'm sure his protection is considerable."

"The Italians work in tandem with the Tierra Kimber government to ensure the safety of Pryce, his family and the staff he employs. When he's in Italy, he's under the protection of the Italian government."

"And they're proposing to just sneak you in?"

"Sneak *us* in, although it's really not that sneaky. Pryce already knows several people are assigned to his protection and he's expecting a mix of men and women. Much of his work takes place in more relaxed settings, and it helps to have pairs working together. We'll mix and mingle as guests at his events, and we're expected to function as knowledgeable members of his staff."

"And you don't think he'll make both of us."

"That's why we're not sneaking. We both run well-respected security operations that Pryce has likely heard of. He'll know who we are from the get-go."

"And you think that'll be enough?"

"I know so." That dark gaze evaluated her once more

and Kensington couldn't stop the light line of gooseflesh that tickled her skin.

This man did something to her.

But did she dare spend time in his company? *Intimate* time that would require them to become allies, working toward a common goal?

Could she really stay away?

Jack glanced around the inner sanctum that was Kensington Steele's office. He'd imagined her repeatedly, here in her element, but now that he had a true picture of her work space he could see where his musings fell short.

In his mind's eye she conducted business behind a small, delicate writing desk. Instead, the large cherrywood monstrosity she currently sat behind looked more as if it belonged in a ship captain's office than that of a modern-day righter of wrongs.

Although he hadn't imagined the desk correctly, he had pictured her space as neat, tidy and efficient and she didn't disappoint.

"What's that look for?" She glanced up from where she tapped on a few keys at the computer just before the gentle whir of her printer started up.

"I took you for the neat and orderly type." He pointed toward the desk. "But I didn't expect you'd sit behind a desk the size of a frigate."

"How else do you think I can file everything and keep it neat and orderly? If I sat at a small desk, I'd have piles everywhere."

"Fair point. It doesn't change the fact that this isn't quite how I imagined you."

"You imagined me?" Delicate eyebrows arched over those expressive eyes.

"Several times."

She opened her mouth, then closed it and shook her head.

"What is it?"

"Nothing."

"Come on. We're going to work together. You need to feel you can talk to me."

"*If,* Jack. If we work together. I haven't made a decision on that yet."

He suspected she'd made up her mind and was simply analyzing how she was going to close the deal. "I thought it was *when.*"

Those eyebrows rose another fraction of an inch. "That's exactly my point. I've not decided yet and your ridiculous insistence on flirting isn't helping."

"And here I thought it was a bit of fun."

At the word *fun* the suspicion in her gaze turned decidedly unreceptive. "If you're after a bit of sport then you've got the wrong girl."

"I'm quite sure I've got the right girl."

Her eyes widened as his words registered and Jack sensed he was in imminent danger of overplaying his hand. "Look. Whatever you need to decide isn't going to be found in this office. Let's get out and you can see my style. See how I work. If you're not convinced we'd make a good team, then you can cut and run."

"I never cut and run."

"Prove it."

Chapter 2

Prove it.

Jack's words still rumbled around in her mind like the silver ball in a pinball machine, racing to and fro and ringing a hell of a lot of bells.

In for a penny, Steele.

"Why are we going to Midtown?" She snuggled into her coat, the blast of heat inside the car welcome after the frigid wind had chilled her as they hailed a cab at the top of her block.

"Come on. Don't tell me a well-heeled city gal like yourself has never been to the diamond district?"

"I've been there. I remember going with my father years ago when he bought a present for my mother."

"Then you can show me the ropes." He shot a meaningful look at their cabbie, and she held any remaining questions. Whatever the man had up his sleeve didn't lend itself to discussion in front of others.

The trip across town passed quickly and in moments they were back in the cold, moving at a fast clip through the steady throng of people that always filled the heart of the city's business district.

"What are you hoping to find?" Her breath puffed out in a fluffy white cloud as they began to pass buildings with bright display windows and heavily padded doors.

"I want to ask a few questions."

"Right. Because we're just going to walk in and ask some of the savviest dealers in the world if the diamonds they're selling are being smuggled."

"That wasn't quite what I had in mind."

"So what are we going to do?"

His smile was broad—bordering on conspiratorial—before he gestured to a door up ahead. "I want to see how fast you are on your feet. Consider yourself suddenly affianced."

"Excuse me?"

The heavy puff of breath that expanded on her words faded from view as Jack pulled her up to a cagelike door and hit the buzzer to be let through. His arm wrapped through hers as he pulled her close.

"Aren't you excited, darling?"

In for a penny.... That crazy voice admonished her once more before a strange sense of fun and purpose filled her. She linked her arm more tightly with his and dropped her free hand to his chest. "Quivering with anticipation, Pookie."

She had a moment of brief satisfaction when a sly grin filled his face before the door clicked open. Behind the bars of the door, they were greeted by an older, slender man dressed all in black. Another large man stood behind him at a respectful distance, the approach surprisingly similar to that of the security team she employed at the House of Steele. "May I help you?"

"We'd like to do some diamond shopping." Jack hesitated a moment before he continued. "Larry Coleman suggested I visit your establishment."

The mention of the mysterious "Larry Coleman" seemed to do the trick, and after a few basic pleasantries, the proprietor pulled open the metal door and welcomed them in, gesturing for them to remove their coats. The large man never moved from his position behind the proprietor as another assistant stepped forward from a small alcove to take their coats. "We're glad you're here, Mr. Andrews. Ms. Steele. What are you looking for today?"

"The perfect engagement ring." Jack's proud voice echoed in her ear as he pulled her close once more. A strange little shiver gripped her. It was silly really seeing as they absolutely were *not* shopping for engagement jewelry—but the moment struck her as momentous all the same.

Shaking off the flutters, she moved farther into the narrow store, following the proprietor's gesture before he turned to face them both at a long glass counter. "What did you have in mind?"

Jack squeezed her hand. "You're on, baby."

His expectant smile had her stumbling for the briefest moment before his words from earlier rang in her ears. *I want to see how fast you are on your feet.* "I'd love to look at something emerald cut."

"Excellent choice. Your long, slender fingers will set off an emerald-cut stone to perfection." The man stepped behind the counter and pulled out a tray of loose stones. She didn't miss his subtle yet assessing glance at the two of them as he unlocked the jewelry case. "May I ask what number of carats you were considering?"

"Six." Jack's voice was deliberate when he spoke, and Kensington fought to keep her jaw firmly hinged.

"Darling. Isn't that a bit elaborate?"

He pressed a quick kiss to her temple before whispering in her ear. "Not for you, my love."

An errant shiver ran down her spine and Kensington pushed it away in the face of whatever charade Jack had cooked up for the visit. She knew her life had been one of distinct privilege—she could hardly claim otherwise—but a six-carat diamond was an extravagance she'd never even considered.

Even if it was all made up and only for show.

The proprietor blinked twice, the only sign Jack's request had him ruffled, before tapping on the counter. "I'll be right back."

They stood close, their gazes bent over the counter as they waited for the man to return. She kept her voice low—a skill she'd honed to an art form years before with her siblings whenever they wanted to eavesdrop on their parents from the stairwells—and a smile firmly painted on her face for the security cameras that were no doubt recording them from four different angles. "You couldn't have started with something a bit more modest?"

"No."

"Jack. This is too much."

The sound of the proprietor returning from the back had him leaning in once more, his breath a quick rush in her ear. "I consider it a worthy investment."

"We have some lovely selections for you to look at."

Kensington tried to keep her mind on the game and *off* the lingering shivers coursing up and down her spine at the close contact and the sweet endearments.

It's all for show. It's all a game. It's just a job.

She kept up the internal litany of admonishments, willing the truth of the words to sink in.

But no matter how rational and calm she fought to stay, nothing would change the fact that Jack Andrews stood next to her, their bodies flush, as they looked at engagement rings.

"The stones are loose but I have a few in settings so you can get a feel for some of the designs. We, of course, are happy to put you in touch with designers should you so choose."

The proprietor separated out a few loose stones on a small velvet square, then added some rings in settings. He selected one and held it out to her. "Please. Try it on. I find brides have a better sense of what they're looking for once they've seen the ring on their hand."

Bride.

The word stuck in her mind, derailing every other thought with a heavy thud.

"Here, darling. Let me help you." Jack reached for her hand, giving it a light squeeze before taking the ring from the proprietor.

The ring slid on, the fit perfect, and before she knew it, she had a six-carat diamond engagement ring winking off her left hand. "It's beautiful."

"No. You're beautiful. The ring dims in comparison."

A tight knot gripped her throat before her gaze slid to Jack's. That knot only tightened when she saw something haunting and serious in those dark depths. She glanced down at her hand once more before the moment could completely overwhelm her.

And was blindsided by a memory.

Even though it had been more than fifteen years, Kensington could still see her mother's diamond as it sparkled from her left hand. Although not as large as this one, she and her sister, Rowan, had always been fascinated by the ring and often begged to be allowed to try it on.

"Someday I'll have a ring like this." She held her hand up to the light, the heavy diamond sliding toward her pinky because the ring was so loose. *"And a big wedding at the Plaza, with Daddy walking me down the aisle."*

Her mother's smile was soft and gentle. *"What about the young man?"*

"What young man?"

"The one you're going to marry."

"What about him?"

"You seem to have a pretty good idea of what the wedding will be like. What do you think he'll be like?"

"I don't know." Kensington hadn't been able to hold back a small giggle. *"I haven't gotten that far yet. I always get lost thinking about the wedding."*

"Let me give you a suggestion, then, heart of my heart." Her mother had reached for her hands and Kensington could feel the slight weight of the ring where it pressed into her the side of her fingers. *"Marry for love."*

"But that's what I'm talking about. Getting married."

A warm smile had filled her mother's face and for the briefest moment Kensington held her breath.

Like her mother was going to share something important.

"The wedding is a wonderful beginning, but that's all it is. A beginning. The marriage will be yours for life. It will be what you make of it."

"I certainly hope it's not full of smelly boys like Liam and Campbell."

Her mother had laughed at that before pulling her close in a tight hug. *"I promise you. When the children are your boys, you'll feel entirely differently."*

Her mother then pressed a kiss to her head and Ken-

sington had reveled in the quiet moment, just the two of them. She loved her family—even the smelly boys despite her protests—but with three other siblings it was rare to get one-on-one time with either of her parents.

She'd pulled back with a start. "How will I know I'm in love?"

"That's the great mystery that no one can explain until it happens."

"What mystery?"

"That even if it seems impossible to imagine, one day you'll meet the right person and you'll just know."

Kensington pulled herself from the memory—one she'd not had in years—as Jack smiled down at her. "What do you think?"

"It's too much."

And she knew her words were about far more than the ring.

Jack squeezed Kensington's hand once more and hoped the gentle reassurance would ensure she stayed with him and in character. They had to see this through and the only way to do that was to keep up appearances. "It's not too much."

He turned toward the shop owner, pleased to see the calculation behind the man's calm gaze. The guy knew a buyer when he saw one.

After a small cough the proprietor gestured to the velvet square on the table. "Perhaps we can look at some of the diamonds, and then we can return to the question of which setting is ideal."

Kensington slipped the ring off and laid it on the velvet square. "By all means."

The owner busied himself with the loose diamonds he'd laid out earlier, displaying them in a single row on the black velvet. Jack marveled how something so small could command such a premium. Even at six carats, the relative size of each diamond was tiny.

Yet despite their size, wars were fought over them and funded by them. Rulers had gone to battle to possess them. Thieves made their lives—or lost them—stealing them.

Gemstones were man's folly. Beautiful baubles that often owned the possessor's soul far more than the possessor owned them.

It made Kensington's reaction to the ring that much more interesting. She appreciated the ring; that was evident. But where most women would be preening under the charade, he sensed a distinct discomfort at the extravagance of the piece.

The jeweler extended a loupe and Jack leaned forward to inspect one of the loose stones. He listened intently as the jeweler described various properties before handing the loupe to Kensington. Their fingers brushed, and Jack held his hand against hers a moment longer than necessary.

The woman was intoxicating.

He'd heard of her, of course. Although the House of Steele hadn't been in business all that long, the Steele siblings had created quite a name for themselves and their family enterprise. Add on that the family name was well-known to begin with and it had been easy to find out more about the delectable Kensington Steele after their first encounter about a year ago.

She was cool, yet he wouldn't go so far as to say icy. Rather, she had a calm, stoic demeanor that didn't ruffle easily. That she'd shown even the slightest stammer over the ring was out of character.

And it gave him a tiny bit of hope things truly weren't one-sided between them.

Which, Jack had to admit, was a rather large change.

He'd spent the first thirty-five years of his life diligently avoiding romantic entanglements, so the fact that he was even toying with this strange attraction to the woman was more than a bit unsettling.

"What do you think, Mr. Andrews?"

Jack pulled his errant thoughts off of the soft sweep of hair that fell over Kensington's shoulder and the graceful arch of her neck and turned to face the jeweler once more. "I think it's time for Ms. Steele to decide."

Her head snapped up from where she viewed one of the diamonds. "Jack. Are you sure? We just started this process."

"When you know, you know."

"But—"

He smiled and tapped on the counter. "Please, darling. You've already made me the happiest man on earth. Now select something that makes *you* happy."

He didn't miss the ever-so-slight raise of her eyebrow, or the hard glint in her crystal-blue gaze, but to her credit, she gave nothing else away.

"I like this one." She pointed to a stone on the edge of the velvet. "It's magnificent."

"As are you."

Without waiting for any further encouragement, he leaned in and captured her mouth for a kiss. The slight "oof" of surprise was the only clue that his actions caught her off guard, and he used that small moment of shock to press his advantage.

The hard wall of the glass counter pressed into his hip and Jack turned them both so they were flush against each other. His hands drifted to her waist and he pulled her flat against him, satisfied when her arms lifted to wrap around his neck.

The tilt of her head and the soft acquiescence of her

lips opening under his gave him the second opportunity to press his advantage. His tongue met hers and a wave of heat and need crashed through his system so hard he had to wonder how he was still standing upright.

He might not have expected her oversize ship captain's desk. And he might not have figured the roses would set her teeth on edge.

But he *had* imagined the power of her kiss.

Rich. Lush. Enticing.

Reality was so much better.

A light cough pulled them both from the moment and he lifted his head and smiled at her before shooting a broad wink to the jeweler. "I'm sure we're not the first ones to do that, are we?"

"Not in the least, sir."

The proprietor's ready sense of humor went a long way toward diffusing the raw need that had gripped him with iron talons. "So what's next?"

"It's time to select a setting."

"Darling." Kensington's voice was a low purr. "Perhaps we can set an appointment and do that tomorrow. This has been the highlight of my day, but this trip was an unexpected surprise. You need to get back to work."

He made a show of checking his watch before nodding. "You're right, as always."

"I'll just wait over there while you finish up."

Her tone was low and quiet, but he took great delight at the small quaver that tinged the edges.

"Slam dunk."

The cold wind wrapped around them once more as she and Jack fought the Midtown rush of humanity. She could practically feel the excitement vibrating off of him. "What could possibly make you think it was a smart idea to spend so much money?"

He shrugged, the casual move at odds with the gravity of what he'd just done. "I can always resell it."

"That diamond was crazy expensive."

"So?" A genuinely puzzled expression filled his features. "It's certainly not going to lose its value."

"Yes, but—" She broke off, well aware she was veering dangerously close to harpy territory. What did she care how he spent his money? And he had a fair point—the diamond could always be resold, so his overall risk was minimal.

A small kernel of disappointment unfurled in her stomach like the first shoots of spring, and she resolutely tamped it down. Today was a charade, nothing more.

Reading anything more into it wasn't only stupid, but it also was a recipe for professional disaster.

Whatever Jack Andrews wanted from her, these strange sparks of emotion that kept swamping her certainly weren't it.

"I just want to know why you ended the fun so soon." He wrapped his arm around her once more as they got to a corner crosswalk.

Shaking him off would be petty, she reasoned, so she stayed put as they waited for the light to turn. "By leaving, now you have a chance to go back. We certainly couldn't ask him his opinion about diamond smuggling on our first visit."

Admiration filled his face in the subtle crease of his smile. "Excellent point."

"Bet you didn't think I had it in me."

"Oh, I had no doubt about that part. I just wanted to see the amazing and awesome Kensington Steele in action."

The light changed and the people around them began

to move, but Kensington planted her feet against the on-slaught. "Are you teasing me?"

"Hardly."

"Then what did you really think about our visit to the diamond district?"

"I think that you really are amazing and awesome."

"Would you be serious?"

"I am serious, but—" He reached for her hand and pulled her along through the crosswalk. "I think we also learned several very valuable things this morning."

"Such as?"

He dug a folded-up piece of paper from his pocket. "Take a look at the provenance on this diamond."

The thin sheet flapped in the breeze as Kensington took off her glove before reaching for the paper. She scanned the contents quickly, not sure of what had him so pleased. "It's got all the basic details of the diamond. The four Cs, its ownership."

He leaned in and pointed toward a small detail at the bottom of the page. Her eyes widened as she finally realized what he was getting at. "It was mined in Tierra Kimber."

"Exactly. That's what we use when we go back. You, my socially conscious fiancée, are going to suddenly get some remorse about that diamond I just purchased."

"And when I show my concern that these diamonds might be a front for war and bloodshed?"

"It will be up to our smart and savvy jeweler to quickly assure you why you've no need to worry your pretty little head about it so he can keep his sale."

"Do you think he knows anything about our problem?"

"Not really. He's a jeweler, not a high-level operative. And although I rarely put anything past anyone, the man's been in a family business his entire life. He's a cog in the wheel, nothing more." He pointed toward a deli a few store-fronts ahead of them. "Let's go eat."

"I need to get back."

"It's nearly one o'clock. You need to eat."

The hand that rested low on her back steered her toward the front door of the deli. "You're pushy."

"I'm not pushy in the least. I maneuver people. There's a difference." He opened the door for her, and Kensington couldn't argue with the warmth that reached out and beckoned them in. "Besides, I'm hungry."

"I'm not easily maneuvered, Jack."

"No. You like to do the maneuvering. It's a trait I can not only relate to, but also admire."

"I do no such thing." The words that left her lips branded her as a liar, but she couldn't hold them back. *Maneuver* sounded so manipulative. And cold.

And she was neither.

She just knew how she wanted things done. How to handle a situation to minimize risk and get the best possible outcome.

"Sure you do. It's one of the reasons we're going to have so much fun in Italy."

"I haven't said yes."

"But you will."

She stopped inside the door, and the urgent need to make her point ensured her feet stayed firmly planted. "This isn't a joke and I'm really not sure I'm going to do this deal with you. We're opponents."

He pressed closer to her as a group of suits bustled past them and leaned down to whisper in her ear. "Then let the games begin."

Chapter 3

Kensington speared a forkful of salad and surreptitiously watched Jack across the table. She was still wondering how her morning had turned into a field trip and a meal, all with a man who got her dander up and her antennae quivering on high alert.

The man was a force of nature—that's all there was to it.

She watched as he polished off a corned beef sandwich with a side of chips and marveled that the broad physique under his suit jacket could be sustained with such hearty lunch choices.

"You haven't said much." His gaze danced over her face as he took a sip of his soda.

"Just processing the morning." A funny thought popped into her head and she set down her fork. "Who is Larry Coleman, anyway?"

"An old friend from college. He's on wife number three

and he's used that jeweler for years. Makes a special trip from Chicago to New York and everything. Based on his repeat visits, I figured I'd get the attention of the jeweler pretty quick."

"You can't be old enough to have friends on their third spouse." The words were out and bouncing between them like an errant ping-pong ball no one could catch.

"When you've got a large bank account and a roving eye like Larry does, thirty-five is plenty old to be on number three."

"Are you on any number?"

Smooth, Steele. Why not just ask him if there was any reason to be feeling guilty for the sexual buzz that's still humming in your veins at that kiss.

"Nope. You?"

"No."

"Ever get close?"

The words were casual—too casual—and she fought to pull her hormones out of the equation for a moment and focus on him. "If skirting the edges of relationships that usually fail between dates five and seven is getting close, then yes. However, I think a more accurate answer is no way."

"Shame."

"Excuse me?"

"It's a shame the five-through-seven guys can't see what I see."

"What's that?"

"A vibrant woman with a lot to offer."

She sat back and tossed her napkin on the counter. "I wasn't fishing for a compliment."

"And I wasn't casting my reel."

"So what's your point?"

"You're a beautiful woman with a wicked intellect to

round out the package. If a guy's cutting and running after a handful of dates, then he's the one with the problem."

She had no idea why she was pressing the issue, but a retort was out of her mouth before she could even think to hold it back. "Conventional wisdom would suggest my career ambitions are the problem."

"Most people who spout conventional wisdom don't have all that much of it."

"Thanks, Mark Twain."

"You're welcome." He snagged the wax paper that had wrapped his sandwich. Casually, he wadded it up, his gaze speculative from across the table, and she suddenly felt like one of those diamonds he'd inspected with the jeweler's loupe.

Her mind raced over the events of the morning. The flowers. His visit to her office. The trip to the jeweler. "What do you really want from me? I'd wager a rather large sum you don't spend your days traipsing through Manhattan with your other professional enemies."

"I never traipse. And I'd hardly call you an enemy."

"We've been up against each other for several jobs. *I'd* hardly call us compatriots."

He snaked out a finger and ran it down the top of her hand, tracing over each knuckle with exquisite care. The sensation was wicked in the extreme, and a tight ball of need centered low in her belly. "We're not enemies. Especially not after what we discussed this morning about the job in Rome. I want your help with the ambassador."

"What makes you so sure I'm your girl?"

"You've got the talents I need. You already know the job and the players. You're smart and you pay attention." He ran that long finger once more over her hand. "And if I play my cards right, there may be a lot more kissing."

She snatched her hand back, unable to bear that seductive touch a moment longer. "This is a job, not a flirtation."

"Can't it be both?"

She bit down on a retort, well aware her actions in the next few minutes would determine the course of their professional—and personal—relationship moving forward. "I don't take assignments because they're fun."

"Why work then?"

"Because it's my job. My livelihood."

"Doesn't mean you can't enjoy the process."

When Kensington said nothing, he pressed a bit harder, his curiosity growing stronger. He could still feel the softness of her skin imprinted on the tips of his finger, and a strange need to understand her better gripped him. "Why were you the one to end up with all the responsibility?"

"In my family?"

"Yes, but professionally, too. The House of Steele's reputation is tied to all four of you, but you're clearly seen as its public representative. I have to imagine that has carried over to the more personal side of your family dynamics."

"At times." She nodded slightly, as if deciding something, before she pressed on. "Do you have siblings?"

"Two sisters."

"How do the three of you get along?"

He thought of the two women he loved to distraction, both of whom were happily married and raising children in the Seattle suburb where he grew up. They'd saved him—ensuring he had a soft place to land no matter how far he roamed—and there was nothing he wouldn't do for them.

"Really well. They're both older than me. They wanted different things but are happy with their lives. And other than constantly pressuring me to settle down and do my duty to populate the world, we're close."

"So they live normal lives?"

The word *normal* caught his attention, and he thought of the unpleasant childhoods he and his siblings had endured. Sidestepping the thought, he kept his voice even and ignored the whispers of the past that skittered around his ankles. "As much as anyone can claim that description."

"My bigger point is, they have families. Regular jobs."

"Sure."

"That is so *not* my family."

Jack couldn't dismiss the feeling that some answer— some clue to who she was—danced just out of his reach. "You say that like it's a bad thing."

"It's not bad—it's just different. We're different."

"Do you support each other?"

"Of course. We drive one another crazy but we support each other without question."

"Sounds like a family to me."

The warmth that briefly tinged her features as she talked about her family faded. "Yes, a family I'm responsible for."

"They're all adults. Successful, accomplished ones. Why are you responsible for them?"

"I need to hold us all together."

"No. You feel the need to be in control, and there's a difference."

A heavy chill that invaded the bones wrapped Giuseppe DeAngelo's body like a tight blanket. He added as much urgency to his steps as his old bones would allow as he walked from the main farmhouse to the vineyard.

The grapes.

Per favore, Dio.

The prayer was a litany in his head, over and over as he shuffled toward his beloved fruit. They hadn't had a winter this cold in years and he was increasingly concerned their methods to keep the vines insulated weren't going to work.

His gaze scanned the rows of grapes, their slender vines covered by geotextile fabrics to stave off the cold. He abstractly wished for one to wrap around himself as he plodded determinedly onward.

Giuseppe bent over the first row he came to, lifting the fabric to touch the vines underneath. His breath came out in heavy puffs and his back ached as he bent forward, but all he cared about was ensuring his vineyard stayed safe. The pain was worth it to protect his grapes.

He ran his fingers over the thick vegetation, his knotty hands trembling as he considered the vines. They'd worked through the previous afternoon to put the blankets into place. The cold vine bent pliably in his hands and he took his first easy breath as he resettled the covering in place.

The grapes were all right.

Grazie, Dio. Grazie.

He puttered down several rows, his actions the same as he lifted the blankets, checking the vines underneath. His breath puffed out in hard, heavy bursts but he paid no attention as he continued to walk the neat, even rows.

The vineyard had been in his family for generations. He'd already made plans to give it to his grandson, his own son off in London having his life's adventures. Adventures that didn't belong on a farm. His Gianni had never been tied to the land, but his grandson, Marco, loved it as much as Giuseppe.

Grazie, Dio. Again, his prayer of thanks and gratitude flooded his mind. His vineyard would live on.

Heavy shouts, muffled through the thick morning air, pulled him from his morning prayers. Had Marco come to help him?

Giuseppe walked toward the sounds, the heavy air distorting them. When he finally reached the end of a row, three down from where he'd begun, he saw he was right. "Marco!"

His grandson hunched over, his hands shoved into the pockets of his black leather coat. *"Nonno."* Grandfather.

"The grapes are fine. The fabrics worked."

"It's too cold out here for you. Go back inside and pour the coffee and I'll join you. I'll be in shortly."

"Bah!" Giuseppe waved his hand and moved closer. Why had he heard raised voices? Marco was alone. "I've been walking these vineyards since I was small. A bit of cold air won't chase me inside."

"Nonno. Please go back in."

Giuseppe shook his head, suddenly aware of the strange urgency that gripped his grandson. Marco shifted from foot to foot, his dark eyes flashing like those of a scared horse. He took the last few steps to the edge of the vines and nearly fell to his feet. "Marco!"

Another man stood a short distance away, a gun wavering in his outstretched hand.

"I asked you to go inside, *Nonno.*" Marco's voice broke before the man holding the gun stepped forward.

"I don't think so. Not anymore."

Giuseppe's mind raced as he took in the scene before him. He'd been so worried about his precious grapes, he'd never realized there was a threat to them far greater than the cold. "What is this about?"

The man with the gun waved it in Marco's direction. "You really don't know? You can honestly tell me you have no idea what's going on?"

"I want to hear it from my grandson."

"I failed, Nonno." Marco lifted his head, his eyes filled with tears. "I failed you and I'm sorry. So sorry."

They were the last words Giuseppe DeAngelo would ever hear.

* * *

Kensington pulled the small bowl of oatmeal from the microwave and padded to the drop-leaf table that filled the corner of her kitchen. She added several scoops of blueberries to the steaming oats, then took a sip of her coffee as her breakfast cooled.

The thoughts that had filled her mind, leaving her tossing and turning until three, didn't fade as she stared at the kitchen without really seeing it. Instead, she saw the hard lines of Jack's face.

You feel the need to be in control, and there's a difference.

Was it true?

On some level she knew that it was, but it wasn't the entire story and it was unfair to paint her with that one-dimensional brush.

Their conversation had spun out from there, each of his questions more probing than the last. She'd made a valiant effort to defend herself, but in the end, none of it had mattered.

None of it had erased that small moue of sympathy that curved his lips in an understanding—and, to her mind, pitying—smile.

"You don't understand, Jack. Do you and your sisters regularly put your lives in danger?"

"They don't. I do."

"My point is, that element isn't a part of your family dynamic. Isn't a part of how the three of you interact in your relationship with one another."

"So you think your family dynamics have some influence on your life?"

"I think everything has an influence on our lives. And I think four adults who consistently put their lives in jeopardy have a funny way of looking at the world."

"You fix the world. And you understand that need in each other. What can be so wrong about that?"

That question had hovered between them for a few moments before she'd managed to excuse herself and grab a cab back to the office, unescorted.

There wasn't anything wrong with how she lived her life. And she was proud of the work they did. Proud of what she, Liam, Campbell and Rowan had created.

But none of it changed the fact that they lived lives outside the mainstream. Campbell and Rowan had both found their way to love, despite the rather evident dysfunction in their lives, but it didn't mean she and Liam were guaranteed the same.

And it certainly didn't mean questioning the shortcomings of her life with a total stranger over lunch was even remotely productive.

"So why are you giving him the satisfaction of giving it one more moment of your time?" She muttered the words to herself before digging into her oatmeal. She'd gotten through only a couple of bites when her apartment doorman buzzed her. She snagged the small phone—connected to her lobby—from the counter. "Good morning, Mike."

"Ms. Steele. I know it's early but a Jack Andrews is here to see you. He said it's urgent."

The urge to say she wasn't available was strong, but it wasn't Mike's problem she was frustrated and annoyed with Jack. Mike dealt with threatening visitors, not ones who simply didn't know how to use a damn phone at six-thirty in the morning. "Please send him up."

She glanced down at her oh-so-attractive flannel button-down pajamas and hightailed it to the bedroom. A pair of jeans and a cashmere sweater lay on a small chair where she'd left them the night before, and she quickly changed into them. A glance in the mirror had her cringing—

seriously, did the man not know you didn't just drop in on a woman?—before she threw up her hands at the loud knock on her door.

Less than a minute later, Jack was barreling into her apartment, his face set in grim, determined lines.

"What's the matter?"

"Have you made your decision on Rome?"

"I told you yesterday I'd think about it."

He moved in, settling his large hands on her shoulders. "Can you speed up the decision?"

"What's happened?"

"Something big and I can't tell you if you're not in. All the way in."

The light flair of flirtation and humor she associated with him had vanished from his face. In its place was a formidable bear of a man. Strength carved itself in the hard planes and angles of his body and she fought the light frisson of anxiety that skated over her skin, leaving goose bumps in its wake.

"Why is this so important to you?"

"You're the one, Kensington. You know the job. You know the players. You know how to play the security detail to maximum advantage."

"I'm not the only professional out there."

"You're the one I want and I don't have time to get anyone else up to speed."

She fought the delicious rush at his words. He wanted her for a job, nothing more, she reminded herself.

And when had she begun thinking otherwise?

In for a penny...

Her grandfather had used that adage so many times that Kensington had adopted it as her own. With one last glancing thought that her sanity must have abandoned her around the time she put the damn ring on the day before, she lifted her head and nodded. "Fine. I'm in. Now will you tell me what happened?"

"The agent the Italian government has in place was shot this morning."

"Was he killed?"

"Almost. It was set up execution-style. The only thing that saved him was a last-minute burst of speed and quick thinking from his grandfather, who had a heavy pair of vine clippers in his pocket."

"And the grandfather?"

"Died before the paramedics arrived."

"Is the agent coherent?"

"Barely. He's been in and out of consciousness all day. We need to get to Italy and find out what he knows, from him if at all possible. Are you with me on this?"

"*Sì*, Signor Andrews. It looks like we're headed to Rome."

Chapter 4

Kensington leaned her chair back and settled into her first-class seat. The day had sped past in a blur—arrangements for the company and her apartment, postponing some meetings, shifting others to Campbell and Rowan, double-checking details and packing all seen to with frenetic motion—and it was only now, nearly midnight by her body's clock, that she'd finally slowed down. Her half-drunk glass of Chianti sat on her tray table next to an unopened book.

Her gaze drifted to the window, the Atlantic nearly forty thousand feet beneath them like a dark abyss.

"You going to get some sleep?"

Jack's words distracted her from her thoughts and she turned away from the window. "Eventually. I don't sleep well."

"You get a remarkable amount accomplished for someone who must be perpetually tired."

She shrugged, not quite sure how they'd drifted—yet again—to one of the odd facets of her personality. "I get by. And coffee's a dear, dear friend."

"Have you tried massage?"

"Yep."

"Aromatherapy?"

"Yep."

"Acupuncture?"

"Not in this lifetime."

His smile was quick and immediate, even as his words were surprisingly gentle. "People swear by it."

She fought the shudder and reached for her wine. "And they're welcome to it."

A wicked gleam lit that dark brown gaze, adding a new dimension to the smile. "Have I discovered something the great and powerful Kensington Steele is afraid of?"

"I'm fine with needles for basic health reasons. To voluntarily have them stuck all over my body? No way."

His gaze drifted, a lazy perusal over her shoulders, and she fought another shiver—this one far more delicious than the last.

How did he manage to do that?

What should have seemed lascivious—or at the least a bit inappropriate—instead made her feel attractive. And, funny enough, cherished.

As if catching himself, Jack's gaze snapped back to his own wineglass as he lifted it from his tray. "I wouldn't go anywhere near it, either."

"Yet you think *I* should?"

"Hey. I'm the idea guy. You need to relax, so I offered up a few suggestions."

"I don't need to relax."

"When was the last time you got eight hours straight?"

"I don't need eight hours."

"Modern medical wisdom would suggest otherwise." He paused and shifted in his chair, that gaze once again direct and all consuming. "So when?"

"I haven't slept straight through the night since I was fourteen."

She saw the question in his gaze—and the ready awareness he'd somehow overstepped—but still he pressed on. "Why is that, Kensington?"

"My grandmother woke me in the middle of the night to tell me my parents had died. I've never slept fully through the night since."

Jack cursed himself a million times the fool for this stubborn line of questioning. He knew he was a ruthless bastard when he got his teeth around something, but even he respected a certain degree of personal privacy.

The loss of her parents certainly qualified on that front.

The proverbial "I'm sorry" sprang to his lips but he kept it to himself. Of all the things he should say, a pithy platitude wasn't it. "That's a long time."

"Didn't anyone ever tell you it's rude to let on you know a woman's age?" A wry smile ghosted her mouth and the urge to lean forward and press his lips to hers gripped him with sharp claws. But again, he held back. Tamped down on the obvious and reached for her hand instead.

"It was more a reference to how young you were when you lost them. And, for what it's worth, I find a few years on a woman gives her character." He lifted her hand to his lips, unable to fully resist. "Makes her beauty more authentic somehow."

Her hand flexed under his, but she didn't pull it back. "I told you at lunch yesterday we weren't going there, Jack."

"Why not?"

"It's messy and complicated, not to mention unprofessional. We're working on a job."

He kept his fingers locked around hers but resettled their joined hands on the small armrest between them. "A job that requires us to have each other's backs."

The lightest stain colored her cheeks and he couldn't restrain the very real interest that tightened his stomach once more. He was interested in her—hell, he'd have to be long past dead not to be—and the time in her company only made it more urgent.

More *necessary.*

"I'm not going to be seduced by some simple words and those come-hither eyes of yours."

Her comment left her open, and he prided himself on being a man who didn't miss an opportunity. "What will you be seduced by?"

"That's not what I meant."

"But I did."

"Why do you keep pushing this?"

Why *did* he keep pressing the issue? And when, exactly, had that little devil planted itself on his shoulder, intent on ruffling her very smooth feathers?

Was it the moment he saw her fluster ever so slightly in her home office? Or was it the moment he stared down at her in the jewelry store, a diamond ring shining boldly off her left hand? Or was it the moment he pressed his lips to hers, the rich, ripe taste a succulent feast?

Whatever the reason, it didn't matter any longer. He was captivated by her. And he'd be damned if he wasn't going to do his level best to show her.

"Because I'm interested, Kensington." He leaned into her, the small space making it a short trip. "Very interested."

He brushed his mouth to hers, the small puff of air against his lips as she sighed the sweetest victory.

The rich Chianti she'd ordered was a bold match for the taste of her. Where he'd had the advantage of surprise while they'd stood at the jeweler's the day before, here he had the luxury of time. The darkened interior of the airplane cabin cocooned them as one moment spun into the next.

Another soft sigh left her lips, the sound echoing in her throat in counterpoint to the increasing urgency of the kiss. Her hands gripped his shirt at the shoulders and he felt the flex of her fingers along the base of his neck.

And then she surrendered.

One last sigh—was that contentment or acceptance?—drifted from the back of her throat. She tilted her head to give him better access before pulling him closer. And the delicious play of her tongue over his had need coursing through his body in hard, pulsing waves.

He *knew* there was a woman underneath that calm, cool exterior very few saw. How enticing, then, that he'd be fortunate enough to get a glimpse.

His hands skimmed the width of her shoulder before dipping down her arm, then snaking over her waist. The firm muscles over her hip bone captivated him and he allowed his fingers to drift over the edge of her slacks. The heat of her skin branded him and the soft flesh sent another shock of need spiraling through his system.

With a last muffled protest from his conscience, he pulled back, breaking the erotic contact.

Those lush blue eyes were wide with shock and need, her large pupils a ready sign of her arousal. "Now do you see why we can't do this?"

"That kiss only reinforced my point, darling."

"Exactly." She shifted and lay back against her seat.

"We've got a job to do and we need to keep our heads in the game. Neither of us have worked this hard to throw it away on a few moments of fun."

She bricked up her personal walls with swift efficiency, her emotions winking out like a light.

And we're right back to that calm, cool exterior, he couldn't help thinking before the urge to bait her got the better of him. "Hide behind your work all you want, Kensington. I'm quite good at multitasking when I put my mind to it. And I've got absolutely no problem juggling my personal life with my professional one."

She sat back up at that, the sexual haze in her gaze vanishing as good old-fashioned ire rose up to take its place. "I'm not hiding behind anything."

"You sure about that? Because I wasn't just kissing myself."

"Oh, for God's sake—enough. We're grown-ups. We can behave like rational, *professional* adults."

"Whatever you need to tell yourself, darling."

"I don't need to *tell* myself anything. I get along just fine."

Jack wasn't sure what it was—the subtle challenge or just this strange madness that gripped him every time he was in her presence—but he knew he couldn't back down. He leaned forward on one elbow, his gaze unwavering on hers. "Know this. When we do make love—and believe me, we will—I'm going to strip away every bit of that prim, proper exterior to reveal the woman underneath."

"This is a ridiculous conversation. Only I choose whom I share my bed with." Her words were flat but the clear notes of irritation sparked underneath each syllable.

"Then you know damn well the next man you share it with is going to be me."

Jack lay his head back on his seat, but just before he

closed his eyes, he had the satisfaction of seeing her mouth screw up in a small, thin line. He was just petty enough— and aroused as hell—to feel a perverse sense of satisfaction.

Served her right.

Now they'd *both* spend the damn flight clamped in the shockingly uncomfortable jaws of arousal, the promise of explosive passion winking just out of reach.

Jack's words echoed in her thoughts throughout the flight and on their cab ride from the airport. The statement that she'd share his bed as if it were a fait accompli. Or worse, as if she had no choice in the matter.

But do I?

That small, irritating voice that had ridden her thoughts throughout the long, overnight flight chimed in with a mad disclaimer.

And a very real part of her knew it was true.

No matter how she attempted to think her way out of this attraction to Jack, she couldn't stop it. Couldn't make sense of this raging need to see where things would go between them.

Hell, she didn't even know the man. How could she possibly think of sleeping with him? Of giving her hormones the upper hand.

The disconcerting thoughts gave way as she finally registered the view out her window. The streets of Rome enveloped them, and it was only when they passed by the Spanish Steps that she began to relax and give herself over to the moment.

Rome.

The Eternal City.

And a personal favorite since she'd been a small child. She, Rowan and her mother had come here when she was twelve for a girls' weekend, just the three of them. It had been a spontaneous trip, in reaction to a weekend her father, Liam and Campbell took on a campout upstate.

Even after all these years, she could still taste the sweet gelato they'd shared in one of Rome's many piazzas. Could still remember her mother's encouragement to lean forward and take a sip from one of the fountains around the city, all which had run with fresh water since the Roman Empire.

And she'd never forget the light gleam in her mother's eye as they'd walked past a gaggle of Italian men who offered up appreciative stares and comments in their native tongue.

She'd been scandalized at the time, and it was only later, as they crossed the Tiber to visit the Vatican, that her mother had explained how the men competed against each other while also saving face by acknowledging the women around them.

"Sort of like how Liam keeps looking at his muscles in the mirror?" Rowan's question had her mother's light laugh floating on the afternoon breeze as they crossed the old bridge.

"It's a bit like that." Her mother pulled both of them close. *"He thinks we don't notice when he does it."*

"That's because he's stupid. All boys are stupid." Kensington couldn't resist offering this tidbit up. It had become her favorite litany, even if she didn't think all boys were stupid. Especially one in particular who'd caught her eye at school.

"No, sweetie, they're not. They're just different from us."

Kensington shook off images of the young boy who'd caught her attention in math class and focused on making her point. "Like this weekend. Who wants to go sleep in a tent?"

She enjoyed the sounds of the city keeping them company and couldn't imagine trading this for a night spent under the stars.

Rowan's argument was swift, winging back within moments. "Hey. I like sleeping outside."

"You can have it."

Her mother tugged them both closer for a hug. "Girls. We're all entitled to like what we like. And your brothers are entitled to the same courtesy. All I'm trying to say is that men see the world differently than we do."

"Is that bad?" Rowan voiced the question first, and for some reason Kensington was glad she had.

Although she had her brothers as ready—and gross— objects of the male species, lately she'd begun to notice that some of the boys at school didn't seem quite so gross. There was Jonathan from math class, who had caught her attention with his cute smile and his big feet that he never quite tripped over. And Jeremy in gym kept teasing her every time they had to partner up for tennis. And there was Paul, who asked her to dance at the last social.

She didn't think any of them *were gross.*

"We're here."

Jack's voice pulled her from her thoughts and it took Kensington a minute to reorient herself. "Already?"

"Already? We've been sitting in traffic for the past half hour." He pointed toward the window. "I thought you looked a million miles away, and you clearly were if you missed the drive."

"I was actually right here in Rome. My mom, sister and I took a trip here when I was a kid and I was thinking about a conversation we'd had."

"It must have been a good one if you're smiling like that."

"Like what?"

"Memories have misted your eyes to a soft, bluish-gray."

The compliment pulled her up short and she wasn't sure what to say beyond a soft, "Oh."

"It's lovely." His dark eyes were inscrutable but it was the husky timbre of his voice that tugged at her.

Not all boys were gross. She'd learned that early and had continued to appreciate the lesson. And with one look at Jack Andrews, she could only concur with her mother's words of wisdom—some of them grew up into dynamic, interesting men.

Their driver pulled up to their hotel on the Via Veneto, the lush accommodations rising several stories above them as they came to a stop. She grabbed her bag but stopped for a moment, unable to hold back a response. "It was lovely. My mother gave Rowan and me several important lessons about boys that weekend."

"Anything you're willing to share?"

The flirtation was as easy as breathing. "Oh, nothing you're not already aware of. Men like to posture and preen in front of women."

The puzzled look that filled the hard lines of his face had her immediately thinking of what he must have looked like as a little boy. "You mean that's some sort of deep, dark secret?"

"It is to twelve-year-old girls who don't understand why strange Italian men are shouting words of adoration at their mother."

"Ahhh. The mating ritual of the European male. I can see how that would be an eye-opener." He paid the driver, and they slid from the car. He reached for her bag before gesturing her forward through the large revolving door that fronted their hotel. "For what it's worth, I avoid showing my appreciation with whistles, catcalls or anything that can be construed that I spend my days hanging around on street corners."

She couldn't resist turning toward him and pushing a bit on the events of their flight. "So sexual innuendo at thirty-six thousand feet is more your style?"

"I prefer to think of myself as a man who takes bold action when required."

Jack pressed a hand to the base of her spine as he guided her through the lobby toward check-in. The heavy width of his palm had sparks shooting up and down her back, and she couldn't hide the small, feminine smile, so like her mother's on that long-ago day.

For all her self-inflicted browbeating in the car, she'd fallen right back into Jack Andrews's orbit. And damn it if she wasn't enjoying the ride.

He pulled her to a halt in the lobby, the bustle of mid-day activity crisscrossing all around them. She nearly stumbled at the sudden stop, but Jack held her in place, his hands firm.

That dark, fathomless gaze drank her in as he stared down at her, and she couldn't shake the very real sense he was going to kiss her again. Her breath caught in her throat for the briefest moment as the muscles in her knees gave way with a light tremble.

But instead of doing the expected, his lips veered off to press against her ear. His warm breath sent shivers coursing through her, but it was the dark, husky words that had heat curling in her belly.

"And I rarely miss an opportunity."

As they moved determinedly on toward the check-in desk, Kensington could only muster up one thought.

Point, Mr. Andrews.

Whatever sexual innuendo had threaded through their travel to Rome, all evidence of it had vanished two hours later as she and Jack sat with the head of the Italian Special Forces assigned to the Tierra Kimber case. Dante Ferrero had the swarthy good looks of his countrymen, set off by a blazing pair of blue eyes that, Kensington was quite sure, had set the hearts of his fellow countrywomen on fire since his youth.

Despite the man's attractive features and intense focus, she couldn't help comparing him to Jack. Where Dante's appeal was nearly blinding upon first notice, Jack's was more subtle. And far more predatory.

He had a masculine grace that was unexpected in a man with such a large frame. And where it would be easy to assume Jack's power lay in his ability to use blunt force, it was actually his more subtle approach—and shockingly sharp intellect—that were the real weapons in his arsenal.

The man was lethal.

And she suspected far too many enemies had learned that lesson a moment too late.

Pulling herself from her reverie, she flipped once more through the briefing packet Dante had given each of them. She needed to shake off whatever fanciful notions had gripped her and get her damn head in the game. Jack Andrews was just a man. A powerful one, yes, but a man all the same.

So why couldn't she keep herself from adding up the various attributes that continued to intrigue her beyond measure?

Focusing on work—the age-old remedy for pushing problems to the back of one's mind—she turned to Dante. "Mr. Ferrero, you and your team continue to maintain Ambassador Pryce is using his position to move diamonds and, based on this dossier, likely drugs, as well. Those are serious charges. I must ask again why you simply don't have him removed from his position. The Italian government is well within its right to do so."

"The benefit of getting to the bottom of the corruption outweighs the potential political embarrassment." Dante paused briefly, as if weighing his words, before adding, "The highest leaders of the Republic are in accord on this matter."

"But what if he's innocent?"

Dante smiled, but the gesture never reached the icy blue of his eyes. "Ever the optimist, Miss Steele?"

"I prefer to think of myself as practical and pragmatic. I rarely have reason to be optimistic in my line of work."

The smile broadened and she sensed an underlying approval in his response. "As Mr. Andrews and I discussed yesterday before your trip to Italy, we've let the ambassador know you both will be joining his security detail. He has no reason to think this is anything beyond routine."

"And he asked no questions?"

"Your reputations precede you both. Ambassador Pryce is delighted to make your acquaintance." Dante nodded slightly. "Yours in particular, Ms. Steele."

Jack's grip on the papers tightened before he leaned forward. "The ambassador does understand we're there as hired employees."

"Of course. But Ms. Steele's reputation is quite… distinguished."

"As an expert in her field, no doubt."

Jack's ready defense opened another soft spot and Kensington fought to keep the discussion on point. "If Pryce knows what my firm is capable of, he must be curious as to why we've been hired, too. Especially as it's really Mr. Andrews who's been given the job."

"Not at all. As I said, the ambassador and his staff have been informed the matter is routine and that senior-level intelligence is being added to his security detail. I think you would call it a 'special assignment.'" Dante hesitated—if she'd not been watching him so closely she'd have missed it. "Again, I must stress, he is delighted you will be there, Miss Steele. Your grandfather's reputation in international circles is well-known and well respected. Further, the details of your beauty have not been exaggerated. Pryce will be delighted to make your acquaintance."

Although she suspected Dante believed he was delivering a compliment, Kensington fought the urge to leap across the desk and throttle him. "I'm hardly here as an escort to the ambassador, Mr. Ferrero. Rather, I'm a paid operative who can either save his ass or put it in a sling. I understand the latter option's not been made clear to the ambassador, but I certainly I hope it's crystal clear to you."

Dante nodded. "As clear as the waters of Lake Como."

"Excellent. I'm glad we understand each other."

While the flash of male posturing—and the clear frustration lingering in the tight lines of Dante's mouth—wasn't lost on her, she'd learned early how to make a hasty retreat. She suspected the good inspector wasn't immune to concern for his team member, so she'd start there. "How is Marco? We'd like to speak with him if we may."

"It can be arranged but it's possible you won't get many details at this point. As of this morning, his medical team has confirmed that he continues to lapse in and out of consciousness."

"Have you accounted for the ambassador's whereabouts on the morning of the attack?" Jack waved the slender file Dante had shared. "Nothing's been updated here since late last week."

"Yes." Dante pulled another piece of paper from a slim folder on his desk. "We also have been monitoring both him and his key staff members for the past three months."

"Is that why the assignment's changed since your original outreach?"

Dante's eyes widened at the question. "I'm sorry, Miss Steele. I don't understand your meaning."

"The request you put to both my firm and Mr. Andrews's firm was to provide security detail to a high-ranking diplomat. Yet here we are, tasked to find intelligence on the same diplomat. None of that was in your original request."

"Are you suggesting there is a problem?" The clipped tones were cold. Why was this the piece that pushed him over the edge? Any hint of politeness had vanished from both his tone and manner.

Deliberately ignoring the censure, Kensington pressed on. "I'm suggesting you purposely withheld information as our firms bid on the project. I'd like to understand why."

Dante sat back, the dismissive move screaming his meaning far louder than his words. "Perhaps Mr. Andrews hasn't found the proper partner for this assignment."

Before she could respond, Jack stood. "I've found the right partner. No need to worry about that."

Dante never moved from his seat. "Are you sure, Mr. Andrews?"

"Quite. What I'm not sure is why your organization thinks that an outside firm is the way to handle this problem. It implies you can't police your own."

Dante's blue eyes flashed with cold fire and he leaned forward at the taunt. "We can handle our problems just fine."

"Yet you've sought my help, and by extension, Miss Steele's, to provide plausible deniability when this eventually blows up."

Whatever else he might be, Dante Ferrero was a cop and it was that trait that ultimately won out. "One of my men is in the hospital, struggling in and out of consciousness and fighting for his life. I want nothing more than to get the bastard who did it, but it seems my government has overruled my eager need for justice. Your firm's investigation adds a certain legitimacy to my concerns about the ambassador."

"And if things do blow up and Pryce is guilty of what you suspect?"

"Then you and Miss Steele have my full blessing to take him down."

Chapter 5

"He's lying."

"No. He's not telling the whole truth. There's a difference."

A light breeze wafted around them as they strolled through one of Rome's many piazzas. Jack wasn't sure if it was the surprisingly nice December afternoon or the presence of a beautiful woman at his side, but he couldn't quite muster up anything more than a subtle annoyance at their meeting with Dante.

Several people sat under umbrellas in the outdoor cafés that dotted the large square and Jack had a sudden urge for a cappuccino. "Come on."

When she only stared at him in confusion he pointed toward the nearest restaurant. "I want a coffee. We'll dissect the good officer's words and come up with our own meaning. We'll also figure out how badly we still want in on this job."

He held up two fingers to the restaurant's hostess before she led them to a small table. Once seated and their cappuccinos ordered, he settled back in his chair.

"I thought I was going to have to separate you and Dante."

The subtle lines creasing Kensington's face softened at the intended joke. "I wasn't that bad."

"You were magnificent. I loved how you went after him."

"Does that bother you?"

"Not in the least. If he's worth his position he knows how to hold his own." Jack leaned forward and tapped a finger on the table. "But you pinned him down. I'm curious why."

"Dante didn't work all that hard on convincing us to stay on the assignment." A small frown tugged at the corners of her mouth. "In fact, it was almost like he was trying to scare us off."

"Remember all that male posturing we discussed this morning?"

"Sure."

"How was our little meeting with the good officer any different?"

The slight widening of her eyes was the only clue his comment surprised her. "Of course it's different. Whistling at a pretty woman and lying about a security problem are two different things."

"Not when it comes to saving face."

Their waitress set down their coffees and a small plate of biscotti, and Kensington waited until the woman departed once again before speaking. "You can't really think they're the same thing."

"Of course they are. His government's running the risk of an embarrassment that will spread through the global community like wildfire. Add on the implications to the drug trade if they don't get this under control and they've got a substantial problem on their hands if Pryce is as dirty as they think."

"And you can honestly sit there and tell me you think that's like whistling at a beautiful woman?"

"It's about power. And position. It's the same."

Her indelicate snort was as spot-on as her retort. "So getting laid and government corruption are about on par in your book?"

"I didn't say that. I said they come from the same source." He leaned forward and snatched a cookie. "Which is where you come in."

"Me?"

"Yes, you. You're the beautiful, brilliant woman who's going to bring it all crumbling down."

"Dante made that point—at least the female point— more than evident. And just for the record, in case there was even the slightest doubt in your mind, I didn't take this job so I could tart myself up and wear a push-up bra."

"More's the pity."

"What happened to admiring my brilliance?"

"Can't I admire both your brilliance and your stunning form? That is why you dress like you do."

"Excuse me?"

The change was immediate and Jack took a perverse satisfaction at how quickly she prickled up. Why did the mention of her beauty bother her so badly? Especially when she made every effort to use those looks where it suited her.

"You're impeccable. I've never seen you in anything that didn't flatter your incredibly elegant form or let everyone in the room know you were a woman. Yet it bothers you when it's pointed out."

"I'm not bothered."

"And that stick that just inserted itself in your spine was all for show?"

She relaxed slightly. "Good posture is a key to a healthy digestive system." She glanced at the cookies as if considering a small square before reaching for her coffee instead. "Besides, the point's moot. *You* were hired. As far as Dante's concerned I'm the pain in the ass tagging along."

"Then you didn't see what I saw."

Her sharp gaze met his with the force of a cracked whip. "Oh, no?"

"That man knows damn well you're the key to this project."

"Then why didn't he hire me?" Sugar dripped from her words, but her smile was all shark.

"That still chaps your very fine ass, doesn't it?"

"Of course it does."

He kept his gaze level on hers, curious to see if she'd give any indication of what went on inside that marvelous mind of hers. "Because you wanted the job or because you hate to lose?"

"Can't it be both?"

"Not if you want to keep your priorities straight and your head in the game."

"My head's always in the game."

"You sure about that?"

Anger heated her eyes to an indigo blue and the bright bustle of the piazza provided a backdrop to the extraordinary self-control she possessed. Despite himself—and the words he wielded to poke at her defenses—he was captivated.

Whatever attraction he'd felt for the woman was nothing compared to the heat that throbbed in his veins at that moment. She was magnificent.

A warrior princess.

And if he wasn't mistaken, she'd grabbed hold of something inside of him he'd thought long dead.

Kensington took a sip of her coffee and attempted to marshal her thoughts. Jack Andrews was a formidable opponent—just as she knew him to be—and her response needed to be thoughtful.

Even if she was vacillating between throttling him and climbing on his lap and kissing him senseless.

Which made about as much sense as this inane conversation they were having.

"You like to win. So do I. I'm not sure why you think it's a silly trait from my perspective."

He shook his head. "I never said it was silly."

"It's implied in your words."

"No, damn it, it's not." She was surprised by how quickly her retort tripped his trigger as he leaned forward with enough force to shake the table. "And just so we're clear, the urge to win never outweighs my focus on the job."

"Neither does mine."

"Then why does it bother you I got the assignment?"

"My brothers, sister and I have worked hard to create a successful business. We pitch assignments we want to win."

"You can't win them all."

"No."

"So if you do understand that and have presumably lost other projects, why does it bother you so badly to lose to me?"

The sudden realization he'd neatly boxed her in should have upset her. If she'd imagined this discussion, she'd have seen it play out with a series of pithy retorts he'd be incapable of volleying back.

Yet so far he hadn't missed one single shot aimed in his direction.

So why wasn't she bothered?

She wanted this job, sure. Was already invested in a positive outcome for their client. Yet that was only the tip of the iceberg.

Jack's succinct assessment of her reaction wasn't far off. It chafed to lose to him. The real question was why. "No matter how hard I push, you just push right back. Why is that?"

"I told you. I'm interested in you. Beyond this job, I want to get to know you. Spend time with you."

"No." She shook her head, working through it in her mind. "It's more than that. Attraction is easy. And it's not worth all the time and effort."

He sat back in his chair, looking for all the world like every other casual male sitting in the café. "I can't agree with you there."

"I'm serious. At its core, attraction's easy. Yes or no. On or off."

A lazy smile lifted his lips in the slightest quirk and a sudden shot of heat arrowed through her belly at the subtle cockiness of the gesture.

But when he leaned forward, those dark eyes as mesmerizing as a magician's, she nearly forgot to breathe.

"Oh, it's definitely on, Kensington."

"Well, turn it off. I'm not going to spend the next week fighting with you on this." The sharp bite in her tone was harsher than she'd planned, but once the words were out she could hardly snatch them back.

"Even if you are interested?"

"I'm more interested in finding out the responsible party

and getting this job wrapped up. You know as well as I do the longer a job takes, the higher the risk."

He leaned forward once more, pushing his empty coffee cup aside. The hard bunch of his shoulders under his jacket drew her gaze before it drifted toward his mouth. A light smile turned up the corners at her scrutiny and she forced her gaze firmly toward his before her body could betray her once more.

"For someone who spends an awful lot of time calculating the odds, you're not very bullish on yourself," Jack said.

"Oh, I do just fine."

"Well, then, let me give you a small bit of advice. One gambler to another."

"What's that?"

"The big score doesn't come around very often. And you'll always kick yourself if you don't bet big when you have the chance."

Whatever she could possibly have said to such a statement was lost as he stood and tossed his napkin on the table. "We should probably get going. I'd like to visit Marco and if his condition is as accurate as we've been told, we may need to wait for a while."

"That means you want to take this job?"

"I want to talk to Marco, but yeah, I want this job and I'm willing to bet big on it. And on us."

Marco DeAngelo lay in his hospital bed, battered and bruised almost beyond recognition. Machines beeped and maintained a steady stream of data on every aspect of his care. Kensington fought the sudden well of tears as she sought the confirmation that his heart was still beating, true and strong.

Crying wouldn't help the man.

Only action could do that.

And the sheer determination to see this job through.

Jack's words still echoed in her thoughts—had kept her company on the entire taxi ride to the hospital—and she was surprised to realize how tightly she clung to them.

I'm willing to bet big on it. And on us.

Us.

Jack's fingers brushed her hand before linking them firmly. His touch conveyed instant support. Belief. Partnership.

The thought caught her up short, battling at her subconscious with swift and immediate impact. For all their talk of partnering on this job, it wasn't until he reached for her that she'd felt it. True partnership.

And for the first time in longer than she could count, she didn't feel like the one who had to keep it all together. For once, she had someone to lean on and help carry the load.

Jack's voice interrupted the thought and she turned toward him, grateful to get out of her own head. "The doctor said it was okay to wake him, but I'm not so sure."

"Let's give him a few minutes." She hesitated briefly before deciding to finish her thought. "Whoever is behind this wanted to keep him from talking."

Jack squeezed her hand once more before he spoke. "They wanted him dead and they damn near succeeded if his condition is any indication."

"I suppose so." She murmured the words before sinking back into her own thoughts. How did someone recover from such a brutal attack and the murder of a loved one?

Yet they did.

And Marco *would* recover, assuming he could get out of the woods and begin healing. People recovered from grief. And they *did* go on. Even if a large piece of them was never the same.

"Are you all right?" Jack turned toward her, shielding her view of Marco with his body. "We can come back later. Go grab another coffee or maybe some lunch."

"I'm fine. It's just…seeing Marco. I can't help thinking of his grandfather." *And my parents.*

"Dante did confirm he knows that his grandfather was killed. Was told early on, during his moments of consciousness."

She supposed there was a strange mercy in that, even if it didn't feel like it. At least he wouldn't wake up to the news. Rather, the horror would be wrapped up as one more piece of his healing.

Was there ever an easy way?

As someone who had lived through it and still bore the scars, she knew the answer was a resounding *no*.

Another layer of those tears pricked hot against her throat when Marco's groan echoed from the bed. She and Jack moved forward at once, but she spoke first. She kept her voice soft yet firm. *"Signore—"*

Marco's eyes snapped open, confusion stamped in their blue depths as his gaze darted around the room.

She kept her voice gentle. *"Scusi, Signore?"*

Marco struggled to sit up, his movements frantic as he sought to protect himself from strangers.

"Dante sent us." Jack backed up her words but made no move to touch the detective.

Marco's eyes never lost their sheen of mistrust but he spoke in flawless English as he stopped his movements. "Then where is he? And who the hell are you?"

Jack made quick introductions before producing additional documentation from Dante. Although the tense set of Marco's shoulders didn't fully fade, Kensington noted the slowing of his heart rate on the monitor behind his head.

They'd passed the first test.

"So you're the hotheaded Americans Dante thinks can fix this case?" Marco reached for the remote on his bed to lift himself to a seated position.

"I'm not sure *fix* is the word I'd use." Jack's broad grin belied the coiled tension she'd felt as they stood before Marco's reclining form. "I think Dante has other plans for us. Your English is excellent, but how familiar are you with the concept of plausible deniability?"

The distinct notes of disgust were evident, even under Marco's many bruises. "Far more than I'd like."

"Then you understand our role in this perfectly."

Marco waved them toward a few stiff chairs that ran along the window. "Why don't you sit down and I'll tell you what I know?"

Kensington took the proffered olive branch and snagged one of the seats, then realized Jack hadn't followed suit. Instead, he filled a plastic cup with water from an icy pitcher on Marco's bedside and handed the cup to the man.

That same arrow to the belly that had pierced her earlier struck once more, only this time it hit a bit closer to her heart. The gesture was simple, really, and shouldn't produce such a reaction, but it did.

Oh, how it did.

Such a small, fascinating insight into the man underneath that cool, competent exterior, but a powerful one all the same. Jack dropped into the seat next to her, oblivious of her scrutiny, which only made it that much sweeter.

"What do you want to know?" Marco set down his now-empty glass. Even with the bruises on his face, it was hard to miss the odd mix of resignation and a subtle hopefulness that rode his features.

"How deep did you get into the organization behind the drug smuggling? Dante's convinced Pryce needs to be watched, yet the ambassador's behavior hasn't rung any bells."

Marco shook his head. "Nor will it. We're convinced he's in the thick of things, but he's not responsible for day-to-day operations."

"Yes, but he can't have that many confidants." Kensington edged forward on her chair. "By all accounts, this operation is small and tightly run. In order to keep it that small, he's got to have a significant role."

"I was in there for almost two months and never detected his presence."

Marco's clear gaze faded as if he'd never been awake and Kensington wondered at the sudden change. Sad memories? Anger at his failed mission? Whatever the reason, Jack's next words were just harsh enough to pull the man back to the conversation. "Do you know how your cover was blown?"

"No."

"So why that morning?"

"I don't know!" Whatever thin thread Marco clung to snapped. "It's all I think of in my waking moments. If I'd sensed. If I'd known. My grandfather would be alive now."

Kensington laid a hand on Jack's knee, but even as she did, she sensed the gesture was unnecessary. Knew it when that same compassion that had him reaching for the water had his voice going gentle. "I'm sorry, Marco. We've pushed too hard this morning."

"No, no." Marco waved a hand and Kensington used the moment to leap up and fill his glass.

The small action kept her busy, yet gave her a moment to gather her thoughts.

This wasn't like her parents. It wasn't the same.

Yes, he was grieving, but Marco wasn't a young man

woken in the middle of the night to find out the news of his family.

Even if he had witnessed the loss of his grandfather.

A hard shake gripped her hands and she quickly set the cup of water on Marco's bedside table.

"Perhaps we can come back tomorrow?" Jack moved to stand beside her, his hand firm on her shoulder.

"Of course." Marco waved a hand. "I'm sorry."

"No, we are the ones who owe you an apology. This is new. Fresh."

"One thing." Marco's voice stopped them.

"Yes?" Kensington saw a flash in the man's eyes and moved closer before she could stop herself. "What is it?"

"Did Dante tell you about the house party? The one at Castello di Carte?"

"He suggested Jack and I should make the house party our first assignment, but he gave no further details."

"It's Pryce's vineyard. It's in the same appellation— the same grape-growing region—as my grandfather's."

Kensington was beginning to get a picture of Marco's involvement in the case and she wasn't entirely convinced Dante had done the young detective any favors. Had Marco simply been an expedient choice?

"Castello di Carte? I'm fuzzy on the translation." Jack's question pulled her from her dark thoughts. Something about the name tugged at the back of her mind. Her own knowledge of Italian was limited, but she sensed that she should know the translation.

"Castello di Carte." Marco's voice was solemn. "House of Cards."

Chapter 6

Jack waited until they were both settled into a cab, their driver practically leaping off the curb before the door closed, when he acknowledged Marco's parting words. "Please don't tell me I'm the only one who thinks the name Pryce gave his vineyard is oddly ironic."

One slender eyebrow lifted at his suggestion. "Ironic or calculated. It could be nothing more than a clever ploy."

"Or a subtly veiled clue."

"Or we're giving Pryce too much credit."

All three options were a possibility, and Jack turned each over in his mind. *Was* Pryce clever? From Marco's account, Pryce was clearly savvy enough to avoid any hint of detection with whatever was going on in the vineyard. And Marco, along with the rest of the Italian Special Forces, was equally sure Pryce was involved up to his eyeballs.

"Something I'm still not fully understanding." The face of her phone lit up and Kensington glanced at it before dropping it into her lap. "Why would Pryce even concern himself with the Italian drug trade? Diamonds, I get, but not the drugs. And I'm sure it's a lovely piece of property, but the man's not *in* the wine industry. The vineyard is small, only one location, so it's not like it's producing mass quantities of wine."

"That could make it the perfect cover. It would be easy to assume the vineyard was a vanity purchase and pay it minimal attention. The rich aristocrat who wanted to own a vineyard and fancy himself a winemaker."

"True." She shifted in her seat, grabbing at a roof handle as their driver took a particularly sharp turn, before pressing her point. "But even if Pryce is looking to run afoul of the authorities, he's not producing enough wine to make it worth his while. How much could he possibly smuggle in a year? Certainly nothing that would make him a player."

Jack turned her words over in his mind. "What do you think he produces in a year? Fifteen hundred cases? Maybe two thousand?"

"At most. It's just not that much when all's said and done. Why would Pryce risk his reputation, his status and his ambassadorship for something that can't be scaled to any real degree?"

A flicker of a memory ran through his mind. "I did some research on the Italian wine industry in advance as I investigated whether or not I wanted in on this job. There are over two million wine producers in Italy, which would make it an easy place to hide any activity. Especially when you add on his built-in diplomatic immunity."

She tilted her head, assessing, then nodded. "There's that, too."

"So where does that leave us?"

"A cheekily named vineyard and a drive to Tuscany for a house party."

His gaze snagged on the phone in her lap, the face once again lit up. "No one leaves you alone on that thing, do they?"

She glanced down and shrugged, but he didn't miss the small smile. "My sister and grandmother included me on a message string tied to wedding planning. Tell me, do you prefer tulle or Irish lace?"

Jack fought a shudder and offered up a quick smile instead. "I'm sure she'll look gorgeous no matter what she wears."

She tapped out a quick reply without sparing him a glance. "Hmm. Clever."

"A man says the wrong thing too many times and he eventually learns."

"Your sisters teach you that one?"

"And a few misguided relationships that didn't end well."

Those magnetic blue eyes lifted off the screen before she added another eyebrow raise to punctuate the moment. "Is the great Jack Andrews suggesting he's been domesticated?"

The shudder that had threatened ran down his spine in full force. He had avoided thinking about old relationships for years and it was hardly the time to start. "Let's just say with maturity and wisdom comes an ability to lead with a compliment. No domestication required."

"Maybe you've just honed that clever tongue to perfection."

He wasn't sure if it was the sad figure Marco had cut in the bed that made him want to reach out and embrace life or simply that elemental tug that wouldn't leave him in her presence, but he leaned forward, mischief brewing in his veins. "Perhaps I can give you a demonstration of just how clever I can be?"

Where he thought he might meet with resistance, he got a loud laugh instead. "You're incorrigible. And persistent. Can't forget that part."

"I'm a man who knows what I want."

Her gaze remained warm but her voice held the steely notes of business. "So does that mean you want this case?"

"Who are we fooling? Was there ever really any doubt? For either of us?"

"Not really."

"So why are we fighting it so hard?"

Jack saw it the moment the meaning underlying his words registered. The humor and attraction flitting across her face expanded with the sweetest notes of delight before she shut it down.

And the light mood in the cab fled right along with it.

An irrational spear of anger pierced the flirtatious atmosphere he'd done his level best to maintain, replaced with a devilish urge to fluster her.

So how was it he was equally flustered?

He'd worked long and hard to keep his relationships with women in check. He never struggled—never lost his balance—yet this one small woman had him in knots.

And he had no freaking clue what to do about it.

He was prevented from saying anything further as their hotel came into view ahead of them. *Just as well.*

"Why are we back at the hotel?"

"We should pack some smaller bags for the drive to Tuscany." He thought of the firearms he'd had sent in advance to the hotel. "Among other things."

"Don't we have to go see Dante first?"

"To accept the job? You want to be there with me for that?"

"Hell, yes." She stopped and frowned. Considered. "But it's probably better if I don't. He's already got a stick up his very macho ass about me. Why don't I stay behind and see what I can dig up on Castello di Carte?"

"You sure?"

"You're not the only one who's learned a few lessons. Besides, if I'm not there you might get a bit more out of the very unhelpful Dante."

"I don't think his reticence earlier was for my benefit."

"Well, it certainly wasn't for mine. Share some of what Marco told us and see if you can uncover anything else."

"Aye, aye, Chief."

She winked as she slipped out of her door. "Don't you forget it."

Jack ordered the driver to wait until Kensington had cleared the front door of the hotel. It wasn't until she faded from view that he took his first easy breath of the day.

Kensington roamed her hotel suite, the plush carpet and vividly colored walls offering little comfort to her jumbled thoughts. Jack Andrews was a problem.

As someone used to solving problems, it was extremely vexing to know she had one she didn't know how to handle. Damn, but the man twisted her up in so many knots she didn't know whether she was coming or going.

And she never felt that way. Ever.

Of course, if she'd just give in to this crazy attraction between the two of them she could put them both out of their misery. Which was the second part of her problem.

Had she ever been this mind-numbingly attracted to any man before? Oh, she'd dated plenty. Each and every one of her dates had been suave and pleasant, self-assured of their place in the world.

And every damn one of them had been as boring and unappealing as day-old toast.

That was why no one lasted past a handful of dates. She

kept them at arm's length and, if she were honest with herself, did it willingly.

Her phone rang—a rousing samba ringtone that she'd associated with Rowan—and she smiled before answering, already anticipating the call with her younger sister. "Hey there."

"You've been suspiciously quiet."

"Hello to you, too. And what do you mean? I'm out on a job. Besides, I told you my feelings on tulle or Irish lace."

"You totally sided with her."

"Um. Yeah. Not only do I think it'll look beautiful on you, but I can't believe you're even trying to argue that one with our very Irish grandmother."

"Finn said the same thing. Some champion he's turning out to be."

Kensington thought of her future brother-in-law and held back the laugh. Although their grandparents had been skeptical about Rowan's new relationship, it was short-lived once they got to know Finn and his fierce devotion to their youngest granddaughter.

And then they fell in love when they realized how crazy Finn and Rowan were about each other.

Add on his Irish heritage that matched their grandmother's, and the initial chilly reception morphed into almost blind acceptance within weeks.

"You totally ignored my other text. The one without Grandma on it."

Kensington thought momentarily about playing dumb and pretending she'd missed the text but dropped it. That tack never worked with Rowan. Hell, it never worked on anyone. "I refuse to answer messages that ask me if my partner's ass is as juicy as it's purported to be."

Rowan's voice took on the slightest pout. "All I wanted

was a simple yes or no. And don't try to tell me you haven't looked."

She had peeked. More than once.

"Come on, Rowan. We're doing a job together. That's all."

"That's what I said about Finn, and now I'm debating tulle or Irish lace."

"There's no debate. Go with the lace."

"You know what I mean, Kenzi."

Kensington fought a heavy exhale—like Rowan would miss *that* through the phone—and also knew protesting too much would only make her sister think she'd won the argument. "You and Finn were meant to be. Since you were kids, really, you were meant to be. Jack's a business adversary. It's different."

"It doesn't have to be. Besides, enemies to lovers sounds like a hell of a lot of fun."

"What have you been reading?"

"Your face every time his name comes up."

Rowan had always played dirty and Kensington could only admire the neat, effective response. "I have an outstanding poker face."

"Not according to Molly. She said you were mad as a nest of hornets over the flowers the other day."

"Office gossip. Nothing more."

"Kenz. Come on. It's me. I'm not taking this back to Grandma or telling Finn. It's just you and me. Can you maybe admit you find him attractive? That you like him, just a little bit?"

"He's an attractive man. A powerful one, in a way that's attractive and not insulting. He respects me. Respects my intellect."

"I'm surprised your panties haven't fallen off due to that fact alone."

"Rowan!" No matter how hard she tried to stay immune, even Kensington couldn't hold back the laughter at that comment.

"You know it's true. You like smart men but most of them don't appreciate that you're a smart woman. Clearly one who does gets you."

"Maybe."

"Oh, there's no maybe about it. So I'm going to give you one more piece of advice and if you're as smart as you think you are, you'll take it."

"What's that?"

"Don't let that brain of yours talk you out of this. You're entitled to a bit of fun and an excuse to let go. Take it, my dear, overanalyzing sister. Please."

"I don't do casual."

"Well, maybe you should give it a whirl. You might surprise yourself by enjoying it."

Kensington struggled for something to say, even as Rowan's suggestion took immediate hold, sprouting deep roots.

"Oh, and one more thing, Kenzi. You still haven't answered my question, which, in my devious-minded opinion, only reinforces my point."

"About what?"

"Jack Andrews's very fine ass."

Hubert Pryce walked the perimeter of his vineyard, supervising the preparations for the weekend's house party. The decorators had been there all day, transforming the property into a lush wonderland of twinkle lights, and he wholeheartedly approved of their efforts.

He swirled his wineglass, satisfied at the rich legs that coated the bowl, visible in the reflection of the bright white lights. The vineyard had been one of his most favorite purchases—a home as well as a good investment—and he never failed to enjoy this particular locale. The fact that it made for an excellent entertaining spot, all while giving him an upper hand with his guests, worked equally well.

Shifting his gaze to the row of grapes beyond the house, he walked toward the land. He had a staff who kept the vines in top shape, but he still fancied himself the brains behind the operation.

After all, it was his knowledge that had them producing some of the region's most outstanding vintages a mere five years after taking over the property. While all his neighbors produced the red table wine everyone in Italy gobbled up, he was already garnering a reputation as Italy's version of a *garagiste.*

Many used the moniker as an insult, but he took no offense. The garage wines—small boutique-sized vintages that commanded a premium—that had evolved in Bordeaux in the past two decades were some of the most sought throughout the world. He was determined to do the same for Italy.

Only he'd do it better.

A light rustling caught his attention and he nearly stumbled over his chief of staff, crouched at the end of one of the rows. "Holden?"

The slender man unfurled himself with quick movements before coming to his full height. "Ambassador. I'm sorry if I startled you."

"I've told you that you don't need to call me ambassador."

"It's your title."

Hubert narrowly avoided the sigh at the young man's rigid formality. "Of course. What are you doing out here? You've made it abundantly clear on several occasions that you're not a wine fan."

"I'm confirming the preparations."

Hubert gestured toward the vines. "In the dirt?"

"I dropped my glasses."

Hubert resisted the urge to laugh. Holden was clumsy, but he managed Hubert's schedule with finesse and an iron fist. "Come. Let's get in out of the cold. The days have been lovely but the evenings grow cool quickly and I'd like to review the remaining arrangements for tomorrow."

"Of course."

Holden kept pace as they walked to the house, his long strides always balanced just shy of Hubert's own. He marveled at the skill—that such a long-limbed, often-clumsy man could control his gait so easily—before abandoning the thought in favor of another glass of wine as they entered the house.

"The special forces team assigned to your detail called. They'll be sending in two new agents."

"Oh?" He stopped himself midselection of several pieces of cheese before focusing on Holden. "What's wrong with the team I have?"

"Nothing, but they're not taking any chances. They also feel the two individuals they've assigned to you have a slightly higher qualification than those who usually manage your security."

"What sort of qualifications?"

"Are you familiar with Jack Andrews or Kensington Steele? Their dossiers were provided late last month."

A vision of lush dark hair and a stunning slash of cheekbone lit up his memories. "I remember Ms. Steele."

"Both have been vetted for their dual ability to blend into the background yet stand out as trusted advisers and respected guests. The police believe you need that additional layer to prevent any unfortunate incidents."

"I'm hosting a dinner party, not playing a game of cat

and mouse." Hubert forced a light laugh into his words, even if something simmered like a fire on low in his gut.

Protection? Additional security detail?

"Is there any reason to worry?"

"Nothing specific, but no one wishes to take chances with your safety. There was an incident at the Cantina DeAngelo winery earlier this week."

Hubert pictured the withered old winemaker who he saw often on his visits to town on the rare weekends he could stay. "I've heard of no incidents. What happened?"

"You didn't know? Signor Giuseppe was murdered."

The simple answer, delivered without any inflection, pulled Hubert up short. "Murdered? What? When?"

"The other morning. They've only released that it was an intruder on his property. I've tried to stress your interests are not the same as the general public, but the police remain stubbornly unwilling to share any further details. They claim it was an unfortunate incident, but no one wishes to take any chances, Ambassador."

"Of course."

It was a long while later, long after Holden had departed back to his room, that Hubert still walked the floors. He'd done a quick computer search on Giuseppe's death and wondered at the limited details. Something like a murder was big news in this quiet part of Italy, yet there had been limited discussion of the matter.

Hell, there'd been no discussion of it. For two days, he'd been oblivious that a man who lived three kilometers away had been murdered on his own property.

Of course, he knew his perception was skewed. He'd lived in the rarified air of international relations for so long, his life was far from normal. Yet it still bothered him that he knew nothing of his neighbor's violent passing.

Had Holden kept it from him? Holden was excellent at

his job, but Hubert knew full well the man managed him. Most of the time he accepted it because Holden Keene got things done.

But now?

Now perhaps it was time to do some digging of his own.

Chapter 7

Rowan's words ran through her head on a loop. A maniacal loop that whispered over and over that she needed to take the leap.

Onto Jack Andrews.

It didn't help the man had sexy forearms, just visible beneath the rolled sleeves of his dress shirt. And masculine hands. And firm, *capable* fingers that flexed on the steering wheel as he navigated them through the Italian countryside.

The fact she was getting flutters in her belly over the man's hands meant this had gone *way* too far.

Desperate for something to say to keep her mind on business, she glommed onto the first thing that popped to mind when she saw the car's brand icon stamped in the center of the steering wheel. "This is quite the rental car."

"I'd say we look the part."

"In a two-hundred-fifty-thousand dollar sports car?"

Jack's grin flashed in the darkened interior. "But don't ya love how she purrs?"

"You do realize this will draw significant attention to both of us."

"That's the whole point."

Although they'd talked about their strategy in broad terms, the opportunity to dive a bit deeper into their approach was a welcome respite from the thick strands of attraction wrapping her skin in tight bands. "The attention's supposed to be on the ambassador."

"No. *Our* attention's supposed to be on the ambassador. Drawing everyone else's away is to our advantage."

"You're not afraid of standing out."

"Darling, it's a fait accompli. You'd stand out if you were wearing a paper bag."

Just like that, those strands of desire wrapped even more tightly around her, nearly choking in their intensity.

Was this what attraction was supposed to feel like? As if all breath were being leached from your body? If anyone had asked, she'd have quickly said she knew what sexual attraction was. She'd had comfortable, enjoyable sexual relationships in her past, and just because she'd been in a dry spell of late didn't mean she didn't like sex.

But nothing in all her thirty years had prepared her for this wild, uncontrollable need that hummed—no, *demanded*—beneath her skin.

She needed to get her mind back on work, so she said, "It hardly matters what either of us looks like. What matters is that we get this job done with a minimum of fuss. Marco's convinced Pryce is our guy and Dante agrees. But what if they're wrong?"

"Wrong?"

"Of course. The worst thing we could do is walk into this job and assume they're right."

"Even if that's why they hired us."

"Come on, Jack. You know as well as I do the buyer's not always right, no matter what they seem to think."

"No, but the evidence against Pryce is pretty damning."

Kensington mentally called up the files she'd reviewed in her hotel room after her call with Rowan. "His vineyard has been the source of suspicious activity. Nothing more."

"Dante said they know there's a drug cartel operating out of the region. Add on Pryce's diamond access in his home country and we've got a winning combination."

"But Pryce hasn't been named with the lot of local thugs. That's the problem. It's suspicious, but it's not proven and that has concerned me about this job from the start. Especially since we become a handy excuse for Dante's team in the event they're wrong."

He lifted his gaze from the road. "You think they're wrong?"

"I'm not convinced they're entirely right."

"You find something on the computer search?"

She thought back over the endless screens of data she'd searched through, including Pryce's college transcripts, a copy of his marriage certificate to his first wife and a copy of his immunization records. The man had high-up connections and several offshore investments, and the lack of anything incriminating had her concerned.

"I didn't find anything. Or let me say I didn't find anything that connects him to something terribly shady. He's paid a bit too much to people in high places and contributed to more than a few widow and orphan funds, but nothing screams drug dealer and diamond smuggler."

"The man's the ambassador from Tierra Kimber. You have to go there. Have to walk into this with the understanding it's not only a very real possibility, but also a sound line of questioning."

She did have to go there but hadn't gotten that far in the limited time she'd had between her call with Rowan and the prep for the trip. "Nothing popped on this review but I'll look harder for that next."

His hands flexed on the steering wheel as he took a turn off the main highway into the town they'd be staying for the night. With almost a will of its own, her gaze riveted itself once more on his body and Rowan's teasing words from earlier came back in full force.

What would be the harm in giving in to their attraction?

She was young, healthy and unattached. And from his work schedule it was evident the man didn't sit in one place for all that long, so there was no reason to think anything would drag out longer than their time in Italy. A quick affair would suit them both.

"You weren't at the hotel all that long. I'm surprised you found as much as you did."

"I was distracted by a call from my sister."

"More discussion of the dress?"

"Among other things."

"Oh?"

She didn't miss the note of interest that sparked in his word and swiftly pushed past it. "She's not sure why I'm not enjoying more of Italy, despite my repeated explanation that I'm working on a job."

"Ah, so that's where the Steele love of fun went. To the baby of the family."

"I'm fun. A lot of fun."

"You sure about that? Because your need to reassure me smacks decidedly *not* of fun."

The light tease was more than evident—in fact, she wasn't sure why she wasn't letting it roll off her back the same way a similar taunt from her brothers would—but something about the joke stung. Way down deep, where it mattered.

And just like their morning visit to Marco, when her tears had welled up without warning, that same hard prickle of emotion spiked the backs of her eyes.

When had she become so serious?

She wasn't lying—she did have fun. Had occasions where she let go and let loose. But how long had it been?

And why did the sudden realization she couldn't remember only make those tears stick stubbornly to her eyelashes before a few spilled over to her cheeks.

"Kensington?"

"Hmm?" She was grateful for the darkness outside the car, but scattered lights throughout the small town ensured she wasn't completely invisible where she sat next to Jack.

And his next words confirmed he hadn't missed the waterworks. "Are you crying?"

"No."

"Kensington." He slowed the car, but there was no place to pull over, which she was incredibly grateful for.

What had come over her? And why was the damn urge to break down and sob so close to the surface? "It's fine, Jack. Just keep driving."

"Did I say something? I'm sure you're a lot of fun."

A small laugh bubbled up over the tears at the immediate concern. She'd seen it often enough with her brothers— men simply did not know what to do with a crying female. "It's not that."

"Something else?"

"It's everything. Marco. The city. Memories. I'm not sure why they've hit me so hard, but there you have it."

As excuses went, it was lame but not entirely untrue. The trip and Marco's loss *had* churned up uncomfortable thoughts.

"Memories of your parents?"

"For what we lost. For what they lost. I know what Marco is going to go through. And although I'm sure his grandfather had a long life, the fact that Marco brought the threat to his door is going to leave a mark. A deep one that won't ever go away."

The raw notes of her sorrow tugged at Jack, tearing at him in small, painful gashes. He'd intended the joke about her having fun to poke at her a bit and lighten the mood, but his words had done the opposite.

Although he knew Kensington's tough exterior likely had its roots in the childhood pain of losing her mother and father, he had also suspected she had a steely core that had nothing to do with loss and everything to do with who she was.

Which made it that much harder to watch her suffer.

"Tell me about them. You talked about your mother this morning. Tell me something else. Something about your dad."

Silence stretched out between them and he feared another well of tears, but when she finally spoke her voice was strong and clear. "My father was scared spitless over horror movies."

"Really?"

"And, of course, all four of his children have a deep and abiding love for them."

"Slasher movies?"

She nodded and he saw the edges of a smile before he heard its match in her voice. "The gorier the better. And if the story's inspired by a spooky legend, we will hunt down every book or website that backs it up."

"Creepy."

"Absolutely."

"So why not just leave you to watch them alone?"

"Because we had Steele movie night every Saturday night, and each person got to take a turn choosing the movie."

Jack saw where this was going as he did the quick mental math. "So four out of every six weeks saw horrifying buckets of blood, guts and serial killers in the Steele family room."

"Yep."

"What did he like?"

"Oh, he regularly made us suffer through foreign films and art house movies. A really lucky weekend was a Hitchcock flick."

"Payback's a bitch."

"But they make for really lovely memories."

The sign for their B and B lit up in the glare of the car's headlights, and her light giggle floated up as he took the turn onto the small street. They'd booked rooms in the same town as Pryce's vineyard. "I still remember the night he had his head buried for two hours in my mother's shoulder."

"If she looks anything like you, I'd say he was a wise man." The small O of her mouth had his own laugh welling up. "Just because I made you cry doesn't mean I have any intention of holding back my interest in you."

"Why do you do that?"

"Do what?"

"Say things that make it very hard to remember why I'm not going to sleep with you."

Need, hot and heavy, drilled itself into his body in time with her words.

"Wasn't expecting that one, were you?"

"Do I lose guy points if I say no?"

"I'd say you just added a few with that response."

"Good. When I have full control over my tongue again, I'll come up with some pithy retort."

He pulled into a small dirt parking lot off the side of the hotel. The moment he cut the ignition, she reached out and laid a hand on his arm. "Thanks."

"For what?"

"For making me remember something good when all I had in my thoughts was the bad."

He nodded, suddenly unable to speak.

And for a man who made a good portion of his living by knowing what to say, that was an unnerving thought.

Holden waited until the château quieted for the night before he headed back downstairs for a glass of bourbon. He had free run of the place, but after his discovery in the vineyard earlier, he wasn't anxious to incite any additional questions. He did have a chance to plant an extra pair of glasses in the dirt in the event he needed a convenient excuse, but it still wasn't worth taking any additional risks at this stage.

Pryce was fairly easy to manipulate, but there'd be several extra pairs of eyes this weekend and he couldn't afford any slipups. The cocked-up shooting at the DeAngelo vineyard had been trouble enough for the week.

Damn Carlo and his hot head.

The thug had shared his concerns about Marco DeAngelo a few weeks ago, and Holden had given specific instructions to wait and play a bit of cat and mouse with the detective. But did Carlo listen?

About as well as Pryce, which was *no, not ever.*

So he now had Carlo in hiding, the man's reckless attack on Marco—who had the damn nerve to survive—putting them all in jeopardy. And to make it worse, now he'd have to go and take care of Carlo in the middle of the plans for the ambassador's house party.

Damn amateurs.

He'd spent his life hiding his true self behind a veneer of competence and, when necessary, subservience. Unlike most others of his acquaintance, he watched and listened and he knew how to patiently wait for the right moment when everything came together.

Like this weekend.

The house party was important, and the individuals invited had been handpicked for their global influence and highly regarded reputations. Although he had his own plans, the chief of staff for the ambassador had opened doors of his own. Tierra Kimber had come up in the world. Once considered a country of little consequence, the rich veins of diamond deposits and the increasing focus on becoming a major player in world politics had caught the notice of people who mattered.

Which meant he had access to all the dark, depraved places he sought.

He had plans and he was so close to seeing them come to fruition. The diamonds he was smuggling out of the country and into the hands of a well-funded terrorist group were going to make him a very rich man—and a powerful one to boot.

So why the hell was he stuck still doing a boatload of dirty work?

His hand trembled slightly as he splashed several fingers of liquor into a tumbler. Here he was managing the hit on a useless underling, ensuring the weekend went off without a hitch and now dealing with the intrusion of Andrews and Steele.

The file on the two security experts was slim—the Italian police hadn't provided any information beyond the basic—but a quick internet search had turned up a fair bit of information on both Jack Andrews and Kensington Steele.

However, because it was all fluff pieces, he was damn sure going to keep an eye on them. No one attained the level of success and reputation they both possessed and managed to erase their digital footprint.

Not unless they did it deliberately.

Which meant he was going to keep very close watch on Mr. Andrews and Miss Steele.

Just like those glasses he'd buried underneath the vines—a prop in the event he needed one—he'd prepare for any eventuality with the elegant duo.

And when they slipped up, which they'd inevitably do, he'd be ready to leap.

Kensington scrawled a few notes as she scrolled through yet another layer of yet another website. The usual insomnia had struck shortly after eleven and she'd been at it for more than three hours already, digging through electronic trails and the story of a life in ones and zeroes.

Yet no matter how she dug, Hubert Pryce kept coming up clean.

"Where the hell are you?" she muttered before reaching for the mug of coffee she'd made from a small travel dispenser in her room. And then nearly choked on the cold, hard taste as it registered.

Disgusted with the fruitless search and the miserable excuse for caffeine, she slammed the lid of her laptop closed and reached for the phone. It was only around eight at home, but even if it had been the middle of the night she'd have no qualms about calling her brother.

"Yo."

Heavy sounds assaulted her ear and she dragged the

phone away to confirm whether she'd hit the correct contact. "Campbell?"

"It's me."

"Where are you?"

"Family night at McBane Communications."

"Why do you sound like you're in the bottom of a barrel?"

Another loud sound echoed through the phone followed by what sounded like several screaming children. "I'm in the dunking booth. Abby's rented out the pier to kick off the holidays. It's a corporate event."

"Got it."

"What's up?"

"Aren't you concerned about getting your phone wet?"

"Perk of marrying into the head of a communications company. The waterproof covering."

"Clever."

"What's up?"

"I'm frustrated and I thought my hacker-extraordinaire brother might have a few suggestions for something I may have overlooked."

"You've got the skill for electronic forensics. I just know how to get in and out of the system."

"Not tonight."

She walked him through the problems she was having, pleased when he immediately clued into what was bugging her.

"That's just it. I can't find a single damn thing this guy's done wrong and I've been at it for a while. Do you think he's hidden it?"

"Wouldn't be unheard of, especially if he's into as many things as he's suspected of. But it's still odd. You know how to find dirt, and the lack of any is a red flag all by itself."

They traded a few more ideas and he gave her a few more strings to tug before they wound down the call.

"You sure you don't want some help?"

"I may need your assistance at some point, but right now let me try these threads. Thanks."

Campbell hesitated for the briefest moment and she thought she might have lost him to a dunking. "I talked to Rowan earlier."

"Yeah?"

"She said you're knee-deep in this job with Andrews."

"We're about to be. We only landed in Rome this morning."

"You doing okay?"

With the skill she'd honed through years of practice, she layered the subtle note of disinterest into her voice. "Of course."

"You're good at that."

"At what?"

"The deflection act. Come on, Kenzi. It's me."

"What do you want me to say?"

"I don't know. Maybe the truth. Are you doing okay? Are you in over your head? Do you need help?"

"What, exactly, did Rowan tell you?"

Despite the four thousand miles that separated them and the screaming families in the background, she heard the frustration loud and clear in her brother's heavy exhale. "Not much. That's what's got me worried."

"Look. I'm not going to have this argument with you." Before he could push back, she pressed on. "You've clearly got a bit between your teeth so whatever I say you won't believe me. And it's after two in the morning here and I'm not in the mood to argue. Thanks for bouncing a few things off me."

A loud grunt echoed through the phone before she heard a big splash of water.

Clearly her brother finally had gotten dunked.

Saved by a well-placed softball was all she could think as she disconnected the call. She tapped out a quick text to tease him about the dunking and confirmed she was heading to bed when she heard a soft knock on her door.

"Kensington. It's me. Open up."

Jack stood on the other side, the soft lighting in the hallway forming a halo around his large form. "What are you doing up?"

"I could say the same for you. And since you've been blowing up my phone for the past three hours with emails, I knew you were still awake."

She gestured him in. "Why didn't you turn the phone off?"

"I never turn my phone off."

"Well, you can turn off email notifications."

"It's fine." He crossed to her computer, his gaze on the small notepad she kept on hand. "You've been sending me updates but I thought maybe you could put it all together for me."

The image he made caught her up short and she had a momentary lapse in thought as she simply stopped and stared at him. An old gray T-shirt stretched taut across his chest, and she could see a small hole at the side of his waist that gave a tantalizing glimpse of skin. Navy sweatpants completed the outfit, and all she heard was the devious voice of her sister as she'd studied the firm outline of his rear end when he'd turned to cross to the desk.

She'd swear the man didn't have an ounce of fat on him. Although his suits didn't exactly hide his taut form, the workout clothes definitely showed his body off to full advantage.

And hoo boy, had her hormones sat up and taken notice.

He pointed toward her notebook. "So what'd you find?"

"Not much." She swallowed hard and fought for composure. "There is simply nothing to be found on this man, no matter how hard I dig."

"I've been doing some digging of my own."

"On what?"

"The timeline since Pryce purchased the vineyard and when the Italians began getting a read on him."

As an avenue of inquiry, it was brilliant. And it reinforced once again just how sharp and on point Jack Andrews really was.

"And?"

"He's had the vineyard for about five years but the issues only kicked in within the past twelve months."

"What changed in that time?"

"I haven't found that yet." He looked up from the notepad. "But I'm here and you're here and two heads are better than one. Especially when one of those heads is yours and has your electronic investigation skills."

She sneaked around him to the desk to get to her laptop. Or at least that's what she told herself.

Until the scent of him filled her senses and heat rose up off his body, practically scorching her.

And the moment she felt all that glorious heat, she knew all the reasons she kept resisting him were baseless.

Without giving another thought to the calm, methodical behavior she was known for, she stepped up on her tiptoes, wrapped her arms around his neck and pulled him against her.

And then she took.

One moment he was looking at lines of scribbled notes and the next he had an armful of woman. Fortunately, no one had ever accused Jack Andrews of not knowing how to take advantage of an opportunity.

Despite the urgent, all-consuming passion arcing between them, he stopped, unwilling to let the moment pass him by. With gentle fingers that might have trembled from the need coursing through his system he brushed a lock of hair behind her ear. "Hi."

"Hi." She murmured the word before the hands that settled around his neck pulled him close.

And then he took.

Her lips were soft under his, the sweetest welcome as she opened her mouth. His tongue slipped inside the entrance, a slow, erotic play that mimicked what he longed to do with their bodies.

He wanted to take things slow—wanted to savor the moment—but the racing of his pulse and that crazy, driving need for her kept pressing him on. The hands that played around his neck drifted, grew more frantic as she ran her fingers down the length of his spinal cord before settling at his hips. With demanding pressure, she pulled him closer into her body, the thin material they both wore doing nothing to hide their mutual desire.

"Kensington." The word—just her name—dragged from his lips as he pressed a line of kisses along her jaw, then down her neck. She tilted her head, allowing him better access, and his body tightened painfully at the soft moan that whispered across his ear.

He wanted this woman. It was so fierce—so elemental—he burned from the inside out.

The desk behind her back provided leverage and he lifted her onto it, then moved to stand between her parted legs. Her thighs rubbed against his hips, telegraphing her need, and in that moment he knew he'd never seen a more beautiful woman.

Bright. Vivid. Passionate.

And his.

The urge to brand her as his own rose up with such a fervor Jack wondered that the feelings could really be coming from within himself.

When had this happened?

And how had she sneaked past the armor he kept in place—firmly in place—at all times?

The jarring peal of a phone tugged somewhere at his subconscious, even as it vibrated against the back pocket of his sweatpants. He ignored it as he continued the erotic byplay of their lips, teeth and tongue.

Until the insistent ringing finally broke through his sensual haze and he pulled away from her on a growl. "What the hell?"

"Jack?"

"Sorry." He ripped the phone from his pocket, intending to throw it across the room when his gaze landed on the number. "It's Dante."

"Now?" Confusion warred with the rapid return of reality as her sloe-eyed gaze drifted to the face of his phone. "Answer it."

"Seriously?"

"Jack. It's after two in the morning." The gentle press of her hands against his chest offered another layer of reality and he fought the urge to growl once more.

"Fine." He hit the answer button with his free hand but kept the other firmly wrapped around Kensington's waist. "This is Andrews."

"There's been another murder."

Chapter 8

The soft light of dawn danced around Dante Ferrero's frame as he stood over the body. The neck was twisted at an odd angle, and even the foggy haze of early morning that had settled over the vineyard couldn't hide the unnatural placement or the bullet hole that speared clean through the man's head.

"You're an awfully long way from Rome." Jack clutched a paper cup the proprietor of their B and B had managed to dig up despite her protests that she had no idea what "to go" meant.

Dante stood up from where he knelt by the body and rubbed his hands together. "And yet clearly not far enough away for this to touch on my case."

"Don't you mean our case?" Jack's gaze drifted to where Kensington stood with two members of Dante's team, her perusal of the body already completed. "You know who he is?"

"Carlo Morelli. Low-level enforcer for one of the region's biggest dealers."

"What'd he do?"

"If I had to guess, I'd say we're looking at the trigger-man who took out Marco's grandfather and attempted to silence Marco."

Jack had suspected as much, but his desire to speculate had vanished the moment he'd heard the words, *"There's been another murder."*

His gaze drifted across the rows of vines. The body had been found at yet another of Tuscany's endless vineyards about four kilometers from Pryce's, in the opposite direction of the DeAngelo farm. The local examiner had estimated time of death shortly after midnight, and it had been sheer serendipity one of the local farmhands had stayed late, carousing with the son of the vineyard owner and stumbling over the body on his way back to a small bunkhouse on the property.

The young man had lost the contents of his stomach along with his buzz and was still crying off and on while sitting on a small porch off the back of the main house.

Jack stood still to absorb the scene. Although there was no one to back up the farmhand's alibi, nor the owner's son's, early review of the site indicated the body had been dumped at the edge of the property. The local police would do their job, but the question of guilt was pointed elsewhere.

On Pryce?

Once more, Jack turned over what he and Kensington already knew of the ambassador. Both couldn't hide the fact that something seemed out of their reach, but what? And no matter how much he enjoyed working with her or how much he valued her insights and her quick mind, had he made a mistake bringing Kensington in on this? They hadn't even been in Italy twenty-four hours and they were dealing with another murder.

Images of the two of them wrapped up in each other assaulted his senses. She was a bright, vivid, *vibrant* woman and his decisions had put her in jeopardy. A sick curdle of fear coated his stomach, turning the coffee he'd drunk over and over in hard, choppy waves.

He'd let her go before he risked her safety. Would watch her walk away, secure in the knowledge she wouldn't be hurt. He knew how to watch those he cared about walk away.

Was more comfortable with that outcome, anyway.

Only this time, he'd live secure in the knowledge she was safe. Protected. Alive.

Dante interrupted his jumbled thoughts. "We texted him a photo and Marco positively identified the man as his attacker."

"Where's Carlo been for three days?"

"In hiding, most likely. Nursing his wounds. Marco's grandfather got a good hit on him with his vine clippers." Dante gestured toward the dead man's bandaged arm. "That's several days old."

"Have you ever seen any problems like this in the region before? I find it hard to believe murderers are running rampant along the countryside."

"Hardly." Dante snorted, his gaze dropping to Carlo's body before he glanced away.

"You said the drug cartel's been here for a while." Jack pressed on, anxious to gather as much knowledge as he could. "Has there been anything like this?"

"No. The guys around here, big as they may think they are, are still small business. The big dealers are in Rome. Milan. The guys out here work a little, manage their business and then play a lot. But when all's said and done, they're small time."

"So someone's trying to up their game."

"Or take out any local competition."

Jack stopped and considered that angle. "You think this is a turf war?"

"It's why we've been watching Pryce so closely. Someone with his power and clout could significantly change the game in these parts. Make himself a player if he chose."

A player in the region's drug trade.

As theories went, it was as good any other, but something still rang false for him. Pryce had shown absolutely no evidence of being a career criminal. So why start now?

"Are you and Miss Steele ready for the weekend's events?"

Jack caught sight of Kensington once more, her phone glued to her ear as she nodded repeatedly to whatever was said on the other end of the line. "Of course."

"There's a possibility things will further escalate during the party."

"We're prepared."

"That's why I hired you. Both."

Kensington still fought the residual effects of nausea at the sight of Carlo Morelli's body. He'd been killed quickly, but none of it changed the fact the man had a bullet in his head.

Their game of "observe and report back" for the weekend had grown considerably more dangerous.

"You okay?" Jack's voice was low but contained a subtle note she'd not heard there before. Fear.

"I'm fine. Not sure I ever want to eat again, but I'm doing fine. I'm sorry I missed the discussion with Dante.

My brother called me back and I made the mistake of mentioning a dead body."

"Isn't it the middle of the night in New York?"

"The Steele family isn't known for outstanding sleep habits. Add on he was still mad at me for not calling him back earlier despite a text that said I was going to bed, and I got an earful. He's now gone from concerned to highly concerned and threatening to tell my grandfather."

"Maybe he's right."

Kensington stilled, his words doing more to effectively silence her than anything else could have. "Excuse me?"

"I'm serious. I know neither of us expected a cakewalk, but this job is more dangerous than either of us anticipated."

"I'm up to the task."

"It's too much. There's too much risk."

She tamped down on the urge to rant and rail, just as she had on the call with Campbell. Yelling got you nowhere and it was an immature reaction to a situation that only served to put the other person on the defensive.

That's what she told herself.

Even as the words spilled from her lips like bullets. "Why the hell do you think this is too much? Are you saying you want me to walk away?"

"Yes."

"Think again."

"This is my job, Kensington."

"Which you've formally subcontracted me on, which makes it my job, too. Don't get cold feet now."

The statement was so absurd—odd, really—but what was even more odd was the image that filled her mind's eye of the two of them standing inside the jeweler earlier that week, a large diamond winking off her hand.

Trained operatives didn't get cold feet.

But those in relationships did…

"This is because of earlier, isn't it? Because of what almost happened between us?"

"No. Not really."

A small tick quivered at the corner of his eyelid and she pressed her point. "Well, what is it, Jack? No? Or not really?"

"You're in danger. I couldn't live with myself if something happened to you."

"That's the risk we take. The risk we both take each and every day based on what we've chosen to do with our lives."

"But I brought you here."

"And I *chose* to accept the challenge."

"Why are you being so stubborn?"

"Pots and kettles." She nearly added the oldie but goodie "if the shoe fits" but stopped at the last minute at the bleak look that rode his dark gaze.

"I'm going to be fine, Jack. We both are. You brought me in on this for a reason. Trust that."

"It's not you I don't trust. It's the situation."

"We're partners. We've got each other's backs. I've got yours and I have every confidence you've got mine."

Somewhere down deep she knew the argument wasn't finished but opted for a hasty retreat when Dante gestured them once more over toward the body.

And even though she knew she was right, she couldn't dismiss the small shot of alarm that slithered down her skin when she turned around and saw Jack standing in the vineyard all alone.

Kensington evaluated her wardrobe once more as she towel-dried her hair. The rest of the morning had gone about as well as expected—which meant she and Jack had gone to their separate corners when they returned to the B and B and hadn't spoken since—and she was anxious to get on to Pryce's *castello.*

The sooner they got to the bottom of what was going on, the sooner they could wrap things up and leave.

Another ending.

Why did it feel like her life was full of them?

She normally resisted anything that smacked of mawkish or maudlin, so it was with some surprise when she sat down hard on the edge of the bed, a silk blouse clutched in her hands like a lifeline.

When had everything gotten so complicated?

At its core, she knew the fact she harbored feelings for Jack contributed to her confusion, but if she were honest with herself, that wasn't the entire problem. Although intense, that attraction to Jack was relatively new.

The ennui and sense of dissatisfaction, however…well, they'd been hovering around her like a blanket for the past few years.

The distinctive ring of her phone—a rousing rendition of the William Tell Orchestra Rowan had programmed on all their phones to signal Liam's call—effectively interrupted her thoughts. It never failed to make her smile that Rowan had tied their older brother to the song best known for the Lone Ranger.

"Liam. Isn't it the middle of the night?"

"Hello to you, too." The cultured baritone of his voice that so reminded her of their father helped banish the last of her scattered thoughts. "And I'm in London right now."

"On what?" She flipped through the mental Rolodex of jobs they had going and puzzled at his location.

"A date."

"Oh."

"Which is only the side benefit of the trip. Finn has a few job leads I'm investigating."

Rowan's future husband had been the source of several strong leads in the past few months and they were nearly to the point of needing to turn down business. It was a funny—and fortunate—position to be in. "Well, don't let me keep you from the latest vapid model-slash-actress who's likely waiting for you."

"My latest model-slash-actress is a lovely young woman named Gemma. And she can wait until I find out why you were spending your early morning hours with a dead body."

Damn Campbell. "Good news travels fast."

"Fill me in."

It was pointless to argue, so she ran Liam through the details of the job—her impressions, thoughts and questions—and was grateful for her brother's steady presence.

"Someone's working behind the scenes."

"Jack and I think so, too. The Italian government's convinced it's Pryce. That's why they have us investigating him, gathering enough evidence so they can swoop in and effectively end the smuggling."

"And then remove him from the position."

"Exactly."

"I don't like that you and Jack are doing their dirty work."

"For a fee, Liam."

A low, barely muttered curse was all she heard before he pressed on. "Not everything needs to come down to money."

"No, but we did make a decision to help people for a fee. That's what I'm doing."

"All while offering the Italian government a convenient

excuse and the ability to publicly deny any involvement. If the government's wrong, you and Jack take the blame."

"I'm well aware of that."

"So what's the upside?"

"Contacts with another government. The opportunity to work with another colleague. And the satisfaction of a job well-done. We don't take the easy jobs."

"Yeah, but when did they get this hard?"

Her brother's words hung there for a moment and she pulled herself from the case she was currently working on. "Is everything okay? Why are you really in London?"

"I told you. I'm relaxing. Mixing a bit of business with pleasure."

"Anything else?"

"Why would there be anything else?"

"You tell me."

"There's nothing to tell except this—watch your back. Andrews has a great reputation but he's an independent. Hell, the man doesn't even have employees—just contracts with a bunch of freelancers for his jobs."

"What's his business model have to do with anything?" As arguments went it was weak—and she wasn't sure why she was defending Jack—but good old-fashioned sibling rivalry prevented her from taking too much advice from her brother.

"He's a lone wolf and he's made quite a career on that. Don't get caught up."

"This coming from the proverbial lone wolf of our family."

She heard the smile through the phone before the whip-quick response. "Takes one to know one."

The heavy knock on the door pulled her attention. "I need to go."

"Be careful, Kenzi."

"You, too."

She disconnected and couldn't help staring at the phone for the briefest moment. Her brother had always been private, but that had only intensified of late. Was he burning out? He'd had several intense jobs over the past year and this wasn't the first time she'd begun to suspect they were taking a harder toll than any of them had expected.

The heavy knock came again, followed by Jack's urgent voice.

"Kensington. Let me in."

She filed away thoughts of Liam, promising herself she'd revisit them when she got home and actually saw him face-to-face, and dragged open the heavy door. "What's the matter?"

"Nothing."

"Then why were you banging on the door?"

"Would you have preferred a telegram?"

His retort was so unexpected she simply stood back to let him in. "You sounded like there was a problem."

He didn't speak until the door closed in his wake. "I'm standing in the hallway, a bag of firearms in my hand and I heard housekeeping coming up the stairs. You'd knock urgently, too."

"You've got guns?"

"Of course."

She knew it the moment the shock coursing through her registered on Jack. The urgent expression he'd worn since she opened the door faded, replaced with grim resignation. "You don't think I'm letting you walk into Pryce's house unarmed, do you?"

"We hadn't discussed it."

"I thought it was a generally acknowledged fact. Did you bring any of your own?"

"No." Her mouth snapped closed, and she had a moment of sharp regret that she'd been so careless and forgetful. It had been a while since she'd been in the field and it showed.

Oh, how it showed.

"Do you know how to use one?"

His question effectively pulled her from her self-recrimination as indignation rose up swift and strong. "Of course."

"Good. Take this." He dropped the Glock into her hands, the heavy weight of it firm in her palm.

"I'm not sure where I'm going to put this with my skirt and blouse."

"Do you have a jacket to go with it?"

"I do, but it's hardly weekend attire."

"Add a scarf and you'll be fine." When she only stared at him, he added a cocky grin. "I've got older sisters, remember? Scarves always bring the party."

"You're a very odd man."

"And your shock smacks of a woman clinging too stubbornly to gender roles."

"Excuse me?" The hauteur was back and she wouldn't apologize for it. "I most certainly do not do that."

"You sure?"

"I was raised at the hands of incredibly liberal parents and grandparents. Everyone got treated equally and everyone was expected to pull the load. Male or female."

He glanced up from where he secured a wicked knife to a sheath on his ankle. "So you don't maneuver people in the ways you think they'll best respond?"

"Is this a job or a psychoanalysis?" She reached for the canvas bag Jack had set on the bed and began digging for a shoulder holster.

"The way we've been dancing around each other, I'd say it's both."

"I'd say it's self-absorbed and irritating."

"If the shoe fits, babe."

"And there you go again with that cocky smile that says you'll keep flirting with me like I'm your latest toy."

The smile fell abruptly. "I don't do that. And you're a smart, savvy woman, not a toy."

"Yes, you do that. The moment gets rough and you crack a flirty joke to swipe at me and keep me off balance."

"I've made no secret of liking you, Kensington. What part of that has escaped your notice?"

Her hands curled into fists but she wouldn't give him the satisfaction of watching her pace the floor like a crazy harpy. "None of it. Especially when you decided to use it this morning to try to convince me to go home."

"This job is more than we both bargained for."

"Would you ever suggest that to someone else you partnered with? A man, for instance?"

"I told you the other day, I avoid partners. I hire operatives and dispense them where they're needed. Clearly it's been a smart strategy."

"So why have you come after me?"

He stopped dragging things out of the bag to stare at her. "This job's bigger than both of us. But with our expertise, together we can get to the bottom of what's going on."

"Yet three hours ago you were ready to put me on the first flight back to New York."

"This isn't about—" He broke off, struggling. "I didn't expect we'd be up against murder by taking this job."

"Yet we are. You know as well as I do that we take what comes in this business. My brother killed his fiancée's half brother a few months ago to protect them. My sister was held at gunpoint in the middle of an Egyptian pyramid. We take the jobs we take, Jack, and we live with the consequences."

Anger sparked in the depths of his dark eyes as he stalked toward her, stopping just short of touching. "I'm well aware of the risks we take and the possible consequences. I'm also well aware you're more than capable of handling them. None of it changes the fact that I put you in the middle of this circus and I feel responsible."

She was working off of nothing more than sheer bravado as anger and that indefatigable stubborn spark arced between them. "I'm responsible for myself."

"Not if I have anything to say about it." His voice gentled, matched only by the hazy need that clouded his gaze.

Shoveling as much resolve into her voice as she could muster, Kensington took a step back. "I've made my feelings clear yet you refuse to move on. Refuse to take me at my word."

"Oh, you've made your reactions quite clear. In terms of what you're really feeling? I suspect it's a lot closer to the surface than you care to admit."

The spot-on character assessment was unnerving. But the realization he'd dissected her behavior so easily was mortifying.

"I can appreciate sexual attraction as much as the next person, but we've got a job to do. I refuse to forget that."

"And there's door number two. Revert to work. Pile on work. Use work as the excuse."

"You don't do the same? You can call it flirtation all you want, but it's not like there's some deep, lasting connection here. Your reputation precedes you. Your skills are impeccable and once a job's done you're on the move. In the past year alone, you've been on five continents. Hell, your own staff is a bunch of mercenaries, by your own admission. People you use conveniently, then discard. Nothing lasting. No commitments."

"You know what's involved in our business well enough

to know there are some damn fine freelancers out there. And I'd wager the House of Steele has done jobs in that many continents, too."

"Yes, but there are four of us. And we've got additional help now, in the form of Campbell's fiancée and Rowan's fiancé. And Campbell's got T-Bone, his right-hand electronics guy. Who do you have?"

"I've got all I need."

"Right. Yourself. You can take care of yourself and control the world."

"I've been doing it a hell of a long time, sweetheart. Don't you worry about me."

Without warning, he reached for her, snagging her off balance and dragging her into his arms. If the night before was a revelation, this was a plundering. Like a pirate at sea, Jack took and took and took and never gave her room to come up for air.

The large body wrapped around her absolutely consumed her. With lips and tongue, with hands and chest, with heat and passion. Through it all, she was unable to say no.

And she refused to pull away.

Just like the night before, Jack drank her in. Emotions he'd never felt before threatened to swamp him, yet he pressed both of them on. Pushed the limits of what had come to life between them, unwilling to play this game alone.

When had this thing—a light flirtation, really, nothing more—turned into a raging, all-consuming desperation?

"Jack." His name tore from her lips, pressed against his own. "Jack."

"What?"

"We have to stop."

"Can't." He captured her mouth once again before murmuring mindless words, as if they could somehow make her understand. "Want you."

"I want—" Whatever protest had sprung up died as she once again kissed him back. Her hands gripped his waist, bunched in the material of his dress shirt where it lay over his hips. Her soft moans listed up the edge of his senses, urging him on, forging this magic between them into something real.

Tangible.

Solid.

"We have to stop." The light press of her hands pulled him from the madness, dangling him just over the brink.

"Why?"

"We have a job to do. We have to get serious about what's to come."

"I'm very serious about this."

"I am…too. I am." She smoothed her hands over his shoulders, the motion doing nothing to cool his ardor. "But we have to focus. This is a distraction and neither of us can afford that right now."

Much as he wanted to argue, he knew she was right. They had to be at Pryce's in an hour. He had every intention of taking his time with her, and an hour wasn't going to be enough.

Hell, an entire week wouldn't be enough.

He took a step away from her before glancing down at the crumpled silk shirt bunched in her right hand. "Sorry."

"It's fine. I wasn't going to wear it, anyway."

"Do you have what you need?" He pointed to the handgun she'd set on the bed next to her purse. "Are you comfortable shooting that?"

"Of course."

"Because I have others."

Her hand snaked out, covered his forearm. "I'm fine. Really. And I'm a pretty good shot. Not quite as crack as my brother Liam but well above average. I can take care of myself."

The words caught him up short. And with it, a memory he'd believed long buried.

I can take care of myself.

His mother had said those same words to him years ago. Just before she left him and his two older sisters eating their breakfast to wait for the bus.

She'd never returned.

He was one of the lucky ones, he knew now, and had avoided the additional upheaval of the foster system or the courts. Kathy was already eighteen and both she and Susan were determined to keep the family together, so she worked and scraped by and managed to keep them afloat and together.

But no matter how hard Kathy and Susan worked to make a life for him—for all of them—nothing could fix his mother's leaving. And no amount of persuasion from his sisters had ever convinced him to stop searching for her.

Which was how Beatrice Andrews became his first job. He'd been twelve when she left, and his father was already a distant memory for all of them, but he hadn't stopped looking for her. Never gave up until that one day at the start of his senior year of high school. He'd gotten quite good in his computer class, perfecting an investigative form of hacking that got him in and out of various state computers while everyone else was still playing around with their C++ programming.

It was there he'd discovered the woman formerly named Beatrice Andrews when she'd gone off the grid. And with a bit more digging, he found the alias she'd taken on after leaving Washington. The one she'd used as she settled into her new life in Santa Barbara.

With minimal additional effort, he'd found her death certificate, written two years after she'd left her children behind to fend for themselves.

"Jack?"

Real concern blinked from Kensington's vivid blue gaze, effectively pulling him from his bleak memories. "Are you all right?"

"Of course. I'm ready to go. You?"

"Yes."

"Then let's get going."

Chapter 9

Wine flowed freely from waiters who circulated around the room and Kensington simply stood still and watched, familiarizing herself with their comings and goings. She'd already identified the kitchen schedule and every entrance in and out of the château. Now she was trying to get a handle on the traffic to and from the wine cellar.

Pryce was proud of his vintages, pouring several years' harvests for the assembled crowd all while highlighting tasting notes for each wine. The polite sips she'd taken from her glass had proved that he had some talent at wine making.

Or directing the winemaker, as the case may be.

Either way, his interest in the art seemed sincere enough.

Her gaze caught on Jack's across the room. They each wore an earpiece but the tight crush in the room had made any real level of communication difficult. What they had been able to convey on chance passes across the room had reinforced each other's intelligence while confirming areas where they still had gaps.

His expression was all business, his gaze ever watchful, but she still couldn't shake her last image of him. That strange look that had come over him earlier in her B and B room. Their kiss had been hot—erotic and all consuming—but it was the bleak look that rode his features after that had occupied her thoughts for the better part of the evening.

Something had triggered that response and she didn't think it was the impromptu rush of passion that had gripped them both.

Although she'd sensed a slight reticence in his personality—more from what she knew of his reputation than from any overt action—she'd assumed that he was a man who kept most people at arm's length. But that look?

It suggested secrets.

Or some long-buried hurt that wouldn't go away, no matter how badly one wanted it to.

She knew that look. She lived with that sort of anger and pain. And despite how deeply she valued her own privacy, she couldn't deny wanting to know more about Jack's past.

"Ms. Steele?" A deep voice, full of the cultured notes of prep school, time in Europe and the distinctly European background of his native country peppered Hubert Pryce's words. "I'm delighted you're here."

"Good evening, Ambassador."

"Hubert, please." The older man took her hand in a firm grip, placing a gentle press of his lips against her knuckles. Although his hair edged toward white, the pale features of his Dutch ancestors were readily evident in his ruddy complexion and vivid blue eyes. "My appreciation for your assistance this weekend."

The acknowledgment of her role gave her the briefest sensation of being off-kilter before she recovered, her smile broad. "It's my pleasure. You have a beautiful home."

"Thank you. I have always loved this part of the world and it delights me to now own a part of it."

She couldn't quite ignore the odd pinch to the base of her skull at his words. As someone who knew she was privileged—had grown up with both the luxury as well as the responsibility—she knew what it was to own things. And never in her life had she fancied herself owning a *part* of the world.

If her parents' early deaths had taught her anything, it was that you simply leased it for a while.

"I can see why. The grounds and your home are stunning."

"As are you, Ms. Steele. Or may I call you Kensington?"

She smiled broadly and hoped like hell Hubert Pryce didn't notice the gesture never reached her eyes. "Of course."

"Your reputation precedes you, Kensington. The Italian police speak highly of your skills and my chief of staff was well acquainted with your talents."

"I'm afraid I've not met him yet."

"Holden's around here somewhere." Pryce gestured with his full wineglass—his fifth by her count—and gave the room a vague glance. "The boy's always running here and there. He ensures I stay on point and make all my appointments."

Boy? The briefing she and Jack had received indicated the man was nearly forty.

"You're lucky to have him."

"Quite."

Pryce's gaze roamed her face, his irises never dipping below her neckline. She had to give him credit for main-

taining the proper decorum, even if his perusal still gave
her the willies.

"May I offer you some of our special reserve label? The
finest of the Castello."

"I'd love some." She laid a hand on his extended forearm and followed him toward the large bar set up on the
far side of the ballroom. "I'd also love to know how you
came up with the name of the vineyard."

"Castello di Carte? Don't you know?"

"Know what?"

Jack's heavy cough echoed in her ear at the blatant lie
but she refused to take the bait, never even glancing in
his direction.

"The name means house of cards. It's a bit of a joke."

She smiled once again and forced the subtle notes of a
purr into her voice. "Oh, do tell me more."

The overwhelming urge to beat something—namely
Hubert Pryce's round red face—coursed through every
fiber of Jack's being. And even though he wished like hell
he could do it, he was also amazed and awed at Kensington's suave handling of the man.

He'd watched her, the cat-and-cream smile that tinged
her lips as she spoke with the ambassador. The lightly flirtatious notes in her voice. The gentle play of her fingers
on his forearm.

She was a virtuoso and if he weren't so damn crazy
about her himself he'd probably enjoy the performance a
heck of a lot more.

Instead, all he had was the increasing urge to punch
something.

A flash caught his attention from the corner of his eye
and he reluctantly pulled his gaze from Kensington and
Pryce to investigate. He'd kept tabs on all the waitstaff all

evening, but the face exiting toward the wine cellar, decked out in waiter's clothing, didn't look familiar.

The slight tingle at the nape of his neck was all he needed to give free rein to his instincts, and Jack headed for the exit on the man's heels. A throng of waitstaff blocked his way—some with silver serving trays either full or empty of canapés and others pouring fresh glasses of Pryce's wine—and he almost lost his quarry a few times, but still he kept on.

The cool winter air greeted him as he followed the man out the back of the château and ran smack into a throng of workers on their break, huddled in circles smoking or relaxing.

"Scusi, signore?" One of the men stopped him, waving a hand to get his attention. "Can we help you?"

"Just taking a break." Jack kept his tone casual as his gaze continued to drift over the huddled groups, but the waiter he'd followed was nowhere to be found.

Another member of the staff tried a fresh tack with slightly more enunciated English. "We are happy to show you back to the party."

"No need." He held up his hands. "I'm sorry to intrude."

He gave the servants' area one long, last look before turning to go back inside. Whatever instinct had him racing for the door had struck equally hard in the man he'd followed. A few whispered murmurs echoed in his wake before Jack stepped back inside the château.

The long corridor that he'd followed out beckoned him, but a small offshoot behind the kitchen caught his attention and he decided to follow it. The house party was going to last all weekend, but this would likely be his only chance to use a cover of semi-drunkenness and a sudden hankering for a tour of the residence, so he took his shot.

Kensington's voice still echoed in his ear, her polite

platitudes to Pryce's increasingly insistent questions grating on his nerve endings. Jack followed the hallway to the end, then headed toward the back of the first floor. The external sounds of the party died even as he continued to hear them through his earpiece and he forced his attention on what he was doing and off the lush, seductive tones of Kensington's voice.

They'd been given a tour of the premises before the start of the party, but the ambassador's private offices on the first floor had been strictly off-limits. He'd not made a fuss at the time, taking the deliberate omission as a sign they were here for the right reasons. Following the hallway, he walked into a library and a small sitting room before he found the office he was looking for.

A large desk sat in the center of the room, its top devoid of anything but a thin laptop, a leather portfolio and a small personal desk calendar. Dark wood bookcases sat behind the desk and an oversize globe sat on a stand by the window. Add on the heavy accents of Louis XIV scattered around the room and Jack figured he'd walked into a designer's version of "Diplomat Decorating 101."

Ignoring the lack of anything original, he crossed to a small credenza strategically positioned between the globe and the desk. A tug on the drawer had it opening easy enough, which was his first clue he'd likely find nothing in the unlocked piece. The fact that the drawer held only packaged, sugary desserts and a few unopened bottles of bourbon only sealed the deal.

"Ambassador, I'm afraid I've hogged far too much of your time." Jack keyed in on the sultry tones of Kensington's voice as he moved to the file drawers on either side of the desk. "Much as I'm enjoying hearing all about the rich landscape of Tierra Kimber, surely I can't monopolize you."

"Of course not, my darling. Which is why I insist you have lunch with me tomorrow. Before we begin the afternoon's activities."

"I can't—"

Pryce steamrolled over her protests. "You must. Now, I'm afraid I do need to excuse myself."

"Of course."

Jack heard a muffled sigh before his name echoed in his earpiece. "Jack. Where are you?"

"Pryce's office."

"What?"

He smiled to himself as the second desk drawer slid out, unlocked just like everything else in the room. "Cover, darling. Keep your cover."

"My cover is fine. Yours, however, will be blown if you're not careful. What the *hell* are you doing in Pryce's office?"

"I had a shot and I took it."

"Well, get out of there. He just left the room to check on something and I have no idea where he's going."

The second drawer turned up nothing and he closed it, then glanced around the room for anything else to search. The oversize globe drew his attention once more and as he stared at it, Jack realized there was a small drawer at the bottom of the thick base.

"I've got one more place to check before I head out."

"Come on. We can do it later."

"I'm here now."

He heard the distant voice of a waitress, offering Kensington a refill on her glass, and knew the woman's presence was the only thing stopping their argument. The globe beckoned and he dropped to his knees before it. He pulled out his handkerchief, intending to use it on the heavy drawer, but the piece didn't budge.

With quick fingers still protected under the cloth, he ran his hands around the base, curious to see if he'd find a key in easy reach, but no such luck. He tried tugging on the drawer once more, testing to see if the stand was as sturdy as it looked, but all he managed to do was spin the globe by a few rotations.

Curious.

The desk and credenza held nothing, but an innocuous drawer in the globe was locked.

"What did you find?" Kensington's voice hissed in his ear and he heard the sharp click of her heels.

"I'm not sure."

"How far down the hall are you?"

"At the end. Why?"

"I'm headed your way."

"No. Stay in the main room."

"Like hell I will."

That same prickle at the back of his neck went off as he imagined her vulnerable and alone in the hallway. "Seriously. I'm finishing up. Go back and keep an eye on Pryce."

"He disappeared and I have no idea where he went."

The sound of her heels continued as a distant click in his earpiece. "And what do you propose to do if you run into him?"

"Same thing you're going to do. Play dumb and admire his artwork."

"There's no artwork in here."

"Then I'll admire his books. Or his furniture. Or whatever the hell else is handy. Just like you would have if you got caught."

Her voice brooked no argument and, yet again, he found himself on that odd precipice between being aroused and fascinated as all get-out and mad as a hornet the woman didn't know how to listen.

Oh, and scared out of your mind for her life. Can't forget that one, Andrews.

The door clicked open and Kensington slipped in, then closed the door quietly behind her. "What'd you find?"

"Unlocked drawers full of nothing interesting and this small drawer I can't get open."

"Did you bring picks?"

"No. Did you?"

"No, but I've got something almost as good." She dragged a bobby pin out of her upswept hair, letting loose a small curl that fell over her cheek. "Let me try this."

He stood back to give her space and light as she matched his knelt pose before the globe stand. "Keep watch on the door."

"And what's going to be your handy excuse after someone walks in?"

She smiled and pulled one of the hoops out of her ear. "Lost earring."

"That works."

Kensington went back to work, her fingers repeatedly plying the lock at different angles with the bobby pin. "How'd you end up in here, anyway?"

"I sneaked out when I saw something suspicious."

Her head whipped up from where she worked. "What? Who?"

"A waiter I hadn't seen before caught my attention. I followed him out back to the waitstaff's break area but he disappeared before I could question him."

"You think he was after something?"

"My instincts went off loudly enough that I wanted to go check."

"At least you had something to do. I had Pryce slobbering all over my hand as he regaled me with all of his feats of diplomacy."

"He's got his eye on you."

"Which I tried to keep in mind—" she broke off as she worked a section of the lock "—as I nearly fell asleep listening to him."

"He's dangerous."

"Which is why there are two of us here."

And there it was again. Complete lack of concern for her own personal safety or risk.

"Come on and get up. I can get my hands on some picks tomorrow morning and we'll do this again."

"I nearly have it."

"We've been missing too long and we need to get back out there. Especially since you've attracted the eye of the ambassador, your new boyfriend's going to get worried if he doesn't see you."

"He went off to take care of—" She broke off as the both heard the lock click at the same time.

Without waiting for her to agree, Jack reached for Kensington, snagging her around the waist and dragging her to the closest chair. Louis XIV wasn't the most comfortable, but it gave him a place to sit as he dragged her onto his lap and plunged his hands into the updo of her hair.

Abstractly he felt the pins give way, pushing at the stragglers to get his hands all over that lush mane. He heard her gasp as he took her lips with his own. Heard an even louder one as his hands settled on her ass as he pulled her closer on his lap.

The door swung open, a soft shout of "Hey!" speared in their direction.

Jack ignored it and tightened his grip on Kensington.

It was time to put on a show.

She thought she was prepared. Thought she knew how to handle the sensual assault that was Jack Andrews. But try as she might—even with a serious threat to both of them standing in the office doorway—she couldn't muster up anything past pulse-pounding attraction.

"Excuse me!" The sharp voice cracked like a whip and she pressed against Jack's chest before adding a rueful smile for good measure.

The ambassador's chief of staff, Holden Keene, stood in the doorway. She hadn't met the man yet, but Hubert had pointed him out while they'd talked earlier.

"Um…um…" She added a quaver underneath the layer of embarrassment. "I'm sorry."

"What are you doing in here?" Holden stalked across the office, his gaze slashing over both of them. Jack kept a firm hold on her when she tried to struggle off his lap, the movement clearly designed to highlight the tight rise of her skirt over her thighs, all while detracting from any noticeable bulges in her jacket where her gun was holstered.

"Jack!" She upped the pitch and added a giggle for good measure before struggling once more on his lap. The skirt rose another notch and she rubbed her thigh against Jack's, hoping to lift it yet another inch or two.

The answering spark of arousal in his dark gaze coupled with a quirk of an eyebrow had her making the movement once more. She couldn't resist tossing him a final, cheeky smile before she turned back to the other man. "Excuse us."

"How did you get in here?"

"Um…" She added the stammer once more but Jack beat her to the punch.

"Come on, mate. We were just looking for a quiet spot."

"This is a major international event, not a cheap motel. Officer Ferrero said the two of you came highly recommended, but I'm not so sure."

Kensington pushed off of Jack's lap and altered her tone, heading straight toward wheedling. "Please, Mr. Keene.

You can't tell anyone. This was a mistake." She tossed her head, shooting a dagger-filled glance at Jack, then turned back. "I have my reputation to consider."

"Perhaps you should have thought of that before disappearing from the party and your posts."

"Of course." She cast a glance down and saw the wash of bobby pins that spread across the floor. Pleased they offered some measure of cover from the one she'd dropped after working on the lock, she bent to gather them up. "Please just give me a moment to compose myself."

Holden stood with his arms crossed as she crawled on the floor picking up the pins. For his part, Jack had already stood and was shielding her body from Holden's view.

As covers went, they'd have put another proof point in the "accidental discovery of a careless couple making out" column if Jack had stayed seated, watching her pick up the pins, but she couldn't deny it felt nice to know he had her back.

More than nice, she admitted to herself, as she snatched the last bobby pin and got to her feet.

"We'll be going now." Jack pressed a hand to the small of her back and escorted her from the room. It was only when they'd reached the hallway that she took her first easy breath.

"Do you think he bought it?"

His fingers flexed on her back as they rounded the corner and headed toward the sounds of the party. "I'd say that trick you did with your skirt had his tongue lolling out of his mouth nearly as far as it did mine."

"Happy to use every asset at my disposal."

"That you did. Admirably."

She glanced at his profile, the strong slash of his jaw tighter than she'd have expected compared to his lighthearted retort. "We're okay, Jack. We got out of there just fine."

"You know he's not going to keep this to himself. How do you think your new boyfriend's going to react when he finds out you were making out hot and heavy in his office?"

"It's a house party. They have to expect a certain amount of indiscreet behavior."

The ballroom doors were ahead, but Jack stopped just short of them. "They're not going to expect it of the ambassador's security detail."

"If we get questioned, I'll say I lost my head. The ambassador did press a lot of wine on me in the past hour."

"You're missing the point. We were discovered. It's going to limit our ability to move freely for the next few days."

"Then I'll just have to work that much harder paying attention to the ambassador's boring stories."

She sailed back into the ballroom, unwilling to continue arguing the point. It might be small and petty of her, but Jack kept saying they were equal partners, yet he wanted to remain in control.

Something was in that drawer and they'd never have found it if they hadn't investigated the study. They'd both gone with instinct and it had paid off. Even if Holden did question why they were in the ambassador's office, he had no proof of them doing anything beyond engaging in an inappropriate make-out session.

They had nothing to worry about.

Holden surveyed the office and checked to see if anything was out of place. Although it was hard to argue with the scene he'd witnessed, he had no doubt Jack Andrews and Kensington Steele weren't in the ambassador's office for an illicit moment of passion.

He walked the perimeter of the room, looking for anything out of place, but found nothing. Frustrated, he crossed to the decanter of bourbon on the sideboard and poured himself a large glass.

He hadn't slept in almost thirty-six hours and he was just tired enough to consider snagging a few minutes of shut-eye. The events of the past few days ran through his mind as he took one of the uncomfortable seats the ambassador believed were evidence of his inordinate good taste.

Whatever.

Holden drained half his glass, then settled his arms on the rests of the chair. What had the two of them been doing in here? Although he'd seen the evidence of their interest in each other with his own two eyes, interest could be faked. Ardor and passion were tools like any other.

Yet…the brief moments he'd witnessed smacked of supreme sexual interest and nothing in the office appeared disturbed.

On a sigh, he attempted to settle once more in the torturous chair. He was tired, that was all. He'd check again in the morning with fresh eyes.

With his lids at half-mast, he reached for his glass once more and drained the contents. It was a play of the light, really, nothing more, that had him leaning forward to see what glittered in the carpet next to the globe.

Curious, Holden got up to see what it was.

A distended bobby pin.

He picked it up and inspected the front of the lock on the globe stand, then stared at the twisted piece of wire.

A twisted piece of wire that appeared to have been repurposed from its original job of holding the long dark locks of Kensington Steele's hair in place.

Chapter 10

The party finally came to a close around one in the morning. The ambassador's guests had happily drunk every bottle of wine he'd served and it was only when a few waved the white flag and headed for their rooms that others reluctantly began to get the picture.

"The ambassador throws quite the party." Kensington flexed her shoulders, and Jack didn't miss the subtle way her hand sneaked into her jacket to touch her gun. "And despite the revelry, it was quieter than I expected."

"Civilized. Some of Europe's finest power players, drinking wine and making deals."

"Exactly." She stared at the canopy of stars above them. "I can't stop thinking about that drawer. What might be in it."

"We've got two more days to find out."

"Holden never returned to the party."

"I noticed that." Pryce's chief of staff hadn't been seen

after discovering them in the office. "I also noticed when he was at the party, he blended in the background. Seems odd that a man like that wouldn't be more ambitious."

"He's paid to aid the ambassador, not do his own thing."

"But at an event like this?" Jack shook his head. "It doesn't play for me. He'd want to advance his own ends, even if his own ends are support for the ambassador, but he was noticeably absent from conversations."

"We need to look into him."

"First on my list for tonight." Jack fought the yawn that threatened and took a deep breath of the frosty night air. Several smudge pots were lit throughout the vineyard and the scent of gas swelled around them.

Another yawn came on the heels of the last and he didn't bother to fight this one. He hadn't had anything to drink since before the incident in Pryce's office, but a week of minimal sleep had caught up with him. "Do you think we should have made arrangements to stay?"

"Where? Every guest room's accounted for as are a few small living rooms that have been made up for guests. Besides, our B and B is just down the road and no one in Pryce's house can even see straight. I'd be surprised if anyone moved after their head hit the pillow, let alone attempt anything."

"So you don't think anyone else is going to attempt a make-out session in the office?"

"Nope. I think we get those honors, Ace."

The moon hung high overhead, illuminating Kensington in a wash of light. Her wry smile was infectious and he felt his mood lighten with each step.

He'd been alone for so long—had run every op with stoic efficiency—it was an odd pleasure to look over and share his observations on the evening's events.

The gunshot rang out, disturbing the late-night quiet

before it embedded itself in the thick bark of an old tree that rimmed Pryce's property. Jack leaped on Kensington, crushing her against his body and cushioning her as they fell onto the patch of hard-packed dirt acting as a parking lot for the event.

"Where'd it come from?"

He was already reaching for the piece in his holster when he heard the heavy thwap of feet echoing away from them. "Stay down."

"You can't chase after them." The words were hissed but he ignored them as he took off in the same direction as the retreating feet.

"Stay there!"

Jack thought he had a decent chance of gaining on the shooter until the long rows of grapes surrounded them and the footsteps became harder to follow. The rich soil that held the vines absorbed sound, as did the plants themselves, and he quickly grew disoriented as he flew down the long rows.

As the sound of the shooter got more and more faint, Jack acknowledged he'd lost the trail. He came to a halt as he tried to catch his breath and assess his surroundings. He hadn't paid any attention to where he was going as the shooter fled, and now he was awfully far away from Kensington.

As the moon slid out from behind the clouds, he realized just how far away he was.

And then he began to run.

Kensington sat up and put the car at her back as she waited for Jack to return. She'd nearly gotten up three times to chase after him but kept coming back again and again to his order for her to stay put.

Was he in danger?

Or would she put him in worse danger if she went charging off?

"To hell with it." She got to her feet and kicked off her heels, ignoring the cold dirt under her toes. She gripped her gun and started in the direction Jack had run.

She didn't get very far when a string of lights lit up the estate. Shouts echoed through the cold air as several of the waitstaff rushed outside. Cries of *"Signore"* and *"Signorina"* rang out as people rushed from the home like a colony of busy ants.

Several of the waitresses she'd seen moving to and from the kitchen surrounded her and she made out "Are you hurt?" and "What happened?" in their steady streams of concerned Italian. She did her best to ask if anyone had seen the shooter, but their concerned voices and focus on asking if she was hurt kept drowning out the question.

Jack strode out of the vineyard onto the back porch where they all gathered, and she let out her first easy breath at the evidence he was fine.

With her limited language skills, she reassured the people around her she was unharmed before trying once more to ask if anyone had seen the shooter. Vague smiles and a sudden inability to comprehend a word of English were the only reactions she received. By the time someone tried to suggest—with large hand gestures and very stilted words in English—that the car had made the loud noise that had brought them running, Kensington knew it was pointless to keep pressing the point.

It was only when Jack's arm came around her and he pulled her away that she finally stopped asking questions.

His breath hovered over her ear. "These people are too familiar with the ways of the world to give you any information. Your only saving grace is because they're familiar with those ways, they're not going to run to their employer."

"Where is Hubert?"

"Sleeping off his drunk, no doubt. It was only one shot and if you missed it, there wasn't anything else to hear."

"True."

He escorted her to her side of the car and she shook her head at the ridiculous selection. Who needed a sports car on bumpy dirt roads while undercover?

But she had to also admit it gave a certain sense of carelessness that only reinforced their behavior in Pryce's study.

"I think you accomplished what you set out to do."

He turned to her as he put the car into gear. "What was that?"

"We certainly made an impression tonight."

The events of the evening continued to keep her company as they walked into the B and B and her limbs shook with the lingering adrenaline. The main lobby was quiet but a fire still burned in the large, cavernous fireplace that dominated the far wall and several bottles of wine and fresh glasses were set out on a small sideboard.

"Join me for a nightcap?"

Kensington gripped her hands together, willing them to still. "I don't sleep well on the best of nights, so yes."

"Good."

She'd left her gun and holster locked in the car and both had gone a long way toward calming her down, but still, the trembles persisted. Slipping off the jacket she'd worn all night to hide the gun, Kensington dropped into one of the overstuffed chairs near the fire.

A large, lazy cat—clearly a full-time resident of the B and B—curled by the fire. As the warmth invaded Kensington's bones, the cat's stretching and purring helped calm her nerves. She had to give the tabby credit—as a species, they certainly knew how to live and take advantage of the moment.

Something she did far too infrequently herself.

"Making friends?" Jack held up two large wineglasses, their bowls full of a rich red that glistened in the firelight. His hands appeared to be tremble-free, a small, irritating fact that had ire sparking over the lingering fear.

"Intruding is probably more like it. I saw him open one lazy eye as I sat down and took it as an acceptable cue to scratch his ears." She took the proffered wineglass and clinked it briefly with Jack's before resettling in her chair.

Although they'd been over it in the car, she couldn't leave the subject alone. "You never saw the shooter?"

"No. I heard him but never saw him. Between his head start and his dark clothes, he had the jump on me."

"You assume it was a man?"

"I got the basic build and heft of his body. It was definitely male."

"It was meant for us."

"Yes." The grim truth painted his face in harsh lines and the hints of gray at his temples seemed more pronounced somehow.

"You still think the ambassador's *not* up to something? A locked drawer and gunshots?"

"I think the ambassador's one of many who may be up to something."

They traded theories for a few more minutes, neither coming up with anything that felt right. "Nothing's tripping my trigger."

"That doesn't mean it's not right."

"No." She swirled her wine, calculated. "But it's off, you know? Everything about this job is just off a bit."

"Yeah."

"Is that why you brought me in?"

Jack's gaze snapped toward hers, quicker than the path of the fire in the grate. "How do we keep ending up back at that place?"

"Because you broke your own personal protocol by bringing me in on this. You're the lone wolf, Jack. Even before we went up against each other, I knew that. Your considerable reputation precedes you. And you've made no secret the past day or so that you'd prefer to be on this job alone."

"I'm concerned for your safety."

"That's not a reason not to want me here."

"It's a damn good reason." He leaned toward her in his chair, the light of the fire sparking off his eyes in tempo with his seething anger. "We both dodged a bullet tonight, which only proves what a damn good reason it is. Don't forget that, Kensington."

"I haven't."

"Then quit looking for problems that aren't there. You researched this job. Went up for it. You were the perfect partner when I realized I couldn't handle it alone. There are too many facets to this one and it needs more than one set of eyes. And unlike the proverbial lone wolf, I know when I can't do it alone."

She wasn't sure why she kept pressing the point—why this persistent need to open him up and look inside kept nagging at her—but she did. She wanted to know. Wanted to know him and what made him the man he was.

The quiet stretched out between them and her gaze traveled over the tabby's black coat once more. As she stared at the large ball of fur, she let her errant train of thought spill out. "Simple creatures, really. They live in the moment and don't seem to worry about much. We could take a lesson."

"I get your point, especially after the last few days, but I don't think you're quite up to the task."

"No?"

"Would you really want to spend your life lazing it away?"

She knew he had a point—and also sensed there was something hovering just underneath the question. "No, I'm not interested in spending my life in idle pursuits."

"And with your family money, you could if you wanted to."

"You don't know my grandfather."

A light chuckle rumbled from his throat. "No lazing for the Steele children?"

"Are you kidding? I could parade a string of men I've done God knew what with and he wouldn't bat an eye the same as if I'd chosen a slothful life."

His gaze narrowed and she couldn't help but laugh at his sudden prickliness. "I'm sure he wouldn't be crazy about the men, either."

"True." She took a sip of her wine, turning over thoughts of her grandfather as she enjoyed the fruit on her palate. "It's always been important to him that my brothers, sister and I are productive human beings. It was to my parents, too, but we never had them long enough to really hear their opinions of us as adults. But my grandparents—" She broke off, unable to hold back the smile. "They definitely have opinions."

"How did you get started with House of Steele?"

"I'd call it a combination of personal initiative and grandfatherly intervention. Oh, and grandfatherly investment."

"I'm intrigued."

She gave him the quick history of how it came about—each of her and her siblings' skills coupled with their somewhat reckless natures had launched them on the path of the House of Steele, a high-end security firm whose first jobs were on behalf of their grandfather's well-connected friends.

"And it grew from there. Although we were all committed to the work, I think I speak for Liam, Campbell and Rowan when I say we never expected the success we've found. Or the incredible number of people who require our services."

"People have issues that need to be dealt with. That only seems to become more the case as one's bank account grows."

"What about you? How'd Andrews Holdings become the security powerhouse it is today?"

Jack's immediate withdrawal was such a surprise, she could only picture a similar reaction if she'd thrown cold water on the sleeping cat. "Same as you, really. An innate skill I've managed to monetize."

"I'd say it's more than that."

"Not really." He took a sip of his wine, his gaze averted, and the tenacity that had been a hallmark of her personality since birth reared up.

"Interesting reaction, Andrews."

"Not really. I've got a business, same as you. You know what goes into it and you know how competitive it is. There's really nothing more to say."

She stared into her wineglass for a moment and let him have his brood. She had a lot to say but she sensed pushing the wrong way wasn't going to net the answers she sought.

"You told me the other day at lunch that your sisters weren't involved in the business."

"No, they're not."

"Why not?"

"They're older than me and had interests of their own.

Both married and wanted families. Unlike your situation, Andrews Holdings hasn't been a family affair."

"How'd you get started?"

"My first job was a missing persons case."

"We've handled a few of those. They're an odd mix of investigation and sadness. Too often those missing don't wish to be found."

"This one certainly didn't."

The reticence was there, along with the very clear instruction not to trespass. Where her normal curiosity would have her pressing, she was surprised to realize her desire to know was steeped in something else.

Interest in Jack. A fascination about what made him tick. And the very real understanding that something in his past has created a dark well inside of him.

"Did you find him?"

"Yes. And it was a woman."

"And did she wish to be found?"

"She was dead, so her wishes no longer mattered. But it mattered to her family. Her children."

"I'd say so. I can't imagine the pain of not knowing."

"Of always wondering." He glanced up from his wine, his eyes cloudy with memories. "It's hell."

"You sound like you have some experience with that."

"I do. The woman was my mother."

Jack cursed himself a thousand times the fool as the words left his lips, but there was nothing to be done about it. Just as there was nothing to be done about the pity he saw flare high and bright in Kensington's eyes.

Just like there was nothing to be done when he'd had to share the news of his mother's life and death with his sisters.

They'd borne it and moved on.

"I'm sorry."

"Don't say that." The words snaked out, whip quick. He didn't share this part of his life for many reasons. The sympathy that lined her face being the chief one.

"Yes, but—"

"Don't."

He stood, effectively ending their conversation. "I'll walk you to your room. It's been a long day and we need to be back at Pryce's early tomorrow morning."

"Jack. I'm sorry I pushed."

"It's fine. Really." He stopped and knew she deserved better. "We all have things we don't discuss, Kensington. This is mine."

"Of course." She nodded. "Yes. Of course."

The walk to her room was quiet and she said nothing before she let herself into her room, the old-fashioned lock clicking securely into place after she closed the door.

"That went well," he muttered to himself after he'd closed his own door. "Like a root canal, only more painful."

Why the hell had he even said anything?

He'd spent a lifetime cultivating the gentle deflections that kept people from digging too deeply. Hell, he was a master at focusing on his female partners, ensuring conversation dripped with his interest and fascination for them, their work, their lives.

Yet he'd let Kensington Steele in.

Or rather, she'd sneaked in, quite without him realizing it.

His phone buzzed in his pocket and he dragged it out, surprised to see the email message. The jeweler he and Kensington had visited earlier in the week was sending his delighted felicitations once again and was inquiring to see if Mr. Andrews and his fiancée had selected a setting for her engagement ring.

He began to tap out a message when an idea got the better of him and he clicked on the phone number listed underneath the jeweler's email signature. Jack made the requisite small talk, all while apologizing for calling the man so late in his evening, but was quickly assured that the jeweler was available to him at any time.

"I do appreciate it. I was called out of town on business unexpectedly and I'm sorry to keep you waiting on our selection."

"Truly, it is no inconvenience, Mr. Andrews. Have you selected a setting?"

"The platinum band layered with baguettes that you sent photos of. That will be perfect."

"Exquisite. Excellent choice."

And also guaranteed to add several thousand to the price. Jack smiled to himself.

Although he and Kensington had intended to get back to the jeweler to discuss the history of the diamonds, their rush to Italy after Marco's attack had prevented a second trip. Adjusting on the fly, he revised his strategy and took advantage of the man's ready salesmanship and late-night follow-up.

Jack gave it another few beats before he dropped his bomb. "I was actually just singing your praises this evening to the Italian ambassador of Tierra Kimber."

"Ambassador Pryce?" An aura of reverence filled the man's words and Jack didn't miss the subtle scrambling on the other end of the phone. The distinct notes of a keyboard tapping could be heard.

Of course, the jeweler had a file on the ambassador. He no doubt kept copious notes on every major player who could potentially be a customer or influence his sales.

"Yes. I shared with him the exquisite beauty of my fiancée's diamond and how pleased I was that it was mined in Tierra Kimber."

"Their jewels are exceptional."

"The ambassador was quick to assure me that he's expediting additional jewels into the market in the coming months. I suggested he speak with you."

The lies tripped off his tongue and whatever momentary pang of remorse he felt at inflating the man's ego and expectations was squashed by the knowledge of how much he'd spent on the diamond purchase.

Still…he'd figure out some way to make it right once this was all said and done.

"Sir." The man's tone grew worshipful. "My thanks."

"It is my pleasure. If you would, I'd be pleased to share the information of your distribution chain to Ambassador Pryce so that he may ensure you're properly contacted."

The man quickly rattled off several names and that slight itch at the back of Jack's neck grew tighter as he jotted down the information. He really would need to do something for the man.

The image of a necklace made entirely of diamonds lit his mind's eye and he settled on a solution.

"One other thing before we hang up. I'd like to purchase a wedding gift for Ms. Steele. I saw a diamond necklace in the case next to the wedding bands."

"The strand of diamonds, Mr. Andrews?"

"That's the one. It will be perfect."

As Jack hung up, the cost of the piece still echoing in his ear, he glanced down at his notes and smiled at himself. He'd made more than a fair trade.

A heavy tray lay over his lap as Pryce skimmed through his morning correspondence. He abstractly added some butter to his toast as he reread Holden's account of the previous evening. The up-and-coming Milanese fashion designer he'd invited had agreed to an export arrangement that was more than favorable to his home country. They'd also secured venture capital for a Tierra Kimber software developer from one of Germany's leading IT specialists.

Excellent.

He flipped to another file and reviewed today's schedule and his gaze caught once again on the names of the security team who'd attend the noon briefing. Jack Andrews and Kensington Steele featured prominently on the list once again.

The knock at his door pulled his attention off the trim figure Miss Steele cut in his mind's eye. "Come in!"

Holden walked into the room, but not before he made a deliberate show of closing the door. "I must speak with you, Ambassador."

"Are we back to that? This is my bedroom, for heaven's sake. You can call me by my name, Holden."

"Have you read my report?"

"Yes. I'm incredibly pleased with last night's outcome. Two of our key objectives for the weekend have been met."

"Did you finish the report?"

Hubert glanced at the slim file. He'd only read through the top sheet so far. "No. What did I miss?"

"We caught a couple engaging in an indiscreet liaison in your office."

Hubert chuckled to himself at Holden's prim expression. "You know we plan for those sorts of impromptu events. Hell, I'd hardly call it a good party if some couple didn't go off and get amorous."

"It was Steele and Andrews."

"Ah." The smile abruptly vanished as he pictured the lovely young woman he'd shared a good portion of his evening with. "When?"

"After you departed to take several investors on a tour of the cellars."

"Have you alerted Officer Ferrero?"

"I was waiting to discuss it with you."

"Have them removed."

"You may not want to do that."

"What the hell, Holden?" Pryce worked to control his voice as he waved the file from his tray. "Is there something else in this damn dossier?"

"No. It's an impression more than anything else. I think they were looking for something."

His neck and cheeks grew hot as a shot of anger lanced through him. "What are you implying?"

"I believe we need to watch them. Keep a close eye."

Although he was embarrassed at the social cuckold, he had nothing to hide. "I've nothing to worry about."

"Still. We can't discount what they're about."

He'd had plans for Kensington Steele. Social plans that would leave no room for the talk of business. Although he'd have enjoyed continuing down that path, the news she had a *tendre* for Andrews—as well as his own history with her family he'd do well to remember—had him switching gears. He'd find out what she was up to instead. "Leave it to me."

Holden compressed his lips into a thin line and Hubert couldn't hide a small smile of amusement that bubbled up at the gesture. "You look just like your mother when you do that."

Chapter 11

Sleep had proved to be its usual elusive self and Kensington had found her way to a small gym the B and B proprietor kept on-site. The room was small, boasting only a treadmill, an elliptical machine and a small weight rack, but it would do. She climbed onto the elliptical, set a thirty-minute workout and then opened her tablet to review her email.

She'd had Liam looking into some background on Pryce with one of his old prep school friends. The man's father knew Pryce and Liam had worked his magic to do some digging.

She scanned through the email and her brother's careful, point-by-point list of details on the ambassador. There were a few new tidbits, including some of Pryce's social proclivities, which ran to a series of mistresses, but other than that she had the same outcome as always.

Nothing new.

Nothing suspicious.

And nothing that would give her and Jack a new direction to explore.

Which only brought her right back to her sleepless night and the endless thoughts about Jack. His mother had been a missing person?

She'd toyed with looking the woman up but something had stopped her. She lived with the fact that she regularly, and with no remorse, dug into the backgrounds of others.

Somehow it felt like a violation to do that to Jack.

Which was likely misplaced sentiment, but she couldn't shake the need to allow him his privacy.

"I was told I'd find you in here." Jack waved from the door, his voice carrying across the small space.

"Couldn't sleep."

"At all?"

She shrugged. "I got about an hour and a half."

"What's that make? Eight hours for the entire week?"

"I'm used to it."

Jack climbed up on the treadmill next to her and set the display. "Do you ever crash and get, oh, I don't know, maybe four or five hours a night?"

"I usually do. It's a tense time and I can't seem to settle, but I'll catch up after we get back to New York."

His gaze roved over her tablet. "You're doing work, too?"

"Reviewing an email from Liam. He did some digging with an old friend."

"I'm guessing by the look on your face he didn't find anything."

"Other than the fact Pryce likes to keep a mistress, a behavior he's maintained for his entire adult life? Nope."

"Maybe there's something in that."

"That the man fears commitment?" She turned it over,

considering, but quickly discarded the notion. "It's a huge leap from philandering to smuggling and drug running."

"Follow the thought with me." Jack moved into a light run, the heavy belt of the treadmill thwapping in light counterpoint to their conversation. "It's a common choice of powerful men. So common as to be cliché and overdone."

Something about the subtle disgust that rode his features at Pryce's choices caused her heart to turn over. "You don't approve?"

"Hell, no. Be with the person you're with or don't. Some things in your life should be all in."

Kensington searched his face, one moment stretching into two.

As if suddenly uncomfortable with her scrutiny, he shifted gears. "It also doesn't make any sense any longer. His wife's been gone nearly a decade. Isn't the very definition of a mistress the fact that they're secret pieces kept on the side?"

"I suppose."

"There's no side if there's no wife. They're just girlfriends he lavishes money on."

"I guess I'm still not following you. I'll grant you that Pryce doesn't have a lot of moral fortitude in his personal life. I still find it a leap that bad relationship choices suggest he's running drugs and smuggling diamonds."

"What if that's the whole point?"

She saw the spark—that illusive moment when two disparate pieces of information came together. "Like what?"

"Like how a mistress would be an awfully convenient conduit for diamonds."

Jack was still puzzling through the idea of Pryce and his mistresses as he and Kensington drove through the gates of Castello di Carte.

After the discussion the night before he'd expected some awkwardness with Kensington, but she hadn't brought up the subject of his mother again and he was hopeful enough to think the subject might have been tabled.

They'd discussed it. He'd put up the neon don't trespass sign. She'd backed off.

Done.

Even if he knew somewhere inside that a woman as bright and tenacious as Kensington Steele never left anything alone.

"I reviewed the schedule." She waved her phone. "The best time we'll have to get back into Pryce's office is just before lunch."

Case in point, Andrews.

"*We* can't go back in there."

"Then *I'll* find a way in. I can still use the earring excuse from last night since I didn't have to use it with Holden."

"You can't go back in there. We'll have to find a different way in."

"The earring's a perfect choice. And I can use the way we got caught last night to play the embarrassment card if anyone shows up." She pitched her voice to illustrate. "I'm so sorry for last night's indiscreet behavior. I just wanted to sneak in and get my earring and sneak out, blah, blah, blah."

"Blah, blah, blah?"

Her eyes were wide as she turned to him. "Well, yeah."

"Does anything faze you?"

"The two of us getting shot at, for starters."

He wondered if that had left as deep a mark as he suspected. Reaching for her hand, he grabbed it and squeezed. "You doing okay with it?"

"I'd feel a lot better if we knew what we were dealing

with. Who sends a warning shot and runs away? It smacks of amateur hour and that has me even more concerned than some trained thug who might have tried to shoot us."

He caressed her fingers once more before reaching for the gear shift and navigating them through the small dirt parking area. "Could just be a scare tactic. Or a warning that our motives aren't quite as hidden as we think they are."

"But why? The vineyard's full of people. There are better ways to scare two people than to start firing a gun."

"If it makes you feel any better, that's my first order of business today. The waitstaff know more than they're letting on." He thought about some of the guilty body language when he'd interrupted the smoke break last night. "I think I can find a few weak links and press my point there."

"You're going to flash those bedroom eyes at the waitresses, aren't you?"

"Whatever works."

"Which is the exact reason I'm going to lead the ambassador down the mistress path."

"Kensington—" He broke off when he saw the mulish expression settle over those gorgeous cheekbones.

"Yes?"

"Be careful."

She laid a hand over his and he took the briefest moment of solace from being on the receiving end. "I will."

Jack's carefully laid plans for the morning were shot to pieces about three minutes after they'd walked into the château. Houseguests milled around, their polite smiles not really hiding the excesses of the evening before. Several members of the waitstaff were the recipients of tongue-lashings for perceived slow service and too-hot coffee.

But it was a particularly unpleasant moment between a contessa and one of the servers over a cappuccino that gave Jack his opportunity.

The young woman was struggling against tears and attempting to shake it off as she walked back to the kitchen with the oversize cup of coffee. Jack gave Kensington a swift nod, suggesting he'd handle it, before he followed.

The bustling kitchen offered little privacy but he ignored the other employees in favor of consoling the young woman. *"Scusi?"*

"Yes?" The softly accented English gave him hope he'd struck gold with a woman he could communicate with.

"I couldn't help but notice what happened." He took the mug of coffee out of her trembling hands. "Are you all right?"

"I'm fine." She swiped at a few tears before taking a hard sniff. "I need this job."

"Of course." He added a conspiratorial grin. "I need mine, too. But come on. Take a few minutes. Plenty of other people are waiting on that bitch hand and foot."

At the tremulous smile and small nod, he gestured her toward the back patio the servants used for their break. Once they were settled on a small bench, Jack pressed his point. "I'm Jack."

"Sophia."

"Nice to meet you."

"You're here with the other woman. The one on security."

He wasn't surprised by Sophia's notice—the servants missed nothing and anyone who thought they did was woefully misguided. He'd gotten more information over the years from those *not* in a position of power than from those who were. "I am."

"Why are you out here with me?"

"You looked like you needed a friend."

"I usually don't cry over cappuccino. That woman was just—" Sophia broke off and looked around. "It doesn't matter. She's the ambassador's guest so she can behave as she likes."

"That's debatable." Jack waited a moment and gave the woman space to dry her tears. He considered how to ask her what else she might have seen when she offered up exactly what he was looking for.

"I saw what happened last night."

"Where?"

"Outside. At you and your friend. We all heard the gunshot."

"Do you know who it was?"

"No. I know it was a man but he didn't look familiar. Some of the men mentioned going to look for him but in the end, no one went."

He knew how hard it was to police one of your own. When you added on the rarefied air of "us" and "them" underpinning the ambassador's house party, he understood why these people were reticent to get involved.

"If you see anything, would you tell me? I won't let on you were my source, but I'd like to know what my friend and I are up against."

"I will. This place." She shook her head. "Something strange is going on here."

"How do you mean?"

"I can't explain it, but it hasn't always been like this. The ambassador. He's got…how do you say? Quick hands." At what must have been a dark gaze from him, she quickly rushed to make her point. "Not dangerous. Flirty. But he's not a bad man. But now? I don't know how to explain it."

"What changed?"

"I don't know. All I do know is things are different here

at Castello di Carte. I don't think I will interview to work another function again after this weekend is over. There are other ways to make a living."

"I'll make sure you're compensated for any information."

She glanced around, her gaze furtive, before standing once more. "This is a good job. Used to be a good job. If you can bring that back, no payment is necessary."

An unexpected rainstorm pulled the party fully inside for the afternoon and by four o'clock everyone had begun to climb the walls. With the action and movement of the night before, he and Kensington had been able to blend into the background, but the rainy weather stifled activity.

He and Kensington stayed on the periphery, moving back and forth between the kitchen and the main ballroom to keep some discernible distance from Pryce and his guests. Despite the constant movement, Pryce managed to corner him for an afternoon poker game and Jack knew he had to comply.

Several men were invited into a game, along with the crazy contessa from that morning, and everyone was quickly seated at one of three tables in the game room. Jack was curious to see how Holden also kept to the periphery of the room but reluctantly joined a table at Pryce's insistence.

Several of the waitstaff served as dealers and the game began with high humor and a lot of trash talk among the players. Whether from the day's boredom or the fresh bottles of wine that began circulating, Jack didn't know, but the games quickly grew heated despite everyone maintaining a veneer of polite gamesmanship.

Although he'd never put much stock in the Hollywood version of poker games—too often there were stretches of boredom, followed by three quick hands—but he couldn't deny what an excellent opportunity the game made to observe the other houseguests.

By his count, every man at the party was in the room, along with the contessa and a few other wives who wandered in and out during the course of the afternoon. By all accounts it would have been a perfect time to go raid Pryce's study if it weren't for the male-bonding ritual currently being played out over the baize.

"Aces over kings," the dealer intoned as Jack pulled in his winnings under the glare of a Brit who'd clearly thought the pot was destined to be his.

A loud guffaw from the table next to him indicated Pryce hadn't been nearly as lucky in his round and the man stood up, a good-natured smile on his face. Jack watched him from under hooded lids, curious to see how the man would handle not only losing, but losing in front of a room full of people.

Oddly enough, he appeared to take it in stride, slapping the winner on the back and excusing himself to the sideboard to open another couple of bottles.

"Andrews? You in?" Jack pulled his attention from his musings toward the Brit who was clearly aching to get his money back.

"Yep. I'm in."

Kensington tried several avenues to get to Pryce's study but every time she made a motion to head that way, something was going on out in the hallway blocking her passage. Several of the wine stewards were rushing back and forth with bottles from the cellar. When they weren't around, the waitstaff was running heaping trays of food back and forth to the impromptu poker tournament in the game room. Even the cleaning crew had been through, using the diverted attention of the majority of the party to get some additional dusting in.

With a sigh and the inner admonishment to get some freaking patience, she explored the other end of the hall, pleased to find a small, rather cozy library. A small table ran along the window and she crossed to it and watched the afternoon rain fall. Her earpiece echoed with the sounds of the game room and she heard Jack's good-natured laugh when he won a hand.

"Miss Steele."

Pryce's voice washed over her and she forced on a smile before turning toward the older man. "Hello, Ambassador."

"You look awfully lonely there, standing by the window."

The light cough that echoed in her ear assured her Jack heard the exchange and she used the moment to give him a sense of her whereabouts, too. "Just admiring the view from this beautiful library."

"Or pining."

He raised his eyebrows on the last word and she briefly toyed with saying something about her trip to his office the night before, but then thought better of it. If Pryce wasn't aware of her late-night visit with Jack, there was no need to offer up the information.

And if he did know, well, she'd bide her time and see how he played things.

"I'm not a woman who pines. It's unbecoming and it causes wrinkles."

His heavy bark of laughter warmed his face and something in the genuine smile she saw there ratcheted down her unease a few notches.

"I thought you were the instigator of the poker game, Ambassador. How is it you came to be in here?"

"I'm horrible at poker and was out of the game within

the hour. Besides, even if I did have the skill, it doesn't do for the host to win at his own game. It looks crass." He gestured toward an elegant old backgammon set, laid out on top of the small table nearby. "Would you care to play?"

She'd played the game as a child with her father and had enjoyed the strategy of it but hadn't played in years. "I'm afraid I'm a bit rusty."

"A quick reminder's all it takes. I find I'm not yet done with games for the day."

She took the seat he'd pulled out for her, settling herself in the plush leather. "Thank you."

One of the staff bustled in with tea and coffee service and she couldn't stop the small smile or the murmured whisper as she stared up at the ambassador. "Somehow I think you knew I was in here."

"I make it a point to see to all my guests, Kensington. Hospitality is essential in my line of work."

She requested tea as it seemed fitting for the bleak day. She also sensed the warmth would go a long way toward assuaging the cold that had settled in her bones since someone fired a gun on her and Jack the night before.

Once the woman left the room, Hubert proceeded to give her a quick reminder of how to play the game and then they were off. Despite their innuendo-filled conversation the evening before, Hubert made for a surprisingly pleasant conversation partner. His knowledge of many things was broad and deep and he knew how to blend amusing anecdotes into his stories.

As they reset the board for a second game, Kensington decided to go for broke. "I hope you won't think me too forward, but where was this version of you last evening?"

The heavy cough in her ear let her know what Jack thought of her direct strategy, but she was glad she'd asked the question.

And she was even more pleased she'd inquired when Hubert stopped juggling the dice, the clicking of the ivory going still in his hand. "Excuse me?"

"Forgive me." She waved a hand, feigning embarrassment at the forward question. She knew she'd pushed too hard, but the open curiosity in his gaze confirmed it had been the right hunch.

"Nothing to forgive. Please go on."

"It's just that you were so serious and, to be honest, a bit creepy last night. Today you're the consummate gentleman with a cache of very funny stories. What happened?"

"You're a direct woman."

One of her less desirable traits, Kensington well knew. "So I've been told."

"You're also rather like your father."

Whatever she'd expected Hubert Pryce to say, a reference to her father wasn't anywhere on her radar. "You knew my father?"

"I did."

"When? How?"

"We had mutual friends at school and I worked with him on a few projects when I was in the early days of my career, managing a financial portfolio in New York."

Kensington mentally flipped through all her notes on Pryce. She knew the man had lived in New York for a time, but she'd had no idea he'd had any interactions with her father. "When was that, sir?"

"About twenty years ago. I can still remember the picture of you he kept on his desk." Hubert leaned forward, his eyes twinkling. "Which is probably why I had that conversational poker up my butt last night. As attractive as you are, I can't help picturing you in that photo. Gangly arms and legs and pigtails."

She knew that photo and still had it in one of the spare

rooms in her apartment. She and Rowan were in shorts and T-shirts, their arms wrapped around each other as they ate ice cream cones at the Jersey shore. "The one with the ice cream?"

"The very same."

"I had no idea you were acquainted with my family."

"It was a peripheral acquaintance and I'm sorry I never got to know Charles better. His and your mother's death was a tragic shame."

A tight knot thickened her throat and she reached for her tea, determined to remove the well of tears before she embarrassed herself.

"There's no shame in grief, Kensington. Never be afraid to hide honest emotion."

"It's been a long time but I can't seem to stop the tears when unexpected memories hit."

"Time eases the pain, my dear. It doesn't remove it."

She ran a knuckle under her eyes, first one, then the other. "No. I suppose it doesn't."

"So." Pryce gestured to the board for her to play. "Now that we've gotten out of the way that I knew you when you had skinned knees, I hope I won't insult you by offering the assurance that my interest in getting to know you better isn't tied to your considerable beauty. I'm intrigued by what you do. Even more intrigued by the connection that brought you here."

"I was told that the Italian police briefed you and your staff on my presence."

"They did. Of course, that was after they failed to tell me that one of my neighbors over the valley was murdered last week. Surely your presence here is tied to the same."

The man's gaze was sharp and it offered a strong reminder that he hadn't reached his position by mincing words or backing down from a fight.

She weighed what to say versus what to omit and opted for a watered-down version of the truth, especially because it was evident Pryce was still unaware of the lone gunshot the night before. "The police are concerned, Ambassador."

"Hubert. Really, haven't we moved past the formalities?"

"Ambassador." She stressed the title with a smile. "There is no overt threat against you, but they'd prefer not to take any chances, either."

"I have security detail from Tierra Kimber."

"Yes, but you're on Italian soil. Officer Ferrero wants to make sure your time here is safe. Mr. Andrews and I are in a prime position to offer that. We know the requirements of your world and we know how to blend in."

"Are you suggesting Officer Ferrero's staff doesn't have quite the same pedigree?"

She smiled at that, hoping like hell the explanation had satisfied him. "Exactly."

"Nor, I suspect, are they in a big rush to disappear as the evening wears on."

Although she loved hearing about her father, she also wasn't naive enough not to know Pryce's march down memory lane was a deliberate move to soften her up.

I know you. Know your family. You can trust me.

But the reference to her liaison with Jack last night was a different sort of maneuver. One that said *you haven't escaped my notice, nor will you.*

"We're both highly capable of staking out your home and ensuring your safety."

"In my private office?"

"That was ill advised, sir." She made a show of staring down at her hands before looking back up at him. "You have my apologies."

"As I told Holden, a liaison or two is expected at a week-

end house party. In fact, it would almost be an embarrassment to go an entire weekend without one."

"Sir. It's not like that."

"Oh, no?"

"No." She stressed the word, even as she fought the
urge to touch her nose to see if it was growing. And fought
even harder the strangely seductive heat in her blood at the
knowledge Jack was listening to every word.

"What's it like, then?"

"Complicated."

Hubert picked up his dice and rolled for his turn. "The
best things often are."

Chapter 12

*C*omplicated.

The thought had kept Kensington company as the afternoon wore on. And although she knew she needed to focus on the task at hand—namely, just how clean or dirty was Ambassador Hubert Pryce?—all she could seem to wrap her mind around was Jack.

As someone who'd always prided herself on having a poker face, it was a bit mortifying to realize Pryce had seen right through the facade when it came to the subject of Jack Andrews. A mortification only reinforced by the fact that she was so distracted she'd gotten no closer to figuring out what was in that drawer in Pryce's study.

The only bright spot in the day, strangely enough, had been the time spent with the ambassador. Although she never had an opportunity to get to the study, several rounds of backgammon had given her some things to think about.

The man had access to the rarefied world of international relations. He also had a personal fortune worth well over two hundred and fifty million. Despite both ease of access and financial backing to run any scam he could imagine, something kept ringing false.

Did they believe him guilty because he was handy?

And if he wasn't responsible, why did all the evidence gathered to date by Dante's team indicate Castello di Carte at the center of what was going on?

Hubert's probing of her relationship with Jack had given her an opportunity to press him on his own past relationships, which was the line that still seemed worth tugging on.

Hubert spoke of his late wife and his grown children but deftly avoided any comment on the purported mistresses. He also spoke of his purchase of the vineyard, and in his stories about making wine over the past several years she heard true joy and pleasure in his words.

"He's had the vineyard for about five years but the issues only kicked in within the past twelve months."

Jack's intel had played in the back of her mind throughout the afternoon. Was there something significant about the gap between Pryce's acquisition of the vineyard and the time the Italian government began to suspect a problem?

Jack strode into the room. She turned from a small sideboard in the dining room, where trays of appetizers and crudités had been set up for the guests to take as they wanted. His hair showed the distinct signs of being run through repeatedly with his fingers and she couldn't hold back the internal leap of feminine appreciation that tingled under her skin.

"Let me guess. You got your clock cleaned."

"How'd you know?"

"Winners usually look a heck of a lot happier and—" she tapped her ear "—I heard it all."

A sly grin lit his face. "If I looked happier, wouldn't that negate the benefits of having a poker face?"

She added a bunch of grapes to her plate. "Not if the game's over and the winnings are in your pocket."

"You've got me there. I started off strong but lost my mojo about halfway through the game as I kept keying into your conversation. By then it was too late to bow out gracefully."

"So you heard our backgammon match?"

Jack had already begun to make himself a plate. "Heard it but couldn't see it. How'd it go?"

"Quite well. He was a perfect gentleman."

"I'd have excused myself from the poker game and ruined his afternoon if he weren't." The words were quiet but lethal and Kensington felt another trip wire go off under her skin that had nothing to do with arousal and everything to do with awareness.

This was a man who played at the highest echelons of their business. He knew how to take care of himself and anyone who got in his way. Which forced her to wonder why she kept forgetting that simple fact.

She fancied herself at the top of her game, too, but the increased time she'd spent over the past year and a half in the office had distanced her from the day to day. Her siblings had taken on their share of firefights and she'd stayed back to man the home fires.

It didn't seem fair. Certainly not to them, but she'd begun to wonder just how fair it was to herself. They'd built a successful business because they took risks, yet she'd taken very few of late.

"You can quit envisioning taking a bite of his heart as your spoils. We actually spoke quite a bit about my family."

"Are you all right with it?"

"I had no idea he knew my father back in the day."

Jack's grip tightened on a small knife before he resettled it back on an oversize cheese platter. "Perhaps the
ambassador knows more than we've given him credit for."

"My thought exactly."

The dining room was quiet so they took a seat and she
filled him in quickly, highlighting her take on the conversation and promising to give the rest of the details later.

Jack glanced around the room before he spoke. "You
get back into the study?"

"No, but we still have tomorrow."

"Things are wrapping up around noon, which means
we don't have much time."

"Then we'll figure out how to get in before we leave."

"Since you've become such good friends with the ambassador, why don't you keep him occupied and I'll take
the study?"

She smiled and batted her eyelashes in an exaggerated
motion. "Are you sure about that? If you leave me behind,
who are you going to make out with if you get caught?"

"I'm not going to get caught."

"You better not."

Although she'd intended to lighten the mood, the gravity of what he was doing left a surprising weight. Sort of
like with her family. Jack took the risk and she stayed safe
mingling with Pryce.

"Why am I getting the sense you no longer like this
idea?"

"It's not the study, per se." She stopped, hesitated.

"Well, what is it? This isn't my first job and there will
be enough confusion tomorrow to blend in. Worst-case
scenario I say I saw someone enter a door down the hallway and wanted to investigate. It'll be fine." He set his
fork down. "But what's bothering you?"

"It was the discussion about my family. Lately I've begun to question my role."

"You're the glue that keeps House of Steele running."

She'd always thought that, but the events of the past few months had shaken her to the core. Her brother and sister had both faced down serious threats and, although she knew they'd come out the other side—knew worrying about them after the fact was pointless—it had shaken her.

She exhaled the words on a heavy rush. "There's no glue if my family's gone."

The light had vanished from her eyes and Jack knew he was treading on sensitive ground. He'd understood the loss of her parents drove her in a very real way, but he clearly hadn't understood the connection between that loss and the next generation of her family.

Her hand was ice-cold when he laid his on top and he quickly twined their fingers together. That lack of warmth and the bleak emptiness in her blue gaze suggested what a fool he'd been to think otherwise.

"Talk to me about it." She tried to pull her hand away but he held tight. "No way."

She stopped struggling but the bleak gaze persisted. "I'm sorry. We're in the middle of a job and you don't need my mental B.S."

"We're partners on this job and there's no one else I'd rather have my back. You're smart and intuitive and you're an incredibly solid partner." He squeezed her fingers to make his point, then pressed on. "What does concern me is the lingering upset you have over your siblings."

"They could have died."

He didn't have all the specifics, but Kensington had mentioned a few times her brother Campbell and her sister, Rowan, had both faced difficult jobs. Campbell's while protecting his now-fiancée, Abby, and Rowan while investigating a tomb in Egypt with *her* fiancé, Finn.

"But they didn't. And from all you've said, they found the next phases of their lives, as well."

"But they could have. And I'd have been sitting home, getting the news through a phone call."

"Just like you heard about your parents."

She went still at his words. "This isn't like my parents."

"No?"

"They were in an accident. They didn't choose that. But with what we do, Liam, Campbell, Ro and I, we're making a choice."

"Seems to me you all do it willingly."

"I'd say so. I can't speak for them, but I know I do."

"And you're happy with your decision?"

"Yes."

"Then why do you assume they're not happy with theirs?"

"It's different."

"We can't live our lives in fear of what might happen. You and your siblings do good work. Important work. Work that changes lives. And obviously their lives have changed in the process for the better."

"And you? Is that why you do it? Why you take the risks?"

The change in subject was so rapid and unexpected, he faltered. "I'm not… We're not talking about me."

"But why do you take risks? What drives you? Your mother?" She stopped, her eyes narrowing. "Or maybe your father?"

The memory of sitting with his sisters over soggy cereal slammed into him with the force of a hurricane making landfall. Their mother hadn't even kissed them goodbye, just said she had to run to the store to pick something up before work.

He and his sisters had taken her at her word.

And that afternoon they came home to an empty house.

To this day Kathy hated to walk into an empty house alone. Susan kissed her kids three times before she left to go anywhere. And him?

He was the consummate professional, in and out of jobs, fixing problems and solving puzzles so others didn't have to come home to an empty house. So others had the satisfaction of knowing the answers to their problems.

Whatever Beatrice Andrews had imagined that day, he believed to the very depths of his soul she never understood what sort of adults she'd create by her leaving.

She was just sick of her children. Sick of being a single mother. Sick of holding any responsibility for anyone besides herself.

They'd paid for her sins.

"I right wrongs. That's what drives me."

Holden bundled deeper in his cashmere coat and tried to ignore the rain that fell in cold sheets around him. The abandoned outbuilding had become a convenient meeting place, but with the number of people on the property he was still concerned with discovery.

Best to keep it quick.

His local contacts hadn't done a great job of providing hired muscle and the thug standing hunched before him was a glowing example. The man's distracted manner was more than evident by his infernal pacing and chain-smoking until he came to an abrupt halt for his payment.

Holden handed over a stack of bills. The man's thick fingers, scarred with working the vines, thumbed through the roll of euros.

"You said two thousand."

"I said fifteen hundred, Nicky."

The guy dragged hard on his cigarette. "You said two if I fired off a shot last night like you asked. I fired off the shot, so I get my payment."

"You fired off a shot that went nowhere and only served to make everyone suspicious." Suspicions he'd spent all day keeping away from his father's attention. Not that anyone had any idea Pryce's assistant was actually his son.

"You wanted me to *shoot* him?"

Holden fought the urge to shake his head and kept his responses short and simple. "Yes."

"I'm not killing anyone."

"My instructions were to incapacitate. Not kill."

"I'm not doing that, either." The guy dragged hard once again. "The maids are talking about him. Several of the girls took a shine to his fancy American suit. They'll notice if he goes missing."

The staff?

The urge to ask who sprang to his lips but Holden held back. These people—these glorified farmers—knew each other. Grew up with each other. Despite loyalty to a quick score and an easy job or two, there was a strange sense of community among all of them.

He'd wait and watch on his own. Just like always.

"All I'm asking is that you put him in the hospital for a few days until we get the latest shipment moved out of here. I've got the cases prepped and my contact assured me my supply should be in by then."

The thug's eyes lit up for the first time since they'd walked into the old outbuilding and Holden knew he'd touched on the man's true interest. The interest that drove him before all others.

Drugs.

Let Nicky think that was what this was all about. Although the drugs were lucrative, they were simply the cream. What no one knew was the extra packets he added before the lid closed and the cases went out. Small packets of diamonds that bought any number of favors across the region.

And his father knew none of it.

Holden reluctantly handed over the additional five hundred before dangling his next carrot. "I can get you a little something extra out of the cut if you'll make an attempt on Andrews again."

Nicky's eyes shifted and Holden knew he had the fish on the line. "I told you I'm no killer."

"And I told you I don't need him dead. I just need him out of the way. Come on. You can do that, can't you?"

Another drag on the cigarette, down to the filter. "What about the woman?"

"I've got plans for her. You don't need to touch her."

"And I have to do it here? The guy—the American—already saw me yesterday at the party and followed me out back."

"Followed?"

Nicky's movements stilled like nervous prey. "I shook him off. It was nothing and he didn't see me last night. I know these vines."

"So you do. And no, I'd rather you didn't do it here. Andrews and the woman are staying at Signora Barone's B and B. Do it there."

"How much extra are you going to give me?"

"A generous cut before it's placed in the shipment."

"How much?"

Holden did a quick calculation in his head before casually tossing out a number. "Twenty grams."

The widened eyes suggested the number was more than satisfactory. "Just take him down?"

"That's all."

"I'll do it."

Holden bundled up and walked back out into the rain, satisfied he'd made a very sound investment.

Kensington reveled in the connection with Jack, their hands intertwined. "Do you ever get sick of righting the wrongs?"

"I wouldn't be very good at my job if I did."

"But in a bigger sense. Like why people screw up their lives so badly." She exhaled on a heavy breath. God, her thoughts were all over the board. First her siblings. Then her work. And now some misguided urge to play police-woman to the world.

Time to get it together, Steele.

"I guess what I'm saying is that I'm fascinated by the choices people make. And because I do so much of our electronic forensics I'm constantly exposed to those choices. Bank accounts and bribes. Mistresses and mad spending sprees. Debts and dumb choices."

"Very little escapes your notice."

"No, not much does, but that's especially true when I'm hunting for financial information."

"How can you do such specialized work and question your role at House of Steele?"

The question was a fair one and as she considered it, Kensington had to admit the problem went deeper. "It's not that I don't value what I'm doing. It's the bigger con-cern that I've been hiding behind the business instead of running it. I've sent my siblings out into danger and gotten too comfortable sitting behind a desk at home."

"So why was this job different? You didn't have to take this. You could have given it to someone else. Heck, you could have told me to go screw myself and I'd have had to find another partner if I wanted one that badly. Yet you didn't."

"I wanted the job."

"Anything else?"

I wanted you.

The small voice leaped up with its sly whisper and teased her. While her first instinct was to deny—even to herself—that she'd taken the job to be near him, she couldn't.

No matter how badly it grated on her, she was intrigued by Jack. Fascinated by him. And the opportunity to work with him and see him in action had been too good to pass up.

In the process, it had forced her to consider the way she'd been living her life. To evaluate everything she'd been doing.

And everything she *hadn't* been doing.

On the top of that list was rounding out her professional life with a personal life that made her happy. When had she stopped taking chances?

And—worse—when had she become okay with that?

"I wanted the job."

A set of loud voices echoed from the hall before a small group came into the dining room for snacks. Kensington glanced down to where her hand joined with Jack's before pulling hers away.

She had some decisions to make.

Chapter 13

The rain had eased slightly as the evening wore on but a day's worth of downpour had turned the parking lot into a mess. Kensington fought the dismay as thick, heavy mud dragged the supple leather of her boots.

And then she forgot her poor, ruined boots as she took in the low-slung sports car, its tires thick with caked-on mud. "Can you get us out of here?"

"Would I betray my ego and my reputation as a world-renowned superspy by saying I don't know?"

"Only if it would betray *my* world-renowned reputation as a calm, cool and collected businesswoman who would never stoop to use the phrase 'I told you so' about this rental car selection."

His grin flashed in the night, lit up by the sliver of moonlight that decided to make an appearance through the clouds. "Let me give it a try."

Ten frustrating minutes later—after she stayed well

out of the way of heaps of flying mud off the tires—she watched Jack leave the car.

"I'm going to go get help. The staff's still cleaning up and someone's bound to be able to lend us a hand."

She followed him back into the house, the heavy suction of her boots clinging to the floor and leaving large muddy footprints. "Jack!"

"What?"

"We can't make a mess like this."

"We can't help it."

She dragged him into a small utility room off the château's kitchen. "Take your shoes off."

"I'm not going to go traipsing through the house."

"It's still a mess. Come on."

The rain really had done a number and she couldn't hide the disgust as she dragged the heeled boots off. "I love these boots."

"Why are you wearing four-inch heels, anyway?"

"I like them."

"And if you'd had to run in them?"

"Then I'd have taken them off. In the meantime, these accent my outfit to perfection."

His gaze ranged over her body and she couldn't ignore the spark of heat that flashed in the small space. "I can't argue with the results but I still say they're impractical."

"Results?" The word was out before she even thought it through.

"Your legs look about a mile long."

"Oh."

"Which, I suspect—" he leaned forward and dropped a hard, solid kiss on her lips "—is why you wear them."

The loss of height had her considerably shorter than Jack and she had to crane her neck to look up at him. "I wear them because they're pretty and fashionable."

"And because they're designed to make every one of us poor schmucks wild with uncontrolled lust."

She giggled at that, her attempts to remain stoic and haughty floating away on the air. "You put far too much motive into a simple fashion decision."

"And for a woman of the world you're decidedly unaware of what you do to me."

The heat that had flashed and flared the past several days spilled over to boil immediately. The small utility room boasted a cubby for storing various hats, gloves and shoes and Jack had her back pressed against the side wall with quick, determined movements.

The hard kiss he'd pressed to her lips was nothing compared to the raging inferno that he unleashed with his mouth. Long, sensuous kisses assaulted her as he pressed his body against hers, his hands roaming over her hips as he dragged her close.

Kensington gave herself up to the moment, fisted her hands in Jack's shirt and took.

The kiss was hot and greedy and what began as something light and playful quickly morphed into something darker. Needier. Reckless.

"Jack." She moaned his name as their lips broke apart, the sound a breathy sigh.

What had he done to her?

And how had she come to need him? To need *this?*

Even as she thought the words, Kensington knew the truth. Knew it down to her toes.

He fascinated her and had from the beginning. Although their personal interactions had been limited, she'd done her homework and researched him, the same as any other business opponent. But what had begun as a deep dive into his company had changed into a review of the man who had created a highly successful business out of nothing.

At the evidence of his raw ambition to make something of himself in a highly competitive—and highly elite— field, something had sparked inside of her. An intrigued layer of interest that had only ratcheted up and up with each interaction.

The hard press of his hands along the length of her spine dragged their bodies in even closer proximity and she fought to keep her wits about her.

They couldn't do this *here.*

But, true to Jack's promise on the flight to Rome, they *would* do this.

She was going to make love with Jack Andrews.

Jack felt the shift in her attention the slightest moment before Kensington pressed her hands to his shoulders.

"Jack." The loud hiss had a smile curving on his lips, despite the increasing frustration riding his body in swift, choppy waves. "Jack!"

He pressed his lips to her neck for good measure—and because he was loathe to let her go quite yet. "What?"

"We can't do this here."

With tender bites, he nipped his way from her jaw to her ear before whispering in her ear. "Why do you persist in this idea that we're the only ones to make out at the ambassador's house party?"

Her fingers tightened once more on his shoulders and she added a heavier thrust to the press of her hands this time. He broke contact, satisfied to see the thick haze that clouded her gaze and the high spots of color that rode her cheeks. "We're here on a job. This needs to wait for later."

Jack stilled at her words, the underlying implication so loud and clear it practically echoed off the walls of the narrow utility room. A response eluded him; all he could do was stand and stare down at her, the heavy weight of arousal dragging at his body like a raging undertow.

He fought for control, grasping at anything he could think of to calm this overwhelming need for her. Before anything truly effective popped to mind, a heavy noise echoed from the hallway and several members of the serving staff filled the hall.

A mix of Italian and English bombarded them and Jack hiked his thumb toward the door. "Car's stuck from the rain."

Within minutes, a team had been mobilized and he had a troop of staff members escorting him back to the car. His shoes still squished from where he had shoved them back on and he hadn't missed Kensington's moue of disgust as she attempted to drag her wet leather boots over wet socks.

He glanced up in the cool night air, the moon shining clear and bright in the sky, almost insulting in the abundant evidence the rain had fully moved on. A hard slap to his shoulder had him turning, and one of the men who didn't speak English was gesturing with large movements for his keys. Jack dug them out and handed them over before walking to the thick cluster of men preparing to push the front of the car.

"This beauty's not made for this." One of the men he didn't recognize from the weekend pointed toward the car. The man shifted from foot to foot, and something in the broad set of his shoulders pinged at the back of Jack's thoughts. Before he could focus on why that slight frisson of unease climbed his neck, the guy who had his keys had the engine purring while sending up a loud shout with the obvious instruction to push.

The line of men surged forward at once, the car's spinning tires quickly gaining traction with the additional weight. With a few last flying gobs of mud, the car sprang free from its rain-washed moorings, a loud shout of triumph echoing in its wake.

He caught Kensington's eye from where she stood on the side of the parking lot, well out of the range of the flying mud. Her arms were crossed but a sweet, witchy smile lingered on her lips and he felt something inside of himself shift.

Attraction, yes, he had that for her in spades. But this was something deeper. Something more permanent. With a quick shake of his head, he did his level best to push it off and focus on the moment.

Their moment.

He'd learned early that doing anything else was pointless, anyway.

Nicky navigated as fast as he could over the back roads of the valley on his Ducati. He'd traveled these roads since he was a small boy, first in his father's lap and later on his bike. The valley had changed. Or maybe he had.

Either way, what had felt like home for most of his life had begun to feel stifling.

A pervasive sense of evil had hung over everything since the ambassador's chief of staff had gotten involved.

He knew the score, some from whispers and some from his role in the local drug trade. Like he knew how the locals had upped their game since Holden Keene had come into the picture. And how it wasn't only drugs moving through the ambassador's vineyard but loud whispers of the diamonds that came straight out of the ambassador's home country of Tierra Kimber, too.

He also knew old man DeAngelo had been murdered. In his own vineyard, no less. Much as he'd like to do something about it, the locals had embraced Holden Keene's enterprising sensibilities. And even he couldn't deny the quality of what was moving through their valley was some damn good stuff. He'd avoided the heroin, having no interest in chasing the dragon, but he did enjoy the quality of the cocaine Keene ensured they all got a good cut of.

Nicky pulled off about two acres from Signora Barone's and looked for a place to hide his bike. Everyone here knew him, and he sure as hell didn't need to announce his presence.

He stowed the bike behind an old shed that had seen far too many winters, then cut through the backyards of the businesses along the main street of the village, keeping to the shadows. He felt a small stab of guilt but quickly pushed it away. The game was bigger than him—way bigger—and he knew it.

So he'd do as he was asked. Hell, he had no interest in ending up like Old Man DeAngelo and, even if he'd wanted to, you didn't say no to Keene.

Besides, the man *had* offered to make it worth his while.

Nicky heard the roar of the sports car as it screamed into the village and he positioned himself out of range of Signora Barone's back patio. He had a small window of opportunity, and he'd be damned if he missed this time.

Jack pulled the car into a small parking space behind their B and B. Kensington had been quiet on the short ride back and he hadn't been able to get a read on her mood. The sense of anticipation that had hovered between them in the utility room had grown stronger and ever more taut, like a rubber band pulled tighter and tighter.

But underneath it all, he sensed something else.

"You okay?" He put the car in Park and turned toward her. Moonlight filtered through the windshield, highlighting the arc of her cheekbone and the subtle sweep of her eyelashes. It was funny, he couldn't help marveling, how she drew him to her and how he noticed the most subtle things.

Eyelashes? *You really are gone, Andrews.*

"Something's out there."

"Where?"

"There." She gestured toward the window, then shook her head. "Everywhere. We've been expecting something and it hasn't manifested. It's like it's waiting for the just the right moment."

For a woman who managed her life and her reactions to situations with cool efficiency, her fearfulness pulled him up short. It was precisely because she didn't overreact that her foreboding seemed so real.

Tangible.

"The past few days with the ambassador have been uneventful. That doesn't mean we won't get to the bottom of what's going on. Dante has us scheduled for an event early next week. We'll have another chance to dig deeper. And don't forget, we still have tomorrow morning."

"I suppose."

More rattled than he cared to admit, he climbed out of the car and crossed to her side. She already had the car's elaborate door swinging upward, one of those long legs he so admired peeking from the door, when all hell broke loose.

The sense something wasn't right hit him mere moments before the loud pop of gunfire lit up the night. Jack dived toward the ground, screaming as he went. "Stay in the car!"

Another surge of gunfire erupted above his head, striking the front of the car. He knew he needed to get to cover, but the second round gave him a sense of where the bullets were coming from and he used the knowledge to his advantage.

With his only thought for Kensington and getting her out of the line of fire, he reached for the piece under his jacket, coming up with the gun as he came to a sitting position, firing in the direction of the noise.

The shooter got one more round off, the bullet whizzing past the roof of the car, before the outline of a large body was evident in the moonlight.

The light that had seemed so insulting earlier was now his friend as Jack took off in the same direction, his gun firmly in hand. Abstractly he heard the click of the door opening and hollered over his shoulder. "Stay in the car!"

The sound of her heel hitting the pavement told him what Kensington thought of his direction, but he ignored it in favor of keeping his quarry in his sights.

A large, oddly familiar body zigzagged through the backyard of the B and B before heading hell-for-leather toward a large fence that rimmed the property. Jack kept moving and fired off a shot at the man's feet. The shot went wide but the fence post exploding under the bullet was enough to startle the man and he lost precious seconds racing farther down the line of the fence.

Heavy breathing and grunting accompanied the gunman's climb as he attempted to scale the fence, and Jack reached him just as the man had a leg over the top. With a hard leap, Jack reached for the man's foot and flapping pants leg, determined to get a grip on whatever he could.

On a triumphant exhale, Jack snagged the edge of the guy's pants but nearly lost his grip as the force of the larger man's body slammed him against the fence.

Kensington screamed behind him, her cries for help doing enough to get several lights to come on in the backyard. The man above him struggled to pull himself over but Jack held on, his grip tight. He toyed with dropping his gun so he could use both hands but he couldn't risk putting Kensington in danger if he no longer had his piece in hand.

But it was that calculation that cost him. The sound of rending material registered as the weight under his fingers lessened with the force of the man's movement.

And then he was gone as his body slipped over the fence.

Kensington hollered out a string of orders as Signora Barone and her son came barreling out of the B and B. Her Italian was limited at best, but she knew the basics and she was able to summon up the words man and gun with surprising alacrity.

She saw Jack struggling with the man at the fence and waded into the backyard, the grass almost as deep and squishy as the mud of the vineyard. She did her best to ignore it, but the sucking pull of the earth kept a tight grip on her heels and it limited her range as she tried to get to Jack.

Every step was an agony as he never seemed to get any closer until—finally—she came upon the fence. Jack was already up and over the eight feet of wood and she fought the increasing sensation that he was in danger if he kept up the chase.

She slammed her feet into the slats of the fence, desperately searching for purchase wherever she could find it. The climb was actually easier than the muddy backyard and she had herself up to the top in moments. As soon as she had a clear line of sight, she searched for Jack. His large form silhouetted in the moonlight as he ran through the property adjacent to the hotel.

"Jack!"

He never turned but kept going, clearly intent on the large, bulky form zigzagging about thirty yards in front of him.

Her gaze stayed locked on the man who had shot at them and she sensed his movements the moment his hand went to the waistband of his pants as he ran.

Summoning up as much breath as she could through the raw fear clawing at her throat, she screamed. "Jack! Get down!"

The loud echo of yet another gunshot went off and she watched in horror as Jack fell to the ground.

A paralyzing fear gripped her and, for a moment, Kensington couldn't move. Could only stare in horror at where he lay motionless on the ground, his shooter fleeing into the dark night.

Somewhere in the depths of her mind she screamed—or was that sound actually coming from her?—before the temporary paralysis vanished and she moved, lifting off the fence with a burst of speed. Her booted feet hit the grass but she didn't feel it as she briefly fell to her knees. Instead, she was up and racing toward Jack.

The wet earth still sucked at her feet and the distance between them seemed interminable, but she plodded on, step by step, as fast as she could go.

Be okay. Be okay. Be okay.

The words were a litany in her head as she ran.

And then she saw the slightest movement—the flail of his arm just before he struggled to a sitting position—and Kensington fell to her knees as she reached him.

"Jack." Her hands flew over him—head, face, shoulders—before shifting toward his chest. "Are you okay? Are you hurt?"

"I'm fine."

"But you fell? He hit you." Her hands never stilled, as if she could reassure herself he was okay simply by touch alone. "Were you shot?"

"Bastard caught the edge of my arm."

"What?" The word came out on a gurgled scream and she dragged on his sport coat to get to the wound.

"Kensington." She continued to drag at his coat, a hard sob rising in her throat as she fought the thick material.

"Kensington!" He wrapped one large hand around hers and held her still, his voice dropping as he tugged her close. "Baby, I'm all right."

From somewhere deep inside she registered his voice and it was enough to still her movements. His fingers were tight bands around hers and she looked into the dark pools of his eyes.

"I saw you fall." The words dragged from her throat on another hard sob. "He shot you and you fell."

"Shh. I'm fine. Look at me. I'm fine."

"But—"

Jack cut her off and pulled her close with one arm, the other hanging at his side. "Shh now. I'm fine."

She wrapped her arms around his waist and clung, the thick beats of his heart pulsing against her chest the sweetest music. He was okay. Or mostly okay.

The heavy thud of his heartbeat slowed along with his breathing as they sat there, wrapped up in each other. He crooned light, soothing words in her ear but his grip never loosened.

That same sense of foreboding she'd felt earlier in the car washed over her once again.

Something was out there.

And it was determined to take them down.

The heavy crack and snap of a fire in the B and B's lobby fireplace did nothing to warm her as she sat on an overstuffed couch. The town doctor Signora Barone called once she realized what had happened had finished patching up Jack's arm, muttering in a mix of Italian and English how lucky the *signore* was he didn't need stitches.

She'd watched the doctor work as Jack's shirt was removed and the wound cleaned, then covered with ointment and bandage. Through each step, her mind raced over the events of the night on a continuous loop, seeking some answer. Some clue to who was responsible.

The gunfire as they left the car. The climb over the fence. The chase across the lawn and then more gunfire.

Each was more tangible evidence of the threat she knew was looming. They'd been lulled into a false sense of security that Pryce wasn't dirty, but what else could they think? The household knew they were leaving—hell, they practically gave them a bon voyage party before she and Jack departed for the B and B. Someone was acting on Pryce's orders from the inside. It was the only answer.

Her gaze dragged to the bandage, bright, stark white against the darker tan of Jack's flesh. She kept trying to reassure herself that was a good thing. That the bandage meant he was well. Whole. Alive.

But with every glance it only served to make the cold inside of her intensify until her teeth were chattering no matter how close she got to the fire.

Jack still hadn't put a shirt on and she watched where he paced on the far side of the lobby, a blanket half on, half off his shoulders, his phone against his ear. Her gaze drifted from him to where the doctor and Signora Barone stood near the check-in desk, murmuring in a heated exchange. Kensington didn't miss the looks either gave her as they spoke, and she turned away from their stares, huddling deeper into her coat.

She should act. Should do something.

Jack was on the phone with Dante, filling him in on the evening's events. Although he'd have contacted the officer, anyway, he rushed a call to the police at the insistence of both the good doctor and Signora Barone.

Jack had been shot and he had his wits about him. All she could manage was to sit and shiver against the blazing heat of the fire.

"Scusi?" The doctor's gentle voice interrupted her thoughts as he wrapped a blanket around her shoulders. "You are so cold."

The blanket did nothing for the chattering of her teeth and the doctor frowned as he sat down next to her. "You had a scare. May I examine you, as well?"

His words registered somewhere beyond the litany of events cycling through her mind. "I'm not hurt."

"In here." The doctor's smile was gentle as he tapped at her forehead. "I can give you something. Can help with the thoughts."

She shook her head, the vague sense she didn't want drugs flitting through her mind, which refused to still.

Why couldn't she get a coherent thought in her head? And why was the image of Jack falling to the ground the only thing she could see? And why did that image keep morphing into the scene of her parents, their car mangled in the Welsh countryside?

"Kensington?" Jack took the seat on her other side, his hand immediately seeking hers. "The doctor's asked you a question."

"What?" She wrapped her free hand around where theirs joined. "What did he ask?"

"He wants to give you something to help."

"No drugs." She shook her head. That would make her fuzzy. They'd given her something to sleep after her parents had died and it had made everything worse. Had made the sharp grief seem distant and she wouldn't go back to that place.

"Then you need to talk to me."

"I'm fine."

A small smile tilted the corners of his mouth and somewhere through her racing thoughts she registered the fact that the gentle smile didn't reach his eyes. "You keep saying that but you're not fine."

"It's just the adrenaline rush. It'll stop." The words were meant to sound authoritative but the hard clattering of her teeth ruined the effect.

"Come here." He pulled her close with his good hand and she wrapped her arms around his waist. His body heat warmed her immediately, the light, musky scent of his skin warming her from the inside out.

Kensington fought the urge to press a kiss to his chest, a lingering sense of propriety holding her back.

"I think we'll be all right, Doctor." She tuned out as Jack spoke over her head. She vaguely heard the doctor once again offer tranquilizers and she felt the subtle movement of Jack's body as he shook his head.

He ran a hand over her hair before reaching around to tilt her chin up. "Are you ready to go upstairs?"

"I think so."

"Can you walk?"

The first spot of indignation filled her chest and she stood up to make her point.

And promptly fell back into a seated position on the couch.

"Oh, oh!" Signora Barone and the doctor surged forward to grab her arms and Kensington fought the light blush that flooded her cheeks.

"I'm sorry. *Scusi.*"

"No, no." The doctor patted her back. "It is the rush of the night. The events. You're safe now."

The doctor stayed by her side as she gave directions

to her room. His words rattled around her head—*you're safe now*—even as she knew it wasn't true. Despite that knowledge, she kept putting one foot in front of the other, her legs growing stronger with each step.

Jack walked behind them under the eagle eye of Signora Barone, who kept a firm hand on his arm. It was only when they reached the doors of their rooms that the older woman finally spoke, her tone brooking no argument.

"Signorina Steele. You sleep with Signor Andrews tonight."

Chapter 14

Jack's eyes widened at the order from their proprietor. Whereas the woman had given him and Kensington the barely veiled fish eye the past two days, now she was practically shoving them at each other.

With a wagging finger and a subtle gleam in her dark brown gaze, her words brooked no argument. "You shouldn't be alone."

He patted the woman's arm. "Nor should you. I've called for security for you tonight. No one will hurt you."

"No one will touch me in my home, *signore*. It is you and the miss I worry for." He meant his touch to be reassuring, so he wasn't expecting the wry smile that winged straight back at him. "Keep her safe."

The adrenaline high he'd subsisted on for the past hour came to a crashing halt and he could barely nod at Signora Barone before reaching for Kensington's hand. "Come on."

It took all his focus, but Jack lifted his shaking hand

and finally got his key into the lock. The heavy old door swung open and he gestured Kensington through, then followed her. He turned to thank the doctor and their hostess, but both were already gone, their footsteps fading down the hall.

He closed the door, not even having enough energy to shake his head at the older woman's change of heart.

Or the underlying message that he and Kensington had brought trouble to her B and B and her village. "We're lucky she's letting us stay. A small business like this. She could have easily thrown us out."

"She might know she's safe, but she also knows whatever's going on in her village isn't good in the long run." Kensington stopped, her gaze speculative as she bent down to drag off her ruined boots. Jack was pleased to see her legs much steadier and her teeth no longer chattering. "Maybe we should talk to her and get her insights. She's got to know more than she's letting on."

"We can't risk putting her in danger." He edged his way toward the bed, toeing off his own shoes as he went.

"We could arrange for her protection. Something more permanent than one night."

Despite the exhaustion that dragged at him, he couldn't hold back a snort. "Yeah, right. You heard where that got me."

He rubbed at his shoulder, the move unconscious until her sharp gaze narrowed in on him. "Are you sure your arm's all right?"

Kensington had her hand on his forearm, brushing back the blanket on his shoulders to get a look at the large gauze that wrapped his biceps.

"I'm fine. It burns like a furnace, but that's about all."

Now that he mentioned it and focused on the wound,

the pain multiplied several times over, the adrenaline let-down going a long way toward amping up the discomfort.

"You took the tranquilizer the doctor offered?"

He shook the small bottle of pills in his pocket. "The good doctor gave me four pills. Two for you and two for me."

The heavy frown and narrowed eyes told him all he needed to know. "I'm not taking those."

"Me, either. I've got headache medicine with a sleeping agent in my bag. That's all I'm willing to take."

"You're a bad patient."

"Right back at ya, Steele."

Her gaze dropped to the bandage on his arm and his stomach clenched when a stark look painted itself across the vivid blue of her eyes. "I don't have a bullet wound."

"I have a flesh wound, that's all. It's not my first and I'm quite sure it won't be the last."

The casual dismissal had its desired effect and he saw color rise in her cheeks as his words registered. With a snap of her heel she turned and headed toward his small bathroom, her words tossed over her shoulder. "Where's the aspirin?"

"Dopp kit on the counter."

His gaze dropped unerringly toward her truly magnificent ass and he refused to apologize for the gentle swell of appreciation that broke through the sheer exhaustion dragging at his system. He might not have the strength to act on it, but a man could admire a beautiful woman, that was for damn sure.

Her voice echoed from the bathroom, breaking the moment. "You have to be the tidiest man I've ever seen."

"I don't like clutter."

Kensington's face poked around the corner of the bathroom doorway. Color had returned to her cheeks and for the first time in too many days he saw the bright light of humor reflected in her gaze. "There's tidy and then there's tidy. I've never seen anything like this. It looks like a cyborg's staying in this room."

"It's no big deal. I like to be neat."

Her grin only got wider. "I grew up with two brothers. *Neat* does not factor into the male vocabulary. What gives? Have you been sneaking out at night and staying in Signora Barone's room, leaving yours pristinely clean? She's got a soft spot for you, you know."

"Are you going to get the aspirin already?" The words came out on a hard clip and he wanted to pull them back, even as the broad smile faded from her lips.

"Sorry. Of course. You're probably in a lot of pain." She came back into the room with the pills and a glass of water in hand. "Here you go."

He quickly swallowed the pills and willed the medicine to do its job against the hot brand that had taken up residence on his arm. And it was only when he glanced up into her face that he was struck by the effect of his harsh words.

The urge to ignore the awkwardness and skip an apology rode him like a horse toward the finish line, but somewhere underneath the pressure to walk away was something more subtle. And far more powerful.

The pressure to stay.

"I'm sorry."

"Nothing to be sorry about. You're in pain."

The truth locked up his throat in a tight fist and he swallowed hard. Once. Twice. Then downed the rest of the water.

"There's a reason I'm so neat."

"Oh?" She kept her tone light but he didn't miss the sharp interest in that indigo gaze.

The words clogged in his throat and he wished for more

water, but he refused to prolong the moment by crossing to the bathroom to get more.

Nope. Better to take the hit and keep on going.

"After my mother left, I thought it was because I'd done something wrong. Wasn't good enough. Clean enough. Neat enough. So I tried to fix it."

"With neatness?"

"And a maniacal focus on my studies. On being a good student. A good brother."

Where he'd anticipated censure—or worse, pity—all he saw was a sweet understanding that tugged at the deepest part of him. "But those things didn't make her come back."

"No."

"So why are you still neat as a pin? And why do you still feel you need to take care of everyone?"

"Some habits die hard."

"I suppose they do." She moved up into his body, her arms wrapping around his waist. She let out a small sigh before laying her head against his chest. "You don't have to be perfect anymore."

And just like that, another layer of his resistance broke, disintegrating into dust.

No one else knew why he was such a neat freak. He'd driven several administrative assistants to distraction over the years with his obsessive need to have his files in order, and his sisters used it as the basis of several family jokes.

But never had he confessed—to anyone—the reason why. That young boy still living inside of him, abandoned over his breakfast. If he'd only cleaned up after himself. If he'd only been more thoughtful. If he'd only not been such a horrible burden.

It all might have been different.

He couldn't go back, but no matter how hard he tried he couldn't quite move past it, either.

Yet somehow, with some miraculous sixth sense, Kensington understood.

The desire to wrap his arms around her filled him, but his bandaged limb would have none of it, so he used his free hand to keep her close to his chest. He closed his eyes and breathed deeply into her hair, the mixed scents of honeysuckle from her shampoo and the cooler, rain-soaked air of earlier reminding him of a spring day.

It felt good to hold her close. He wanted to do more—wanted to do all—but for now, this was enough.

She pressed a kiss to his chest, her lips lingering over his heart, before she pulled at his waist "Come on. Let's lie down. We're both dead on our feet."

He let her lead him toward the bed, the light pressure of her fingertips on his flesh going a long way toward waking him from his stupor. And once he had her next to him, her length nestled firmly against his body, he pressed his lips to hers. Tentative, then more urgent, as the taste of her dragged him under.

Kensington responded immediately, her mouth opening under his as their tongues met in long, luxurious strokes. She was the finest wine, the richest meal, and he savored the moment. Savored what flared between them, a blazing inferno that neither seemed able to quench.

She broke off the kiss first, but he didn't miss the underlying air of regret. "I want you, Jack. You have to know that."

"A man never tires of hearing it."

She settled a hand against his cheek. "Know it's true. And know that I want you more than I could have ever imagined. But we can't tonight."

He opened his mouth to offer up a token—and tired—protest when she pressed on.

"I won't have the ugliness of tonight be the backdrop

for the two of us together. I want you, too. But tonight isn't the time."

With one final, lingering kiss, he pulled her under his good arm and settled her against his chest. "Go to sleep."

The featherlight snore that rose up to greet him was possibly the first time she'd taken an order from him since they'd begun working together.

With that thought keeping him company, Jack drifted to sleep right beside her.

Kensington awoke slowly, the hard male chest under her hands captivating as she traced lazy circles over warm flesh. Bright sunlight filtered through the windows but it wasn't enough to chase the chill of a cold December morning and she burrowed more deeply into Jack.

Danger lurked outside the room. They'd known it before they even set foot in Italy, but the events of the past few days confirmed it.

So who had identified the two of them as targets?

She replayed her conversation with the ambassador the day before. He'd mentioned her father and her picture when she was small. He'd also spoke of pride about his accomplishments, of how he hoped to raise the global profile of his home country and of his love of wine-making.

Over and over, no matter how she sliced it, she struggled with the image of the ambassador as a criminal mastermind running drugs and diamonds, all the while ordering a hit on Jack and her.

She didn't doubt his ability to be ruthless, but something rang false every time she attempted to tie him to their investigation.

As if he read her tumultuous thoughts, Jack shifted, pulling her closer. She snuggled into his warmth, the heat from his body branding her with its intensity. Despite the very real desire to go back to sleep, the combination of warm male and her thoughts on the ambassador had her mind shooting from topic to topic, clearly finished with sleep.

When her thoughts landed on her clothing situation— and what could her hair possibly look like at this point?— she struggled to hold back a groan. She'd had the foresight to remove her boots when they'd come in, but the rest of her was fully clothed in her outfit from the ambassador's.

Nice one, Steele. Walk of shame clothes and you didn't even get to do the deed.

Not as if they could have. She pictured the two of them the night before—ragtag and falling asleep on their feet— and knew whatever was to come between them would have to wait.

"You awake?" Jack's voice was thick with sleep and his arm tightened around her shoulders before pulling her close. "What time is it?"

"I'm guessing about eight or nine."

He stilled his movements, his gaze shooting up to hers. "What?"

"Yeah, we probably overslept, but I can't seem to get myself motivated to get out of bed at the moment. The ambassador will have to wait."

"That's not what I meant."

When he continued to stare at her, she could only wonder if he needed another round of pain meds, despite his protest the night before to avoid the stronger stuff the doctor had given. "What's the matter? Does your arm hurt?"

"Is it really eight o'clock?"

She twisted in his arms to take in the small bedside clock. "Eight forty-two to be exact."

"You know what this means?"

She turned back to snuggle once more. "We're late.

And I'm a bad, bad employee for not feeling any remorse about that fact."

"Kensington. It means you slept through the night."

The lazy haze that tantalized her with sleep vanished as she sat up. Her mind flew through the evening's events and all the evenings that had come before. No matter how tired she ever was, her ability to sleep vanished somewhere around three or four in the morning.

Yet here they were.

She shook her head, trying to dislodge the rising thought that she'd just slept through the night for the first time since she was fourteen. "I don't believe it."

"Did you take the same stuff I did?"

"No."

"And I know you refused the tranquilizers."

"Absolutely."

"So this was all you, baby."

Tears clogged the back of her throat at the endearment, the moment filled with so much unsaid she was afraid to shatter it. But even as she resisted, she couldn't hold back the words. "No, Jack. It was you. You gave me that."

She leaned back over him and pressed her lips to his. Every kiss they'd shared before had been full of subtle power and the shifting sands of trying to figure the other out, but this kiss was different.

This kiss was filled with promise. With light. And with joy.

One tender moment spun into the next, fragile threads that forged the strongest bond.

And somewhere, deep down inside, in a place she wasn't quite ready to examine yet, Kensington knew she loved.

Holden rattled the pages of his newspaper and made a show of reading it while his father preened over several of his guests. The damn house party had stretched on interminably and he was glad every one of these foolish asses would be gone within the next few hours. Their gazes had grown too sharp and he knew several were whispering of the gossip that had gripped the village last night.

Two of the party's guests had been shot at.

Damn fool Nicky.

Did he have to give the man a detailed plan? Yes, he wanted him to shoot at Andrews and Steele. And yes, he wanted him to hit Andrews. But he sure as hell didn't want Nicky to get into close enough range that he barely escaped unidentified.

Imbecile.

He'd been crystal clear about his plans since he'd started down this path two years ago—get close to his father, gain his trust and use that to set up his future. He'd had enough of playing local kingpin in Tierra Kimber. He wanted more and he was in a position to have it.

The diamond mines in his home country were incredibly productive, a new vein discovered just a few months back. The rich deposits were putting Tierra Kimber on the map in more ways than one and he had every intention of using that to set himself up.

Assuming his relations with the locals didn't ruin him first. The reports had been sketchy and he avoided showing too much interest beyond the ambassador's safety, but if the retelling of the previous evening was true, Nicky had barely escaped detection.

Of course, Andrews was cagier than he'd initially given the man credit for, Holden readily acknowledged, but none of it changed the fact that Nicky was utterly useless.

The urge to take care of that problem as he'd handled the others was strong, but again, he forced himself to relax. A rampage through the village, killing yet another low-level employee, would hardly meet his carefully prepared ends. Nor would he escape detection forever if he didn't show some restraint. He'd made his bones functioning as a shadowy figure in the background, manipulating situations for his own benefit.

Drawing too much attention to himself wasn't going to get him anywhere.

And much as it would please him to take out every one of these stupid locals he was forced to deal with, he had to admit they served a purpose.

They were his eyes and ears and they'd also begun to associate him with a rising prosperity in their criminal activity. With that association, his actions had begun to take on grander importance that worked to his advantage.

He made it a point to oversee the specifics of the shipments—especially the monthly shipments that contained the diamonds—and he also traveled in his role as chief of staff. He hated rusticating in the country and simply tallied his days here as part of his personal investment in his future. And the truth was, he needed people here in the village. Although he didn't trust *them,* he did trust he'd put enough fear into all of them that they'd do as he asked.

Oh, yes. His efforts over the past eighteen months were finally beginning to pay dividends. And even his more tedious activities—this weekend as an example—had begun to bear fruit.

The conversation at the table shifted once more, and his father's guests grew more heated in their speculations of what was going on in the village.

Rising crime. Poverty. Degenerates who drank too much of the wine that was in ready abundance. Thought after thought was offered up with no understanding of what was truly happening. Oh, their sharp gazes and worried frowns implied a sense of vigilance, but the houseguests of Castello di Carte had become surprisingly lax about their personal belongings, thinking themselves above the danger.

Holden fought the small smile that wanted to break out, taunting them all. He'd already procured for himself copies of several office keys, a few computer log-ins and the calendar of when a rather prominent telecommunications owner would be out of the country.

A good businessman took every opportunity afforded him and Holden knew he was the best.

"Mr. Keene." The light, tinny voice penetrated his newspaper and Holden lowered the paper to greet the old biddy who ran one of the major wineries in the region. The contessa was a local legend, both for her imagined sense of royalty and her very real power as a major player in wine.

Whereas most of the local producers managed the endless supply of table wine that filled Italy, the contessa had managed to create an international business, a well-known label and one of the most in-demand Chiantis in the world.

And his father kissed the woman's ass as if she were turning that damn wine from water instead of growing it like everyone else.

Holden lowered his paper and fought the light shudder that ran down his spine at her razor-sharp gaze. "Yes, my lady?"

"We were discussing the incident in the village last night. Is there any mention of it in your paper?"

He shook his head, even as he knew the question was a tactic to engage him in the discussion. "This is a European financial daily. While exciting news for us, they're not interested in the drama in a small Italian village."

"Perhaps they will be when the broader implications of what is taking place here gets out."

The contessa's words beat against him like a hailstorm

and he fought to right himself against the deluge. "I'm afraid I don't understand what you mean."

"No? You manage the ambassador's schedule with an iron fist. Surely you're aware of the security measures in place for his visits here."

"I am well aware, ma'am."

"Then you know as well as I do the situation here in our quaint little countryside is anything but normal. To think, people getting shot at in the village. And this on the heels of Signor DeAngelo." She shook her head and added several tsks for good measure. "It is shameful."

"It is a sorry state of affairs. These locals here, clearly there is some nonsense brewing between them all. It doesn't concern us or the ambassador." He shot his father a meaningful glance, pleased when the old man took the hint.

"Mr. Keene is right, my dear. These things do not concern us."

Indignation flashed in the woman's eyes and, with it, a knowing air that sent another shiver racing down his spine. "I run a business in this region. Of course it concerns me."

"And for that you have my sympathies. But the ambassador must focus on his own challenges. We maintain security here at the vineyard and I suggest you do the same. Minimize your role in the local politics."

"Fascinating position for someone whose interests clearly lie here in my country."

His father coughed and Holden didn't miss the implacable order to change the subject, but he wasn't quite ready to let the matter go. The pompous, self-aggrandizing biddy had been under his skin all weekend and he was done placating her. "Your country, yes. Not this region you call home. Castello di Carte is the ambassador's place to relax.

To enjoy the fruits of his labor. Surely you're not suggesting that change."

His father jumped in, the peacekeeper as always. "I think you misunderstand the contessa, Holden."

"That, sir, is a matter of perspective. However, I think perhaps I should excuse myself to deal with your guests' departures."

He stood, carefully folding his paper before dropping it to the table. He had no idea why the contessa had engaged him in conversation, but because the haughty woman had looked down her nose at him the entire weekend, he had no doubt she had some motive for the discussion.

To make a point in front of her fellow guests? Or was it something deeper?

She did have connections in the region and she surely knew the major players—both good and bad—who operated here. Did she have suspicions about him?

Or had someone talked?

The questions in his mind vanished as his phone began to buzz. The motion sensor he'd placed in his father's office had been triggered and he used the "call" as a chance to excuse himself and the overbearing glances of the contessa.

Servants blocked his way as he barreled down the back hall toward the office. Between the upcoming departures and the large number of people all eating breakfast, he nearly collided with two rolling pieces of luggage and a woman bearing a tray overladen with serving dishes. She let out a shriek as she struggled to hold on to her cargo and he just missed knocking her against the wall.

Damn incompetents.

Again, the thought filled him of how useless these people were. They spent their days serving others, seeing to their happiness.

What a waste.

Holden came upon his father's office door and waited just outside. The door was open and he hesitated a moment to catch his breath. Andrews would be on the other side of the door. He'd bet the next shipment on it.

Already envisioning the exchange, Holden came to a hard stop when he saw Kensington Steele on the other side of the room on her hands and knees before the heavy globe his father kept in his office.

"Excuse me?"

She glanced up but stayed in position on the floor. "I've lost something. I think it's under here."

"This is the second time I've found you in the ambassador's private office. What part of private have you missed?"

A small smile hovered around her face and she tossed her hair back as she sat up on her haunches and gestured toward her ear. "I'll spare you a long, detailed apology about how embarrassed I am for the other night, even though I'm mortified. I lost an earring and this is the only place I can think to look for it."

"Returning to the scene of the crime?" He stalked toward her, curious when she never moved from her subservient position on the floor.

"I've looked everywhere else. I'd normally not care so much but they were my mother's."

"Perhaps you should have thought about that before you and Mr. Andrews slipped in here the other night."

"I know." Her eyes dropped to the floor and, once again, he questioned her complete change of heart. Every time he'd seen her throughout the weekend, her posture and attitude had dripped with authority and a barely veiled haughtiness she couldn't remove from those vivid blue eyes.

Yet here she was, prowling around on the floor like a humble servant. "Did you find it?"

"I thought I felt something just before you came in."

He moved closer, satisfied when the first notes of alarm darkened those guileless eyes. "By all means, then, don't keep me in suspense."

She bent farther, her arm snaking underneath the heavy base of his father's globe. His gaze flicked over her luscious form and the well-sculpted derrière that rose into the air. Perhaps he'd been too dismissive of her...

"Got it!"

She crawled backward, dragging her hand from underneath the pedestal. His thoughts drifted from her exquisite form to the exceedingly strange coincidence that she'd have lost an earring under the one place he stored anything sensitive in the château.

"I'm sorry to have intruded in the ambassador's private rooms." She got to her full height, that wariness still evident in her gaze. "I'll excuse myself now."

He moved into her space and inhaled her scent. The lightest sheen of perspiration was visible along her hairline and he reveled in her discomfort. "I hope you got what you came for."

She lifted the earring. "I most certainly did."

"Have a safe trip back to Rome. I understand from the lieutenant you and Mr. Andrews will be supporting the ambassador at this week's event at the Palazzo Altemps."

"We'll be there."

He leaned forward and whispered in her ear. "I look forward to seeing you then, Miss Steele."

Her steps across the office held the decided notes of urgency and he stood in place several moments after she'd left. He didn't think she'd return, but no use taking any chances.

Just like the other night.

He was right to have removed everything from the small

drawer at the base of the globe after discovering Steele and Andrews the other night. He wasn't a believer in co-incidence.

Nor did he believe—not for a minute—that Kensington Steele had lost an earring.

Chapter 15

Jack took his first easy breath as Kensington maneuvered the sports car back into the city. They'd spent the past two hours going over and over the details of her exchange with Holden Keene in the ambassador's private office and he had only grown more uneasy with each passing kilometer.

The bastard had threatened her.

Oh, it was subtle, by Kensington's telling, but it was there all the same. "He whispered in your ear."

"Jack, I've told you already. Holden just creeped me out. I'm fine."

"Let's walk through it one more time." The bastard had scared her, that much was true. She'd played it cool, but he'd heard every word through his earpiece and he hadn't missed the wide-eyed stare that filled her face when she returned to the common area of the château after casing Pryce's office. Nor did he miss the tense set of her shoulders, which didn't relax until they were well away from Tuscany.

"I've already taken you through this. Look. When we get to the hotel in Rome I'll spend some time digging into Keene's background and we'll take it from there. I'd also like to talk to Marco again if he's up for it and see if Keene's ever tripped his trigger."

Marco was a good idea and further proof she was thinking much more clearly than he was. "Take me through it again. Maybe you missed something."

"Damn, you're bossy. Is this some sort of lingering male frustration because I told you I'd drive so you could rest your arm?"

"This is good old-fashioned male frustration because he threatened you."

He shifted in his seat, the discomfort of his arm only adding to the ire pulsing under his skin. Keene had scared her and that was unacceptable. Until the moment Keene caught him and Kensington kissing in the ambassador's office, he'd ignored Pryce's chief of staff. The man blended seamlessly into the background, his dossier in the file on Pryce minimal and functional. He hadn't looked closely enough at the man.

Holden Keene was a threat and Jack knew his ire at the situation was mostly directed at himself. It was his job to account for every threat and he'd not taken this one seriously.

Worse, he'd nearly missed it.

"He didn't threaten me, which I've explained to you for the past two hours despite the fact that you heard him as clearly as I did. It was just something I felt in his demeanor and attitude."

She could downplay it all she wanted, but it didn't

change the outcome. Or his anger. "The bastard invaded your space and whispered in your ear. I'd call that a threat."

"You get in my space and whisper in my ear."

"Not funny."

"Well, lambasting me for two hours hasn't been a picnic."

That's how she saw it? "You're not the one I'm mad at."

"I told you. Once we get to the hotel I'll start digging into Keene. I don't know why I didn't think to run him earlier, but we'll fix that. I already sent Campbell a note to run whatever he could find and I'll follow up in some of the standard databases I use. We'll figure out who he is and then we can decide what to do about him."

"This isn't about Keene."

Traffic had come to a standstill and she used the lull to turn fully toward him. "It's as much about him as anyone. And it explains why we keep coming up empty-handed when we look into Pryce."

"Damn it, Kensington, I'm mad at myself!"

The words rushed out, loud enough that a few people on the nearby sidewalks turned to stare.

"Jack?"

He slammed a hand on the dash and attempted to organize his thoughts. "I left you to go in there and face Keene alone."

"It was a house full of people."

"And he had you alone. Down the hall and out of sight from all of us."

Images had filled his thoughts on an erratic loop. Her descriptions of the encounter. Keene's thinly veiled skepticism that she'd left anything behind. The words he'd whispered to her before she left.

I look forward to seeing you then, Miss Steele.

He just bet Holden Keene did.

And he was the bastard who had left her to face it alone.

"You're overreacting to this. Nothing happened to me, and he seemed to buy the earring bit. The fact I left the door open had to work in my favor. Keene can act as suspicious as he likes, but I was out in the open for anyone to see. That hardly screams stealth and secrecy."

"Yet you still got the feeling he was skeptical." She nodded slightly before turning back to maneuver through the now-empty intersection. "*And* the drawer was empty when you picked the lock."

"Nothing so much as a paper clip inside."

"Who locks a drawer they're not using?" Jack mentally flipped through all the unlocked drawers they'd discovered on Friday night.

He didn't buy the coincidence that all of Pryce's key folders, full of his business concerns and political discussions, were wide-open, yet a small innocuous drawer was locked?

No way.

"Keene could have removed any files in there between catching us in the office and catching me this morning."

"A definite possibility."

"Or we have to accept that it's just an empty drawer."

"Not likely." He didn't buy that for a minute, but he had to include it in whatever conclusions he attempted to take away from the weekend. He'd already missed one obvious clue—he needed to stay on his game and evaluate all the possibilities.

Her voice was quiet as she shifted the purring car, maneuvering them effortlessly through Rome's narrow streets. Was there anything the woman couldn't do? "I don't know why you keep focusing on the negative when all I see is a huge positive."

"Forgive me if I fail to see any upside."

"That's where you're wrong. Up until this morning we had no leads and no freaking clue what direction to turn. And now we have Keene."

The situation was somewhat fantastical all on its own—a well-respected ambassador suspected of abusing his political power to run drugs and smuggle diamonds. But what if the problem really did lie deeper inside Pryce's staff? "He's flown under everyone's radar. Neither Dante nor Marco have mentioned him."

"Which means he's likely playing us all, including the ambassador."

Kensington slowed once again for a group of tourists and he didn't miss the worshipful looks several teenage boys shot the car as they crossed in front of them. "I'm not ready to let Pryce off the hook. Are you?"

"No." She eased across the street, the city traffic forcing them into a slow crawl. "But it does make a bit more sense since we can't seem to get a feel for any wrongdoing on Pryce's part."

"The man hasn't gotten his position because he's been a choir boy. If anything, the fact that we have questions about Holden only makes the ambassador look more suspicious. You're the one who's suddenly developed a soft spot for the man."

"Not a soft spot. Just a sense, really."

"Because he knew your father?"

"No!" She turned onto the Via Veneto. "No. Of course not."

He trusted her implicitly, but he'd also sensed a widening sense of acceptance toward Pryce. "Your mind and your objectivity are the two best tools someone in our business can possess. Until we fully rule him out, Pryce is still a suspect."

"I know we haven't worked together that long, but I think I'm above a lecture."

"I'm looking out for my partner."

"Yet I'm forced to point out that you've got the gun-shot wound."

He couldn't hold back the smile at the quick riposte. "Touché."

Traffic continued to crawl and he weighed the pros and cons of his next comment before simply diving in. "That's the first time you've mentioned last night."

"I mentioned last night when I told you I'd drive this monster to give you some relief from your wound."

"Don't talk about The Contessa that way."

"You named the car?"

"Of course. She's beautiful."

If Kensington's jokes had fallen flat earlier, he was pleased to see his got a small rise out of her. "If she's so beautiful, why'd you name her after that old lady at Pryce's house?"

"Recent company excused, The Contessa sounds like a hot car's name."

"Whatever. But for the record, I'd have gone with Scarlet or Katerina or Sophia Loren."

"I suppose Sophia Loren is somewhat appropriate since we're in Italy." He hesitated another moment before pressing on. "I was actually talking about the fact you slept through the night last night."

Her face remained curiously blank, without a clue to what she truly thought about spending the night wrapped up in each other.

Kensington fought the urge to gulp in great breaths of air as Jack's words hovered between them in the narrow interior of the car.

How did she explain last night? And what did she even think about it? Although the evening before had been heavy in her thoughts as she dressed that morning, some of its impact had faded in light of the exchange with Keene. Yet here Jack was, bringing it all back up again.

"I suppose it's simply proof that I finally found a job that actually tired me out. I don't want this to ruin my street cred, but although I've been in tough situations before, I haven't actually ever been shot at."

"Let's hope last night was the first *and* last." His words held dark overtones and his face remained limned in hard lines. Clearly her third attempt of the afternoon to ease the situation with a spot of humor missed its mark.

Three strikes and you're out, Steele.

"Do you want to talk about it?"

"Getting shot at?"

"Sleeping through the night."

Jack Andrews wasn't the only one who could do implacable and unmoving. She had no interest in digging deep into her psyche and figuring out what had changed.

None whatsoever.

"What is it about the freedom of a foreign country? Seems like we're both unloading a lot of baggage on this trip," Kensington said.

"Don't brush this off. Last night was a big deal. On a lot of levels."

"It was for me, too, but let's not make it more than it needs to be. We were both exhausted when we dropped into bed. It obviously caught up to us."

"You've never been tired before?"

"As a matter of fact, I'm tired of this conversation." The words lashed out, whip quick, and she didn't wait to see if they'd hit their mark.

"Talk to me."

"What do you want me to say? That last night was a revelation? That I'm suddenly free of the demons of my past? It was one night, Jack. That's all."

"You're the one who hasn't slept through the night in over fifteen years."

"And you're the one who keeps preaching I need to keep my head in the game."

As excuses went, it was lame but effective. He had lectured her more than once, the admonishment not to let her guard down around Pryce as recent as the past few minutes. But even as the self-righteous anger seethed through her, she knew it was something more.

The night before had made her vulnerable in a way she'd never expected. Funny that she'd been prepared to have sex with him, but sleeping in his arms had actually been even more intimate.

She'd let her guard down and she still hadn't figured out how to get it back in place. Especially because Jack had several no trespassing signs of his own.

"What are you getting so prickly about?"

"This from a man who got upset because I told him he was too neat."

"That's different."

"How?" She turned into the long, curving driveway of their hotel, the activity under the porte cochere like a hive of bees, all busy with their work.

"It just is."

She slammed the car into Neutral and pulled the parking brake. "So my life's an open book and yours is a well-guarded secret? I don't think so."

Jack was prevented from saying anything by the arrival of their bellman, and he jumped out to direct the man with their bags. She dealt with the valet and it was several minutes later before they were walking back toward the hotel's elevators.

"We're not done discussing this."

"We are for now. I want to unpack and do a bit of research."

He nodded and gestured her toward an open elevator car. "Then don't let me keep you waiting."

The unpacking took all of five minutes and a shower to freshen up another ten. Which meant she had nothing but an empty hotel room and a computer to keep her and her unruly thoughts occupied.

Who did he think he was? And when had she ever let someone get to her so badly?

Those probing questions and "talk to me" tone of voice. Like he had any business asking those questions, especially when he was locked up tight as a drum about his own issues.

Kensington stopped midstalk across the room and set her brush on the small desk that sat on a far wall. Since when did she get mad about other people's personal business? She and her family carried more than enough of their own baggage—both by circumstance and by the fact that they kept the day to day of their lives private.

She had no right to expect anything less from Jack.

With a hard plop on the bed, she forced herself to calm down. Whatever else she was mad about—and she had a right to plenty—expecting a quid pro quo over personal demons and secrets wasn't who she was. Jack had a right to his past and his privacy, just as she did. Getting mad because he was uncomfortable discussing it was hypocritical and petty.

Even if you are thinking of sleeping with the man?

The low knock on her door interrupted her thoughts. "Kensington, it's me. Open up."

A quick glance down at her robe showed the sash firmly tied and the terry cloth wrapped up to her neck. With a check mark in the decent column, she tightened the belt once more, then reached for the door. "Hi."

"Hi." He leaned against the doorjamb, that large frame seemingly eating up all the space.

And taking up all the air.

The breathy quality of her voice—when she finally found it—only supported the notion. "Hi."

"Can I come in?"

She stood back and gestured him in. "Sure."

Jack opened his mouth, then closed it, then opened it once more before he paced the small expanse of the room. If he didn't look so uncomfortable she might have smiled at how sweet he looked, fumbling over whatever it was he wanted to say.

"You're entitled to your privacy." He stopped in front of her, close enough to touch even though he kept his hands at his sides. "I'm sorry I didn't give you that."

The urge to touch him—to close that distance—had her fisting her own hands at her sides. "That's funny, because I was just thinking the same thing about you and how incredibly curious I've been about your background. You've a right to your privacy, too."

"We make a pair. I don't think I've ever met anyone as prickly as me." His dark hair stood up at the ends— must've been running his fingers through it again—and those lightly edged silver tips drew her attention.

Were they caused by stress? Or by the simple fact he'd seen far too much of life at far too young an age.

"Then clearly you need to spend more time with the

Steele siblings. We've all got a pretty good grip on stick-up-the-bum syndrome."

"Sounds painful."

She laughed at that, the lift of his eyebrows going a long way toward easing the tension of their mutual apology. "At times."

They stood there for the briefest moment, his head bent toward hers, her lack of heels causing a noticeable difference in their height. Her breath caught once more in her throat as their gazes met and everything they'd faced the past week simply faded away.

Both of them kept their hands at their sides, but the air between them began to vibrate with need. Heat arced off his broad shoulders and she had the damnedest urge to reach up and touch him. To trace those hard, capable lines and slowly strip his shirt off to get to skin. To wrap her arms around him and let the moment take them wherever they were meant to go.

Deep down inside, she knew what was to come. It was inevitable.

And so very right.

The heat from his body was no match for the inferno that blazed in the depths of his dark brown eyes, turning them nearly black in the light. But it was the gentleness she also saw reflected there that took this attraction between them from simple need to a complex vortex of emotion that demanded from both of them.

If the emotional intimacy in the car was painful in its intensity, this was its antithesis.

With nothing but impulse and the deepest sense that the moment was right, she lifted her hands, tracing a path over his shoulders. Lifting up onto her tiptoes, she pressed her lips to his, soft and seeking, the moment full of only one question. His arms came around her and as he crushed his mouth to hers, Kensington got her answer.

Against the press of his lips, she whispered hers in return. "Yes."

A million thoughts filled his mind as her arms wrapped around his neck.

Kensington.

She was the breath that filled his lungs and after waiting longer than he thought himself capable, she'd come to him. That simple fact meant more to him than he ever thought possible.

Abstractly he felt the tight tugging in his arm where he'd just placed a fresh bandage over his wound, but the pain was nothing compared to the demands of his body. Nothing compared to the need that drove him to make this woman his own.

"Are you sure?"

"Yes."

There it was again. That one simple word, so full of acceptance and promise.

The tie on her robe slid through his fingers and within moments he had his hands over the warmth of her flesh. A light moisture from the shower still sheened her skin and the scent of her rose up to greet him. The subtle suggestion of orange blossoms from her shampoo battled with something darker and more seductive. Something uniquely Kensington.

He traced a finger down her neck, over the top of her chest, stopping when he reached the curve of her breast. The bright light of afternoon filled her hotel room and the look on her face was unmistakable as it tilted up toward him. Voice husky with need, she whispered his name as his hand closed over her flesh, his thumb and forefinger coaxing the nipple into a tight point. He captured her other breast, satisfied beyond imagining when she leaned into him.

A subtle sigh drifted from her lips as she closed her eyes and tilted her head back. He leaned forward and pressed a line of kisses along the slender column of her throat. The lightest tang of salt tinged his tongue and he lapped like a cat licking cream at a small bead of water that drifted from her still-damp skin.

Shifting, he dropped his hands to her waist and moved her toward the bed, following her down onto the mattress as she pulled him on top of her. The slender lines of her body cushioned him until he turned them so they were face-to-face. Warm and responsive, she moved in his arms, her soft sighs and light moans urging him on as he explored her.

His fingers drifted from the heavy globes of her breasts over the flat planes of her stomach before settling between her thighs. Her eyes widened at his touch and she gripped his shoulders as he delved into the warmth at her core. Her soft cries encouraged him and he kept his motions firm against her pliant skin.

"I want to watch you, Kensington."

"Jack." She uttered his name on another breathy whisper and her gaze locked on his. "It's too much."

He increased the pressure slightly, pleased when another layer of passion filled that liquid blue gaze. "You're so beautiful. Show me what you feel."

Before he could say another word, he felt her clench around his fingers, the sensation matched by the pressure of her hands on his shoulders as her world shattered.

Long, gorgeous moments passed as he dragged every ounce of pleasure from her flesh.

And as she drew his head down to hers for a long, soul-searing kiss, Jack felt the hard, unyielding part of himself crumble to dust.

Kensington kept her arms locked around Jack's neck, desperate to show him with her kiss what he did to her. She wasn't an innocent, but she was cautious about who she let in.

And never before had she experienced anything like this.

He'd branded her, plain and simple.

Branded her with his words and his touch, with his lips and his gentle, determined push to take everything she had and more. Her body still quivered from her explosive orgasm at his hands, delicious shivers quaking through her nerve endings as the rush subsided.

He lifted his head, the smile on his face broad as he looked down at her. For a moment, Kensington simply looked her fill, silence more powerful than any words. Bright sunlight filled the room, the vivid light of a late-winter's afternoon bathing them in its glow.

She ran her hands over his shoulders, surprised to realize he was still covered. "You're wearing too many clothes."

"I had impeccable timing finding you just after your shower."

"I'll have to remember that." With nimble fingers, she tugged at the hem of his T-shirt, dragging the material up the thick lines of his body. The same heavy ropes of muscles she'd admired that morning flexed under her fingertips as she removed his shirt.

When she reached for the snap on his slacks, he stilled her hands with his. "I'll get it."

"Spoilsport."

A lopsided grin filled his face as he rolled off the bed. "Eminently practical. You make the wrong move and I may ruin what's still to come."

"Well, when you put it that way—" Kensington left the word to hover there and lifted her arms in a stretch. A shot of heat arrowed toward her core at the appreciation she saw reflected in Jack's eyes at the sensuous movements.

"You're really trying to kill me."

"I'd prefer to think of myself as opportunistically taking advantage of your current weakness."

His pants fell to the floor and he kicked his legs out of them before reaching for the waistband of his briefs. His heavy arousal was evident through the material, but even that didn't prepare her for the sight of him fully naked.

Magnificent was the only term she could come up with as her mouth went dry and even that adjective was inadequate.

Wholly inadequate, she was forced to acknowledge as he came down over top of her once more.

"Now," he pressed his lips against her ear as his body pressed against hers, "what was that you mentioned about opportunity?"

"Let me see if I can refresh your memory." She pressed against his shoulders until they lay on their sides facing each other, then snaked her hand down between them, capturing his thick erection. His body tightened reflexively, but it was the sharp intake of breath as he pressed himself into her hand that had her smiling.

"I think opportunity just knocked." His voice was dark and heavy, arousal vibrating in every word, but she couldn't hold back the joyful shot of laughter that lit her up.

"You're a funny one, Andrews."

"And you're amazing, Kensington Steele."

The light humor faded as the demands of the moment caught them both. She wanted to stop and savor the feeling of simply being together but knew the need that had gripped both of them demanded satisfaction.

She ran her hand over the length of him once more, the throbbing flesh in her fingers and the sheen of sweat that broke out over his flesh ready confirmation of Jack's pleasure.

With tight strokes, she demanded all.

And only when she'd pressed him to his limits and beyond did his hand wrap around hers, his breath strained and his words ragged with need. "Not yet."

Before she could coax him further, he'd shifted, reaching for his pants on the floor. A lightly muttered oath when he fumbled his wallet had her smiling, the sweetness of the moment not lost on her.

He was as affected as she was.

His hands shook when he surfaced from his hunt through his clothing and she took the condom from his hands, the light tremble in his fingers warming her as she tore the foil. She made quick work of the condom, surprised to find her own fingers trembling as she covered his length.

And then she gave herself to the moment, wrapping her arms around him, and simply hung on for the ride.

The passion that he'd kept tightly leashed shattered and he filled her in long, sure strokes. Pleasure spiraled through her body, taking her up and pressing her on once more with its raw power. She met him, her hips rising to meet each of his thrusts, matching the rhythm he set for them both.

Kensington was vaguely aware of the soft cries that escaped her throat as the pleasure built, but she was too lost in the moment to concentrate on any one piece of the sensual onslaught. She pressed her fingers into the hard globes of his buttocks, pulling him closer each time he thrust.

And only when the telltale signs of her response began deep inside—and she felt him answer in the further tightening of his muscles—did she let go, reaching once more for the exquisite pleasure only he could give.

A heavy, exultant shout matched his last thrust and she took him in, welcoming his heavy weight and complete vulnerability in her arms.

As they lay there wrapped up in each other, their breathing still heavy with exertion, she marveled at what he'd drawn from her.

A desire she'd wondered herself incapable of swamped her in a tangle of thoughts and needs and feelings, thick with all the things she'd worked so hard to keep buried. With a surprising amount of ease, Jack had opened the tight lock she kept around her heart.

And Kensington wasn't sure it could ever be closed.

Chapter 16

Kensington awoke slowly, the dark sky outside her window the only proof that they'd slept. The days had gotten progressively shorter as winter descended and she estimated the subtle twilight still outside her window meant it was late afternoon.

Her stomach let out a loud growl and she amended her estimate to early evening.

The hard lines of Jack's body cradled her and she ran her index finger in lazy circles over his biceps. His flesh was soft to the touch, but the muscle underneath was firm. Implacable.

Just like the man.

Her eyes adjusted to the dim light and she used the quiet moments to observe him at her leisure. He was a big man—broad and capable—so it was with no small measure of surprise to find him so fit. Now that she'd seen and touched every inch of him, the long ropes of muscles over his large frame indicated a man who kept himself in prime condition.

Unable to stop herself, she shifted her explorations to the muscles over his stomach. She traced the lines of his ribs, then moved on to the curved muscles above his belly button. The hard, muscular ridges contracted at her touch, the warm flesh puckering slightly with goose bumps.

"That feels good but it tickles." His hand stilled her movement as his lips curved into a smile against her temple.

"I'm sorry I woke you."

"I'm not." The smile broadened before he shifted and nuzzled his lips to her neck. His hand stayed solid over her palm before he pressed her to explore farther south.

A different line of muscle greeted her as her fingers closed over the long length of him and she couldn't hold back a smile of her own. "Calculating, Mr. Andrews. Nicely done."

She traced him from base to tip, the sharp intake of breath and the tightening of those stomach muscles she'd so recently explored the very real evidence of his arousal.

"You know—" she whispered the words against his earlobe "—I'm not sure all this activity is good for your wound. You really should be resting."

His hand covered hers once more, his fingers holding her firmly in place before he rearranged them against his body. "Woman, if you leave this bed, I'll simply drag you right back until you finish."

"Well, then. It's a good thing I wouldn't do that."

The darker thoughts that flitted through her mind earlier vanished under the sexy banter. The time in his arms—and the sheer joy of being together—was better than she could have imagined.

"You wouldn't?"

"Absolutely not. I'm a woman who sees every job all the way through to the end." The breathy, seductive words were a revelation and Kensington couldn't hold back a smile.

But it was the complete abandonment to the moment—and the joy of playing the temptress—that had a sense of freedom coursing through her veins as she made good on her promise.

Jack poured a rich red Chianti into Kensington's wineglass as she finished up her order. Once their waiter departed, he handed her the glass, then lifted his own for a toast. "To an amazing afternoon with an amazing woman."

A light blush crept up her cheeks as she clinked her glass against his. "I'll second that."

The blush only heightened the healthy pink glow in her cheeks and Jack was absurdly pleased to know he'd put it there. He had no idea where the caveman urges had some from, but he had no interest in changing his attitude. The woman had gotten into his blood and he felt too damn good to question the reasons why.

"What did Marco say when you talked with him?"

The sudden shift to business had him faltering for a moment, but he quickly righted himself. "He's feeling better and he's happy to talk to us in the morning. He's also sick to death of his hospital bed and sounded like he's more than ready for something to occupy his mind."

"Good. That boredom's a sign he's on the road to recovery." Kensington tore off a piece of bread from a hot, crusty loaf their waiter had left behind and toyed with the edge. "What did he say when you told him about our suspicions about Keene?"

That dull edge of annoyance sharpened ever so slightly and he tried to push it aside as he reached for his own piece of bread. They did have a job to do and he'd called Marco while she'd gotten ready for dinner.

So why did her interest prick at his ego?

"It was a surprise to him. Apparently he had vetted Keene through several sources early on and nothing popped."

"Maybe he wasn't looking in the right places. I'll take a look when we get back to the hotel."

"I had other ideas for when we got back to the hotel."

That blush returned, but with it a subtle darkening of her eyes. "We can't lose focus on this. I appreciated the afternoon distraction, but I need to get those runs down on Keene. I'll carb load here at dinner and then get to work."

Distraction?

"You sound like you're running a marathon." His words came out with a clipped edge he hadn't intended and he reached for his glass of water to sooth his throat.

"A mental one, at least."

"For the record, I don't know that you're going to find a heck of a lot on Keene. The man hasn't tripped anyone's trigger for a reason."

"I have my ways." Her eyes twinkled over the rim of her wineglass before she took a sip.

"Yeah, well, clearly so does he."

"Way to motivate your partner, Jack." She tore off another piece of bread before offering him a small smile.

"Am I a partner or a distraction?"

The words shot out as if from a cannon, landing squarely in the center of the table. A dull, oafish sense of playing the fool flooded his senses but there was no way he could take it back.

"I'm sorry if my multitasking offends your manly sensibilities."

"It doesn't."

"Oh, no?"

"Of course not."

"I have brothers. I get it. I should be sitting here in a rapturous glow, staring at you with adoring eyes with nothing on my mind except how fast we can get back into bed."

Even though she'd practically hit a bull's-eye, he couldn't quite acknowledge he was that big of an ass. So he reached for her hand instead. "I wouldn't mind a bit of adoration. Especially since I can't seem to get my mind off of anything but you."

"Oh." The teasing note left her eyes, replaced by a light sheen of tears. "That's so sweet."

"Until I messed it up by acting like a caveman."

A lone tear slipped down the side of her cheek and she brushed it away before that gorgeous smile returned to light up her face. "I like your caveman. And I had an amazing time this afternoon and I'm quite anxious to repeat it. You know, in case you were wondering."

He hadn't asked—or sought—approval from a woman in his entire adult life, so the fact that he felt such an overwhelming sense of relief was as shocking as it was awkward. "I had an amazing time, too."

"Then we're agreed."

"On what?"

"On how it's time we refocused on this case. There'll be time enough for—" she broke off as if suddenly aware of the permanence her words implied. "There'll be time enough for talking about us when this is finished."

"If you want to get all girly about it and, you know, talk about your feelings. Sure. We'll discuss it then."

The joke hit its mark and her tossed napkin hit him square on the head. "Ha ha, Mr. Caveman."

Their waiter arrived and placed their steaming plates of

pasta on the table. He refilled their wineglasses, then departed after the assurance they didn't need anything else.

Jack dug into his pasta, the luscious smells redirecting some of his earlier angst toward his growling stomach. "My sisters will probably give you the third degree, but I'll get them to go easy."

"What?"

He had his pasta twirled around a fork and halfway toward his mouth before he realized Kensington sat and stared at him, her plate untouched. "What is it?"

"You want me to meet your sisters?"

As he listened to his own words wing back at him, he knew with absolute certainty he wanted to bring her home to meet his family. "Well, yeah. They're nosy as all getout but they're wonderful. They'll love you."

"I'd like that. Very much."

A few hours later, after pasta, cappuccino and a shared tiramisu that would make angels weep, Jack wrapped his hand around Kensington's. "It's a cold night—you sure you don't want a cab?"

"No way. I need to move after that huge dinner, which I so elegantly ate all of, and it's a pretty night."

He nodded and they started off, strolling hand in hand along the winding streets that made up Rome. The air was crisp and sharp, the night sky winking above them.

"Did Marco say anything else?"

"No, but he did promise to put out a few feelers. I got the distinct feeling he was thrilled to have something to keep him busy."

"I can't believe they haven't released him yet."

They entered the long common area of Piazza Navona, their steps leisurely. People were out and about, but foot traffic was definitely light for a Sunday evening in winter and Jack couldn't get past the simple joy of taking in the night air with her.

It was almost enough to forget the events of the past few days. The gunshots and the discovery of Keene's potential involvement in what was happening in Pryce's own home.

The memory of how close they came—and how vulnerable they had been—had his gaze sharpening on the edge of the square. "The Palazzo Altemps is just outside the north end of the piazza. We should take a few minutes to check it out, without Dante and his men swirling around us. See if there're any areas we want to call to his attention so he can beef up security for Pryce's event."

"Agreed, but can we stop at the fountain first?"

She wrapped her arm around his waist and he used the movement to pull her close under his good arm. "What would a trip to a Roman piazza be without a visit to a fountain?"

"Exactly."

They kept up their stroll, the warmth of their connected bodies staving off the cold. The air around the running fountain was cool when they approached it, the slight mist from the water icy on the night air.

Kensington pointed toward the large statue, an obelisk standing tall from its center. "This is one of my favorites. It can't compete with the Trevi Fountain, but it's pretty great in its own right."

"This fountain had a lot of controversy when it was unveiled in the seventeenth century."

"Funny how no one likes art when the people are starving."

He stared down at her, fascinated again by her depth of knowledge on so many subjects. "You know that story?"

"Oh, yes. Bernini created the statue for Pope Innocent the Tenth, but it was done at the expense of the Romans as a public project. Rome was experiencing a famine at the time so spending money on some carved rocks wasn't anyone's idea of a good time."

Kensington linked their fingers before dragging him around the perimeter of the statue so they could see the fountain from each side. Four rivers were represented in the statue, signifying the four continents where the papacy had influence at the time it was created.

Although beautiful, Jack couldn't see how the statue could take precedence over people's basic right to food. "A monument to vanity."

"Albeit a functional one." Kensington pointed toward the water pooling in the base. "The fountain did, and does, provide running water to the city's denizens."

"A modest distinction at best when you have nothing to eat."

"The powerful want what they want. Isn't that what keeps us in business?"

"Is that how you see what we do?"

"Don't you?" She looked up at him as they strolled from the fountain toward the museum where Pryce would hold his next event. "The wealthy live by a different set of rules. They see the world as theirs to control while most people are simply at its mercy."

"Interesting opinion from one of the women who controls it."

A light snort escaped her lips and she waved a hand. "Hardly. I know I lead a comfortable life, which I'm grateful for, but I don't have the sort of power that drives global events or rules an entire city."

"No, but you do have the power to bring one down. You realize that, don't you?" A light prickle of awareness lit up his spine when her eyes grew wide with the implication of his words.

"Is that how you see what we do?"

He'd never put it in such deliberate terms before, but the truth was he did see his role that way. His business was all about uncovering secrets and lies.

"Don't you? Look at why we're here. We're in a position to investigate and ultimately depose a global leader if the suspicions about him are true. What we find can disgrace his ambassadorship and ripple through his country on many levels. At a minimum, the sheer embarrassment of what Pryce has done is going to do damage."

"We don't know it's him."

"But we know enough to sense it's him or someone close to him. By virtue of what we do, we're in a position to make waves and rattle chains."

"Yes."

Hesitation dripped from her words and Jack was intrigued despite himself. "So why the reticence?"

"I guess I've always seen my role as more discrete than that. Separate. Riding in to the rescue, then riding off again."

"Is that the job, or you?"

He wasn't sure where the question came from, but the light stammer in her words was proof positive he'd overstepped. "Does it have to have a definition? I have a set of skills and so do my siblings. We do the work that needs to be done and we've got the connections to make it happen. It's as complicated and as simple as that."

Jack suspected it was a lot more complicated than she let on and nearly said as much when the light prickle that had tripped his trigger a few moments earlier coalesced into something more distinct.

And far more threatening.

"What is it?" Kensington's gaze drew sharp at his motions but he kept his hand firmly pressed over hers, moving them forward. "Keep walking and don't look back."

"Jack?"

"I've got a funny feeling."

The piazza was long and oval-shaped and they'd nearly cleared the length of it, the street access to the Palazzo Altemps in sight. "What kind of funny feeling?"

"Like we're being followed."

The arm she had around his waist tightened reflexively as she burrowed against his chest. "Did you see anyone?"

"No, but I need you to look now. Giggle at something I'm saying and run your hand over my cheek. When I press you against that wall over there I need you to keep an eye on the street."

"I'm not tall enough to see over your shoulder."

"Well, I'm sure as hell not putting your back to them."

"There's no choice and we need to know what we're up against." She lifted her hand to cup his cheek, the light carefree giggle that erupted from her throat at decided odds with the words that followed. "Do it now."

He knew it was useless to argue and they didn't have much time to waste, but a slick layer of fear coated his tongue as he dragged her back against his body. The moment he had the wall at his back, he angled around her as far as he dared, then dropped his mouth to hers.

The shot of heat—so uniquely Kensington—coupled with the adrenaline roaring in his blood disoriented him for the briefest moment before he righted himself and opened his eyes. The north end of Piazza Navona spread out before him and he scanned the area in quadrants, checking off areas in his mind as he surveyed the landscape.

First quadrant, second, third. All produced nothing beyond average citizens of Rome or a few late-season tourists.

He'd nearly given up on the hunt when he saw the man, leisurely out of place with his back to a wall about thirty yards from them.

"You see something?" Kensington whispered the words against his lips while shifting her arms around his neck to hide the fact they'd stopped kissing.

"I think so. I'm going to turn you around and I want you to take a look also. Stand to the side and I won't get in the way."

He kept his moves easy, his gaze never wavering from Kensington's. "To your right. About one o'clock."

"I see him."

"And?"

"He's watching us and it doesn't have that voyeuristic edge that you'd expect if we were just two people kissing in the square."

"He's on the hunt."

"Yes, he is."

She allowed her gaze to travel over the man once more. He wore a leather jacket and he leaned back against the thick, stone walls of one of the many buildings that dotted the piazza, one booted foot up behind him, balancing him against the wall. Cigarette smoke swirled around his head and he looked for all the world like a man out enjoying the cold evening.

Had they seen him before?

A mental loop played through her mind of the last several days, but nothing registered. "He doesn't look like anyone from Tuscany."

"Pryce and Keene likely have a higher-caliber group of thugs right here in Rome to do their bidding."

"We need to flush him out. See what he knows. You've got your gun, right?"

Jack's harsh cough stilled her. "As a last resort, yes."

"I think we've run out of options."

A wry smile ghosted his lips. "Are you always this bloodthirsty?"

"I am when I think someone's going to shoot first."

The small smile vanished and she was gratified to see she'd made her point. He glanced down between them. "Gun's in my coat pocket."

"Well, then. Let's go ask our friendly neighborhood stalker a few questions."

The walk across the remaining yards of the piazza felt endless, but she stuck by Jack's side, determined to see this through. Despite the sarcastic tone, she was nervous and only grew more so as the man's steely-eyed gaze never wavered.

"Who are you?" She eyed his stance, curious that he never shifted from his insouciant pose against the wall. "What do you want from us?"

"I'm someone tasked to keep an eye on you at the orders of a very powerful man." Although his words held the thickness of an accent, his English was flawless. "I think you underestimate your opponent, walking brazenly about as you do."

Jack's words were even in tone, his own stance relaxed when he spoke. "Your boss has nothing to fear from us."

"And I'm here to see that it stays that way."

"Your boss has made some exceedingly poor decisions." Kensington floated the thought, curious to see if the man took the bait and indicated who he was working for.

Pryce? Keene? Both of them?

"Decisions that are none of your business. You're outsiders and you have no reason to be here. Take your ideals and your flashy attempts at providing security and leave."

"We were hired to do a job, guarding the ambassador, and we'll see it through." Jack maintained that nonchalant tone but Kensington didn't miss the subtle shift as he put his body between hers and the man. Although unnecessary—just like his attempts to protect her during their kiss—she couldn't deny how good it felt to have his protection.

The man cocked his head as he exhaled a steady stream of smoke into the crisp night air. "I find it humorous for all your supposed skills you don't understand the game you're really a part of."

"Game?" The nonchalance vanished from Jack's words, replaced with a harsh bite. "I fail to see any humor in the analogy."

"Because there is nothing funny about the situation you both find yourselves in."

Kensington pressed against Jack's side, sensing something deeper behind the man's words, even if it wasn't immediately evident. "We'll finish the job we came here to do."

"Even if it costs you your lives?" The man took one last drag, then threw his cigarette to the ground, grinding it under the toe of his boot.

Jack moved forward another step. "Again, I'm sensing threats you're in no position to make."

The man never moved, but a broad smile spread across his face. "Events were set into motion long ago and you can't stop them. And make no mistake about it, you will die trying."

Chapter 17

Die trying. Die trying. Die trying.

Kensington shuddered, the man's words playing on a continuous loop through her mind. She and Jack had long since returned to their hotel, yet the threat lingered. She'd already taken a long hot shower and changed into the warmest pajamas she'd brought on the trip, but even the fluffy fleece did nothing to warm her against the cold thoughts.

"Got it." Her brother's voice snapped through her phone and she pulled her attention back to the call.

"Got what, Campbell? You're working on, like, four things simultaneously."

"The cameras from the piazza. I got a clean read from the bastard's face and I'm running it through facial recognition right now. I'll send you what I find."

"And the other things?"

"T-Bone and I have been digging on Pryce's financials for days. Same as you found before. Nothing's popping."

"And Keene?"

"Nothing there, either. You sure that's his name?"

Her brother's words unleashed a torrent of expletives as Jack let himself into the room, two cups of coffee in his hand. "What'd I miss?"

Kensington hit the speaker button on her phone before focusing on her computer. "Damn it to hell, I do not believe it."

"What don't you believe?"

Campbell's tinny voice echoed from the speakers of her cell phone but it was Jack who picked up the conversation. "She's typing furiously and muttering more of those dainty words I never thought I'd hear cross her lips."

"Bite me." Kensington shot back the words as she logged on to one of the databases she paid through the nose for each year.

"You must be Jack. Campbell Steele here."

Jack and her brother traded pleasantries—nonsense words that faded as she focused on the screen.

Layers. It was all about layers, and she hadn't dug through the right ones.

Events were set into motion long ago and you can't stop them.

The thug's words came back to her as she typed, digging as fast as she could.

"This is about as fun as watching paint dry, Kenz. Want to tell me what you're looking for?"

"I'm so stupid." She shook her head, wondering if it could be that easy. "How could I have missed it?"

"Missed what?" Jack's voice layered over Campbell's continued muttering about how single-minded she could be.

"It's been right in front of us." She looked up and gestured Jack toward her screen. "Remember what the thug said—things set in motion long ago?"

"Kensington!" Campbell's harsh tone echoed through the room.

She tossed a glance at the phone but reined in her irritation at the interruption before she spoke. "Would you calm down?"

"Would you tell me what's going on?"

"Keene. You were right, Campbell. It's not his real name. It's just like Abby and her brother."

The muttering through the phone—a lovable quirk of her brother's she'd learned to ignore—stopped as he went quiet. "What do you mean?"

"We missed the signs when you were in Paris because the threat against Abby was a half brother she didn't know she had."

"Yes."

Her heart turned over at that single word. Although Campbell and his fiancée, Abby, were dealing with it, she knew the trauma of the previous September still lived with both of them. Abby's half brother had kidnapped her and it was Campbell who'd killed the man, removing the threat that hung over both of them.

How odd, then, that such a horrible experience would ultimately shed the light they needed on Keene and Pryce.

She tapped one more set of instructions into the database, then directed Jack's attention toward a specific point on her computer screen.

"Holden Keene is Pryce's illegitimate son."

"The weekend went well. You continue to prove yourself an incredibly valuable asset, Holden." Pryce handed over the last of the paperwork they'd reviewed, then steepled his fingers over his desk. "I'd like to formally announce you at the charity event at Palazzo Altemps tomorrow."

"It's been a pleasure to work with you, Ambassador, and I appreciate the praise. Much of Tierra Kimber's growth in global public opinion is directly attributable to you. For that reason, I would prefer to remain in the background at tomorrow's event."

"Holden." The ambassador let out a soft sigh and Holden knew what was coming. "You may dispense with the formalities. You are my son. A relationship I'd like the entire world to know about. Why must you insist upon hiding it?"

"When I came into your employ we agreed these were my wishes."

"Yes, yes." His father nodded. "But I'd hoped you'd come around in time. I'm proud of you. Proud of your accomplishments and your mind and your talents. I missed that for too long, which was my mistake, but I'd like the chance to make amends."

I just bet you would.

Holden tamped down the thought, anxious his true feelings not show in his body language. The old man hadn't been proud of him years ago. Oh, sure, he was around and available, but he'd kept Holden and his mother hidden away, unwilling to publicly acknowledge them.

It was all well and good he wished to do so now, but too little, too late, as the saying went.

He had plans and part of what made them work so well was the fact no one knew who he was. Keene was the name of the man his mother eventually married and it had been to his benefit to keep the moniker, distancing himself from Pryce.

The man might want a chance to make up for his youthful hubris now, but Holden had long ago stopped seeking his father's approval. In fact, it shocked him how much more appealing it was to consider the ultimate destruction of his father's good name.

Pryce.

Oh, yes, he'd paid the price. Holden had lived in the shadows, the illegitimate bastard who was never good enough, all while Pryce's three other children were feted and groomed for something more.

Funny how all that time and effort hadn't paid dividends, old man.

One son had wasted his life racing cars until the sport took his life. Another had far too big a fondness for the ponies and not enough for any degree of labor or effort. And Pryce's youngest, a daughter, was content to smile on the arm of one bachelor after another, refusing to settle down or do anything beyond spending her days at the salon.

So now Pryce wanted him?

Wanted to tell the world how proud he was.

Too little, too late.

Tierra Kimber sat on some of the richest veins of diamonds anywhere in the world. With his own personal connections and the added grease working for the ambassador provided, he was well on his way to building his own empire.

The diamonds moved a pretty penny, financing any number of nefarious schemes throughout the world. All because they fit nice and neat into bottles of barely drinkable table wine.

But the real beauty of it all was that he was virtually untouchable. The wine was his father's. The vineyard was his father's.

And Holden had put enough safeguards in place that at any point anyone caught on to what he was doing, it would be his father who'd take the heat.

Yes, he was smart and enterprising. The bastard son who'd made good.

And he'd be damned if he was going to let Hubert Pryce take the very best of him now.

"She's different. I can hear it in your voice. Tell me about her."

Jack held back the sigh at his sister's demands and buckled down for the third degree. The nine-hour time difference between Seattle and Rome ensured she was wide-awake and in the prime of her day.

Which, knowing Kathy, meant she was rarin' to go, full of questions and would not be put off.

He'd learned long ago not answering when either of his sisters called did him no good, they just kept trying, so when her name filled the screen on his phone he'd opted to bite the bullet and answer.

And wished he'd just accepted the barrage of text messages instead.

"Her name's Kensington Steele. She's working with me on my latest job."

"You've never worked with anyone before. And since when do you hire anyone beyond mercenary thugs to help you out?"

"This job required special assistance."

"How special?"

"She manages a firm like mine. They specialize in high-end security and deals. I needed a woman on this to look convincing."

"You've needed a woman for some time and for reasons a hell of a lot better than appearances." Kathy's words were far too knowing, but the sentiment underneath was all big-sisterly concern. "Sounds like Ms. Steele fits the bill."

"Kath." He hesitated for the briefest moment before plowing ahead. "How do you know she's different?"

"There's something special in your voice, Jackie. I can hear it when you say her name."

"What's that?"

"Happiness."

Jack ignored the uneasy sentiment that arose but before he could say anything, Kathy pressed him further. "You deserve to be happy. And you deserve something more than that job of yours."

"I like my job."

"I'm not suggesting otherwise, but it can't be everything."

Although he generally avoided even thinking about his feelings let alone discussing them out loud, Kathy had caught him at a weak moment. At least that was what he told himself. "What makes you think I'm unhappy?"

"Oh, babe, no matter how big you get, you're still my baby brother. You think I don't know or understand the hell you live with? The hell you've had to live with?"

"It's fine. Mom was a long time ago."

"Yet she's like a ghost you can't shake loose. You're entitled to happiness. To sharing your life with someone. And there's someone out there who will be committed to doing their part to share it with you."

"Kensington isn't about Mom."

"I never said she was. *You* did, little brother."

Clever.

He ran his hands through his hair, tugging tightly on the ends. He'd come to hate his mother for leaving them, but he still struggled to talk about her.

Whereas their oldest sister, Susan, had struggled for years with the effects of their mother leaving, Kathy had been more pragmatic. After her initial grief of their mother abandoning them, Kathy had moved on, refusing to mince words about Beatrice Andrews.

So why couldn't he figure out a way to do the same?

His mother had nothing to do with his relationship with Kensington. Frankly, his mother had nothing to do with nothing.

Not any longer.

So why couldn't he bury the ghost?

"Listen. Much as I'd love to hear more about this amazing woman, I know when to cut bait. And I'm being summoned from the living room to help decorate the tree."

"Really?"

"Please don't tell me you've forgotten it's December."

Maybe he had. Or if he hadn't forgotten the month, he had skipped over the major holiday part of it. Just as he'd missed Thanksgiving with his family because he was pulling back-to-back jobs that didn't allow for any time off. "I know what month it is."

"Did you book your tickets here for the holidays?"

"Not yet."

"Then I'll leave you with one last thought—consider bringing a guest."

Jack hung up the phone and wondered why it felt as if he'd been put through the ringer, even though he'd never moved off the small love seat in his suite.

Kensington reviewed the notes she'd made on the small tablet next to her computer. Holden Keene, born one Holden Pryce Abernathy. Birth certificate for said child originally listed no father but was later amended to reflect Hubert Pryce.

She kept scanning, reviewing the information she'd already committed to memory. Education at the best schools, all paid for by Pryce. Genius-level IQ, testing off the charts relative to his classmates and the general population of Tierra Kimber. Natural aptitudes for geology and politics and an active refusal to be photographed.

Although he'd not fully escaped photographic capture, she'd run the images she did have back through the same imaging program Campbell used and was surprised to find subtle differences that would have made any standard database kick out errors.

Sculpted changes to his ears and subtle alterations to his teeth and chin were prevalent in a majority of the photos.

"Don't like getting your picture taken, do you, Holden?"

When her computer beeped it had completed the last task she'd put to it, she shifted gears and ran through the remaining information on-screen. No known siblings from his mother's side, despite her remarriage to Theodore Keene, but Holden had three half siblings through Pryce's parentage.

Because she'd already run Pryce's children, she didn't pay them much mind, but she couldn't deny the direction her thoughts turned as she opened up a new search query.

Jack had excused himself earlier to talk to his sister, and the sibling connection reinforced a thought she'd had earlier.

She was curious about Jack's mother.

She'd long ago stopped feeling guilty for digging into the people who were part of the jobs she managed, but she had made it a personal policy to avoid looking up those she knew. People didn't live perfect lives, a truth her access to information indicated with shocking regularity.

So why did she feel the urge to go against her instincts on this one?

She loved Jack.

Funny how after fighting it for so long, the reality was so easy to embrace.

For so long she'd lived with the fear that she wasn't capable of sharing her life with someone. That a husband and family simply weren't meant to be hers. And that the damage inflicted by such deep, expansive loss at a young age left a hole that couldn't be filled.

How wrong she'd been.

She loved Jack.

And because she loved him, she was deeply curious about the events that had shaped who he was. He wanted her to meet his family, yet he refused to say anything about his mother beyond the basics he'd shared. He'd not even risen to the bait when she asked about his father and could only suspect the man had never been a part of his life. Factor in that he lived his life with a vague sort of recklessness, the evidence of that behavior currently sitting on his biceps in a healing gunshot wound, and she was desperate to know what made him tick.

Maybe if she understood what shaped him, she'd understand how to love him.

And maybe you need to back away from the computer, too.

That small voice that whispered that she needed to leave well enough alone and let Jack share when he was ready was loud, but the blinking cursor and ready curiosity that was a hallmark of her personality steamrolled over the privacy barrier.

Before she could second-guess herself further, she tapped in Beatrice Andrews's name and known family members and waited for what was to come. And was beyond shocked when the results streamed across the screen.

A well of tears lodged in a tight ball in her throat as she read the reports of his mother's death, bludgeoned in her bed by the man believed to be her second husband.

Jack had found that. Discovered this horrible news as

a child, hacking away into a computer database seeking information.

This was what had shaped him. Not only had Beatrice left him and his older sisters behind, but she'd lost her life so violently. A senseless act that tossed away any ability for her to right her wrongs against her family.

"Kensington? Are you all right?"

She hadn't even heard the door unlock and then Jack was at her side, kneeling down before her. With her one hand she closed the lid of her laptop while dashing away tears with the other. "I'm fine. Fine."

"What happened?"

Tell him!

Her conscious shouted the words, but try as she might, they wouldn't come.

"Nothing. Nothing at all."

"Why are you crying?"

"It's senseless. So senseless."

He pulled her to her feet and wrapped her up in his arms. The steady thud of his heart against her chest reassured, even as it seemed to issue an accusation.

You had.

No right.

To spy.

Shaking off the strange thoughts, she pressed her lips against that sure, solid beat and prayed she could love him enough.

Jack couldn't understand what had Kensington so upset, her murmured words making little sense as she clung to him. She'd seemed fine when he'd left her to take the call from Kathy, so returning to find her crying—especially because he'd spent the past fifteen minutes working through the emotions churned up by his sister's questions—was unnerving.

He tilted her chin up with the tip of his finger. The tears had stopped but her eyes still held a watery glaze that turned those blazing blue irises the color of the Mediterranean. "Shh. It's going to be fine."

"I know." She nodded.

"Did you find what you were looking for?"

The question had an odd expression flitting across her face—was that guilt?—before she tamped it down. "Keene is Hubert's son. I found the information to prove it."

"Yet they don't acknowledge each other."

"Nope."

"Is there the chance, even if it's remote, that one of them doesn't know?"

"I'd say yes but the birth certificate was amended when Holden was about five. Pryce signed notarized papers ensuring he was added to a formerly blank reference to birth father."

"There goes that theory."

"Jack."

He pulled his mind from the situation of Pryce and Keene and shifted his gaze back toward hers.

"Make love to me. I don't care about anything outside these four walls right now. Not Pryce or Keene. Not our job. Just you."

The change was such a shift from their dinner, he couldn't resist poking her ever so slightly. "What happened to the all-business-all-the-time speech I got at dinner?"

"Can't a girl change her mind?" One lone index finger trailed over his jaw before running down to settle on his chest.

"Just so long as you let me keep up."

Without waiting for further instruction, he scooped her

up and crossed to the bed, laying her down on the center of the blankets. The world outside could wait. For now, he had a warm, willing woman in his arms and he refused to let the opportunity pass him by.

He covered her body with his, stripping her pajamas with quick, efficient movements. He shucked his own T-shirt and jeans, then returned to her warm form, her arms open and ready for him.

No matter how heated his fantasies had been since meeting her, nothing could replace the reality of making love to Kensington. She was an eager lover, as willing to give pleasure as to receive it.

The minutes spun out around them like a tapestry, woven together with soft sighs and heated glances, slow caresses and carnal exploration of each other. Over and over, they plied each other with an aching tenderness that demanded all.

The gentle lovemaking he imagined in his mind was quickly overruled by the intense needs of his body, only driven more so when she rose up over him after sheathing him in a condom. He gripped her hips to help her set the rhythm, her soft curves rising above him in an erotic display of physical beauty.

He reached for her breasts, caressing her hardened nipples as she pressed herself into his palms. The tight fit of her body dragged him through his paces, the look and feel of her in his hands the sweetest aphrodisiac.

She screamed his name on a hard cry as her pleasure crested and he reached once more for her hips, driving upward into the tight sheath of her body before he gave in to his own release.

Pleasure radiated through his body in heavy, greedy waves and he buried his face in her neck as he rode the last, all-consuming need for possession.

"Kensington."

He whispered her name, unable to put to words what she did to him.

Or how badly he needed her.

So instead, he simply held on and hoped what he held in his heart was enough.

Kensington slowly came back to consciousness as if surfacing from a deep sleep. She reached out a hand for Jack's warmth, then woke up faster when she realized he wasn't in bed with her.

She sat up and a quick glance at the clock showed she hadn't slept that long, only a few minutes at most. Her body still tingled from the aftereffects of making love to Jack and a subtle stiffness had settled in her muscles. She lifted her arms for a stretch as Jack came out of the bathroom, that gorgeous form now clad once again in his jeans.

"Now who's all-business-all-the-time?" She couldn't quite hold back the complaint at the evidence he'd at least partially dressed.

"Hey now. I had an idea and I can't very well sit around naked."

"Suit yourself." She reached for her pajama top where it had settled on the end of the bed and dragged it on. "What was your idea?"

"I want to do a search on what countries Pryce sells his wines. That should be readily available on his site. I also want to check a few distribution contacts our jeweler readily provided."

"Our jeweler? The guy we acted for in New York?"

A large grin spread across his face. "Was it *all* an act?"

"You know what I meant. When did you talk to him?"

"I forgot he'd called me the other day. I buttered him up with some nice words about Pryce and how delighted he was to share the quality of his country's diamonds with the world. Then I promised I'd connect them."

"How are you going to do that?"

"I can't." He shrugged. "So I made another purchase that assuaged my conscience and made the entire ruse worth his while."

"You bought something else?" She knew she should really do better than letting her jaw drop like a country bumpkin, but he'd already spent a considerable sum on their first visit.

"Well, I was buying practically wholesale."

"Jack!"

"What's your password?"

"Sherlock." Whether it was the distraction of his imagined purchase or the sight of his bare chest peeking over her laptop, Kensington didn't know. She only knew the answer was out of her mouth before she remembered what she'd left posted on the screen.

"What the hell is this?"

Chapter 18

"Jack. I can explain."

"*This* is what you were crying about before?" He pointed a finger at the computer as he stood and slammed the chair backward with his foot. The chair rolled on its wheels before crashing against the wall behind him. "You spied on me?"

"No!"

The lighthearted banter between them had fled, along with any sense of lingering warmth from their lovemaking. "So you just happened to put my mother's name into a computer program, uncovering the results of how she met her untimely demise."

"Would you listen to me?"

"Why? Because you were so honest with me? Spying on me like I was one of the common criminals you investigate?"

"It's not like that."

"Then what was it like?"

"It was a query into your background. Something you did on me before this job even started."

"It's not the same and you know it. I looked into your business and you know damn well you did the same. I looked into the basics of your background. I did not go digging to find your parents' death certificates."

The barb lodged just under her heart and no matter how she spun it, nothing changed her actions. Knowing that, she fell back on the only thing she had left.

The truth.

"I wanted to know more about you. With all those little details you keep locked up so tightly it's a wonder there's any air in there."

"So you ask, Kensington. You don't spy on me to get information."

She whirled away from him, grabbing her pajama bottoms from the foot of the bed and dragging them on. When she turned back around, her ice-queen shield was firmly in place. "Since you won't let me explain I'd like you to leave."

"Right. Sure. Slap up that brick wall when something gets hard and uncomfortable."

"It's not like that!"

"Then what is it like?" The anger of betrayal shifted to something else entirely. Like several coals burning inside a furnace, he dropped the one labeled duplicity and snatched up the one labeled confusion right along with its counterpart, misdirection.

"You won't talk about it. About the shadows in your eyes and the betrayal that lives under your skin like a brand. I wanted to know and I had the means to find out."

"Instead of asking me."

"Would you have told me what really happened?"

Although it didn't lessen the choice she'd made, he had to admit—even if only to himself—that he'd have played it off. Would have made some excuse to keep from telling her about his mother's sordid end.

An end he discovered while sitting in a school computer lab, desperate for information when he should have been studying for a history exam.

So instead, he clung to his small moral victory. "None of it matters because you had no right to go there."

Kensington snagged the largest to-go cup of coffee she could find in the lobby of their hotel, preferring to drink her caffeine straight instead of doctored with milk and sugar.

She'd take all the fortification she could get.

Jack had left after their heated exchange and an hour later she was still pacing her room when Campbell had called with the results of further digging into Holden Keene's background. Unable to hide the tears once her perceptive brother started asking questions, she'd had to sit and explain all over again what she'd done.

Although Campbell had kept his censure to a minimum, in true Steele fashion he didn't let her off the hook, either. *The man's right, Kenzi. You had no right to look into his background.*

Damn it to hell, she knew that. She knew she'd done wrong. Had known it the moment she'd hit Enter on the search query. And still, somewhere inside of her she was glad she knew. Glad she had some clue into what made Jack Andrews the man he was.

And what demons he fought on a daily basis to keep to the strict code he chose to live by.

"Morning." His large, oversize cup matched her own as he came up beside her.

"Car's waiting for us."

"We're not going that far."

"Dante thought it was best."

"Fine."

She wasn't interested in arguing with Jack and the inspector was adamant they take transportation provided by his team. With a swift turn on her heel, she crossed the remaining length of the lobby and saw the car waiting at the edge of the hotel's parking area.

She gave a small wave to let the man know they were coming and took a step across the lot before a heavy weight tossed her to the ground, cushioning her as they fell.

Before she could orient herself, the air came alive with gunfire and the heavy press on her back didn't lessen. Screams lit up the morning breeze in counterpoint to the gunshots and she heard the heavy roar of an engine whiz past them on the asphalt.

"Kensington! Are you all right?"

She rolled to her side, Jack's weight making it difficult to move until she pushed at his shoulder. "What happened?"

"I saw the flash of the gun in the morning sun just in time to knock you down." He kept a hand on her shoulder, heavy with pressure. "Stay here."

"Like hell."

He dragged the gun from his waistband. "Stay down. Dante's men are providing cover."

She glanced in the direction of the driver and saw two other men at his side. A third was on the ground clutching his shoulder, blood pouring onto the sidewalk. "Someone's hurt."

"Not fatally. Dante's men can take care of themselves."

"Would you stay here and wa—" The words floated

onto the air as he was already racing toward the officers with his gun drawn.

Heart in her throat, she nearly ignored the order not to follow, but another car pulled out from across the street, racing away down the Via Veneto. Insistent shouts had several of the officers scrambling into their cars to give chase now that the immediate threat had passed.

Jack returned to her side along with one of Dante's men. Someone she vaguely recalled being introduced to on their first day crouched down next to her. "Are you okay?"

Her blood throbbed in her ears and she barely heard the question, but she didn't miss the concern in the man's eyes. With a nod, she took his hand as he helped her to her feet. "Fine. I'm fine."

Dante marched over, his phone pressed to his ear, a string of what she assumed were Italian curses dripping from his lips in a steady stream. "They escaped. Changed cars along the way."

"Did your men get any sense of who they were?" Jack's gaze drifted back toward the street before facing their small circle.

Dante shook his head, another stream of raw language peppering the silence before he answered the question. "No, the car was already abandoned and burning when they reached it."

"These guys move fast." Kensington thought about the speed with which everything happened. "Which means we're dealing with more than garden-variety thugs."

Dante pointed toward his car. "Let's go to my office. I'm going to rescind our working arrangement. You're both free to leave Italy."

Jack hadn't gotten past the raw, acidic anger that had accompanied him since discovering Kensington's snooping efforts, but he had calmed several degrees by the time they were seated in Dante's office. A steady stream of officials had come in to visit with him and Kensington, each offering apologies for the extreme danger this job had put them in, before departing to make way for another bureaucrat.

"Are they afraid of lawsuits?"

"Among other things," Jack answered. "Your family's well respected in Europe and it wouldn't do well for the granddaughter of a prominent Englishman to die in their country."

"So glad to know my family tree's the only thing keeping me alive."

"I'll keep you alive." He might be mad—madder than he'd ever been in his life—but he'd die to protect Kensington Steele. He didn't need the damn Italians to do it for him.

"Looks like neither of us has a choice. If Dante's bosses have their way, you and I are on the next plane back to New York."

"You're going home. This has been my job from the beginning and I'm seeing it through."

If he'd waved a red flag in a bull's face he'd have had a milder reaction than the virago before him. "You can't honestly think I'd walk away from this job."

"Why wouldn't you? There's nothing but danger."

"For both of us."

"Yes, but I took on the contract. I'll see it through."

Sparks practically leaped off her as she stood to pace the office. "You know, if I thought this was about last night I might have more sympathy for your point of view, but I don't think that's it at all. I think you're scared to death of what's between us and this is the convenient excuse you've been waiting for to get rid of me."

"I'll be back in New York within a few days. We'll pick back up then and figure out what's going on between us."

"We won't pick back up because I'm not leaving. This job has required both of us from the start and now that it's gotten to its most crucial point I'm not bailing."

"You're my subcontractor. I can call you off the job at any point."

She threw her arms in the air. "And we're back to that. Right where we started several days ago, practically in this very office."

"We're back to that place because I never should have listened in the first place. This job is dangerous and every step closer to finding out who's responsible has increased that danger. I couldn't forgive myself if something happened to you."

She stopped pacing, her gaze searching as she stood before him. "Trying to control the situation again?"

"Trying to keep you alive."

"Jack. He's escalating. The other night at Pryce's. The thug last night in Piazza Navona. And now this. It's coming to a head and we're the only ones with enough knowledge to stop it."

"What knowledge? That Keene is Pryce's son. That's interesting but hardly incriminating."

"So the fact that Holden Keene's made several large deposits in an offshore bank account doesn't interest you?"

"What?" He stammered at the sudden change in subject.

"Or the fact that he's traveled to the region where some of the richest veins of diamonds sit in Tierra Kimber four times in the past year?"

When the hell did she find all this out?

"*Or* that the rumor in Tierra Kimber's capital city is that a large shipment is going to drop in the next week?"

"When did you get all this?"

"Last night. Campbell found some of it and I found the rest. I didn't sleep last night."

He saw the evidence in the fine lines and dark smudges that rimmed her eyes and fought down the sharp stab of guilt that he was responsible for her lack of sleep. She might have spent the past fifteen years unable to sleep through the night but the prior evening's lack of rest was entirely his fault.

"Don't you see? It's Keene. And either Pryce is in cahoots with him or is about to be the victim in whatever his son has planned. Either way, we need to see this through."

"Dante and his superiors want to send us home."

"We both signed all the usual waivers. They can remove us from their payroll, but nothing says we have to leave. This job is ours, Jack. We have to see it through."

The events of the night before faded in the face of her urgency. "We're already late for Pryce's event today, Jack."

"Which works to our benefit. We've got our clearances and no one's expecting us. We'll sneak in and get the lay of the land."

Excitement filled her cheeks with a pink glow. "Are you actually excited about this?"

"I am excited about putting this bastard away."

"Let's go." She settled a hand on his arm, the subtle pressure effectively holding him still. "I need to say something."

That same shaky panic that had filled him when he saw the screen on his mother reared back up at her words. He knew he'd overreacted. And on some level he understood why she'd pried.

But it was so ugly. So degrading. And no matter how many times he told himself he'd grown old enough to get past it, nothing could change that his mother walked out on him when he'd still needed her, leaving his older sisters to take care of him and forcing responsibilities on them when they should have been off enjoying college and the start of their lives.

"Okay."

The lines around her eyes deepened as she stared down at the ground before glancing back up to hold his gaze. "I'm sorry for what I did last night. I had no right to pry and I know that. I even knew it when I did it, but I ignored the very loud voice in my head telling me to leave well enough alone. I don't expect you to forgive me, but I need you to put it aside until we see this through. Can you promise me you'll do that?"

"I've got your back."

"I've got yours, too, Jack. Even if you don't believe that."

He stilled at her words. He trusted her with his life—and likely a hell of a lot more—but they both needed to focus. "We need to tell Dante we're not leaving."

"He's not going to be happy with either of us."

"So he won't be happy. He hired us for our skills. It shouldn't surprise him we want to see this through."

When she only nodded, he followed her from Dante's office and hoped completing the mission was the right decision.

The Palazzo Altemps was one of the buildings that made up the National Roman Museum and as they passed through its doors, Kensington could only wish they had more time to spend amid the splendor. Despite several visits to Rome she'd never been to the museum. The physical architecture of the site was breathtaking.

Jack let out a low whistle as they sneaked in a back entrance, moving in and among the serving staff. "Pryce must have pulled a few strings to hold his event here."

"He has arranged for the exhibition of several pieces of Tierra Kimber art along with a very generous gift to the museum of five flawlessly matched diamonds."

"Seems like a big outlay of cash just to hold a party."

"The party's window dressing. The real point is that he's making Tierra Kimber a major player in the local economy. The diamonds alone will up the visitor count to the museum from both tourists and locals."

"It doesn't provide a half-bad cover, either."

She hadn't factored in that piece, but now that he mentioned it she was again reminded of how well she and Jack worked together. They each saw different pieces of the puzzle, and because of that, they worked through the answer so much quicker together than alone.

Her parents had been that way. As individuals they were very different, yet together, they seemed to become more than the sum of their parts. They brought out the best in each other. They worked with each other and they had a true partnership.

She'd spent her adult life comparing men to the ideal she held in her head, yet when someone who fit the ideal came along, she'd fought the slide into love.

Even the night before with the background check on his mother. She knew better. And she also knew how she'd feel if the situation were reversed, yet she'd done it, anyway.

Was it a subtle sabotage? Some deeper unwillingness to keep herself from being happy?

The sounds of the luncheon event pulled her from her maudlin—and half-formed—thoughts and she threaded through the active rush of serving staff in Jack's wake. He'd pointed toward the door to a large ballroom where the noise originated, positioning himself at the servers' entrance to scan the room.

"Is Pryce in there? And Keene?"

"Both at the head table."

"Any signs of any of our friends from this morning?"

He shook his head, his voice grim. "No, but watch your back. I'd wager they're more likely to end up out here than in there."

Her hand went instinctively to the gun settled in the holster wrapped around her upper body and she also felt the reassuring weight of the clutch piece in her boot. The wicked sticker could do some damage if all hell broke loose, and it was easier to disguise in the fake lining of her boots than another gun.

The lightest shadow of movement hit her peripheral vision and she turned to see two large men sneaking through the doors of the kitchen. She tugged on Jack's suit jacket. "Behind us."

He turned just as another guy barreled through a door farther down the hallway. "Let's move. We need to follow the two you just saw."

"What about the other guy?"

"One problem at a time."

"So we split up. Go after both of them."

She didn't miss the mulish set of his jaw. "I'm not leaving you, Kensington. How many different ways do I need to explain that?"

"We need to neutralize the problem. Only going after one set of men leaves the other to finish up whatever they're after. Come on, Jack. We're either in this or we're not, but if we're not then we might as well go the hell home. We'd have the same results."

"This is why I work alone."

She saw the chink in his armor—it was slight, but there all the same—and dived in. Going on nothing but instinct, she wrapped her arms around him and pressed a hard kiss to his lips.

His arms wrapped around her and in that moment, Kensington knew the sweetest victory.

They'd come out on the other side of this.

They had to.

Every instinct he possessed protested pulling away from Kensington and sending her after the retreating thug. Before he could do anything about it, he took off after the two others, the taste of her still on his lips.

Damn fool woman.

Even though he knew she was right.

They were operatives and they needed to see this through. He had faith in her skills—as much as he did his own—and it was time to start trusting that simple fact.

The hallway snaked several times, as if the ancient building held secrets it was unwilling to share. Following along the wall, he kept out of the way of servers and other museum workers bustling about, his strides long and purposeful.

No one questioned him and no one would, he knew, so long as he kept moving forward.

Kept watch ahead.

The sounds of the event faded along with the smells of lunch as he took what had to be his eighth corner.

The force of two bodies had him slamming against the wall, the impact knocking his head back into the thick plaster. Adrenaline kicked in to neutralize the pain and he fought the stars in his eyes to plow into one of his attackers. His movements were fast enough to catch the guy off guard, but there was no way the second guy didn't have the advantage.

He doubled over as the thug number two's fist connected with his solar plexus, the abrupt lack of air dropping him to his knees.

Before he could stand again, pain shattered through his skull and everything faded to black.

Chapter 19

Kensington kept to the wall, snatching a chef's coat off a rack as she passed a small changing room near the kitchen. As disguises went it wasn't much, but she didn't need much. All she needed was enough of a distraction that her quarry didn't immediately identify her as the nosy bodyguard assigned to watch Pryce.

She had no doubt every goon in the place knew exactly what she looked like.

She stuffed her hair in the neck of the jacket as she walked but left the white canvas open at the front for easy access to her gun.

The man slid out an exterior door and she followed, not surprised when he ran toward a sedan, similar in make and style to the car that had sped off this morning.

Although that car had ultimately burned to a crisp, their fleet of getaway vehicles was obviously an homage to uniformity. Dragging at her coat, she pulled out her gun and aimed for the wheels as the car maneuvered through the narrow alley. Gun up, she sighted her gaze and it was only at the last moment, when the goon opened the back door to climb into the car, that her gun fell, clattering to the old cobblestones beneath her feet.

Jack was slumped over in the backseat, his eyes closed as if asleep.

Before she could retrieve her gun, or race after the car or even scream, the sedan was gone.

And so was Jack.

Jack fought to surface against the pain in his skull, but all he could muster was a heavy moan. A hard kick to his shins was the only answer he got for his trouble and he couldn't hold back another dark cry as pain radiated up his leg.

"Shut up." The words were delivered with all the warmth of an iceberg and Jack struggled to open his eyes.

Where was he?

And where was Kensington?

His lids popped open at the thought of her, but a quick glance around the moving car only showed the thugs who'd attacked him in the hallway and the man Kensington had followed.

So where was she?

Even as he thought it, he rejoiced that she'd avoided the same fate. If she wasn't in the car, she had a chance.

If she wasn't in the car, it meant she was likely still alive and undetected by the bastards who held him captive.

Forcing himself to stare out the window, he fought the wave of nausea that threatened as he watched the passing scenery and took note of where they were going. The fact he had no hood on didn't bode well for their expectations on him getting back to the city, but he'd worry about that later.

In the meantime, he needed to reserve his strength. He needed to focus.

And he needed to figure out how the hell he was going to get out of this.

Kensington fought the nauseating waves of panic in her stomach. The image of Jack slumped in the backseat with all those thugs haunted the back of her eyes, burned there with unblinking clarity.

She raced for the door to the ballroom, the loud clapping and excited voices a direct counterpoint to the sheer terror she felt, and she used every breathing technique she could think of not to hyperventilate.

The ambassador sat at the front of the room, his table full of smiling faces and impeccably dressed guests. Everyone's attention was turned toward the stage and it was only as she got closer that she realized one of the seats was empty and Holden Keene was nowhere in sight.

Instinct had her heading for the ambassador and she let it carry her onward. Ever since the discussion about her father she'd sensed something in Hubert Pryce that was innately kind, and, out of options, she opted to trust her gut and trust Pryce.

He glanced up, his smile broad as the crowd roared at something the luncheon emcee said in Italian. She could only assume her features spoke far louder than her words ever could have because the man stood immediately and walked toward her, gripping her arm.

"Miss Steele. It's a surprise to see you today."

"I need to talk to you. Where's Holden?"

"His phone rang and he stepped out to take a call."

"What was it about?"

"Miss St—"

She cut him off, plowing forward with as much clarity as she could muster. "Where did your son go?"

Subtle red splotches lined his cheeks and the ambassador sputtered. "How did you know?"

"Hubert. I need your help. Now."

Kensington didn't wait for a response; she simply grabbed his hand and dragged him toward the exit.

Holden drove the roads out of the city at a sedate pace, satisfied that his plans were all coming together. Shipments of drugs had already begun their distribution throughout Italy, the packets of white powder floating inside each bottle of red amounted to a tidy sum for those preparing to take delivery.

But it was the shipment headed out later that night that he was most excited about.

He tamped down on the celebration since he had to deal with Andrews first. There'd be time for celebrating later. First, he was going to kill Andrews and then Steele when he found her.

And then there'd be no one left to question him.

No one left to put any further kinks in his plans.

He had a terrorist already lined up and waiting on the opposite end, ready to take control of the diamonds in exchange for a rather tidy sum. The man would smash the evidence of the wine as soon as he'd retrieved the special packet at the bottom of bottle number seven and burned the crate it came in. And Holden would have the second half of a several-million-dollar payment sitting in his bank account.

Easy peasey.

Just like killing Andrews.

And for this one, he would do it himself. The damn man

shouldn't have even made it to the event. But everyone he'd sent after Andrews had botched the job.

Well, no more. He'd handle it and remove the threat of discovery once and for all.

The Italian police thought they were so smart hiring Andrews. Thought he wouldn't notice when one of the world's most renowned security experts suddenly showed up at his father's weekend house party.

Amateurs.

He'd worked too long and too hard to see his efforts crumble now. Events were in motion and his father was set up to take the fall. Just as he'd planned.

"What is this about?"

"Your son. He's been moving diamonds and drugs through your wine shipments."

"Holden? My chief of staff, Holden?"

"Look, Ambassador. With every possible respect, I don't have time to argue with you. His thugs got to Jack and they mean to kill him. I know it."

"What thugs? My regular security detail has impeccable behavior and they're still inside."

She fought the scream welling in her throat, knowing she had to keep it together. If she wanted to discover where Keene had taken Jack she needed to stay calm and work the information out of Pryce.

Piece by painful piece.

"Your son has his own team of crackerjack security men, all of whom look like tanks and carry about as much artillery. They just captured Jack and have taken him."

"No." Pryce shook his head once more, but she saw the truth alight in his eyes. His face crumbled at the news. "Not my son."

"I'm afraid so, Mr. Pryce."

"Why?"

Wasn't that always the question? Whenever something bad happened—unexpected and horribly, terribly wrong—the first question anyone had was why.

"I don't know. But I need your help getting to Jack before it's too late."

"Too…" Whatever he was about to say next faded as Pryce realized the implications. "Come with me."

Jack dragged at the bindings around his wrists, but they were tight and strong, implacable knots that weren't going to come loose with a few simple twists and tugs. The goons who'd knocked him out had done the tying and he'd done his level best to piece together their conversation in Italian as they'd trussed him up.

Other than Keene's name, he had no more knowledge than he'd started with, but he knew he needed to figure something out. Holden Keene's arrival wasn't going to bode well for him.

Images of the past week with Kensington filled his mind's eye as he fitted the rope against the frame of the chair he sat in. The position was painful as hell, especially when he started moving his arms, but he persevered. He needed to loosen the bonds and he had to ignore the pain in his arm from his healing wound.

The anger that had left him so bereft the night before faded in the very tangible reality that he might never see her again. Yes, she'd made a mistake, but she'd owned it and explained why she'd done it.

And she'd apologized.

Wasn't that enough?

His hands stilled as that simple thought washed over him. Forgiveness. He'd wasted years of his life wrapped up in anger and pain, unwilling to forgive himself. Or his mother. Or the cruel circumstances that had left him and his sisters alone.

Oh, he'd made a good show of it, but deep down inside, where it truly mattered, he'd harbored boatloads of ill will and anger.

The moments he'd spent wrapped up in Kensington—from the simple joys of sharing a meal to the sheer elation of making love to her—had shown him something else. Had cleared out the ugly and made room for something good and new.

He'd found love.

With renewed purpose, he went back to work on the bonds. He'd wasted so much of his life waiting for what he'd found with Kensington.

He damn sure wasn't going to die and miss out on all the fun.

Kensington took the turns as Pryce prescribed, heading farther and farther out of the city. "How far did you say this place was?"

"About twenty kilometers outside Rome. It's a small vineyard I bought first, before Castello di Carte."

She stared at the odometer and hoped like hell Pryce had guessed right. She'd already called in the location to Dante amid the man's protests to leave the situation to them, but she'd hung up on him and kept driving.

The older man beside her had wept openly when she shared what they thought Holden capable of and he'd continued to shake his head, soft sobs escaping in heavy breaths throughout the drive. "What have I done?"

"You haven't done anything."

"I did. Early on. I should have claimed him. Should have let him know what he meant to me. But I always put my other children first. I let the stigma of illegitimacy stand in the way of love. Of caring. Of being a parent."

She left him to his words, the desperate need to get to Jack consuming her as she flew over the highway in Pryce's luxury sedan. The car had pickup, she'd give it that, but oddly enough, she found herself wishing for the sports monstrosity Jack had insisted on.

What if they didn't get there in time?

Holden had a strong lead on them and Jack and the thugs were even farther ahead.

What if they were too late?

The question burrowed into her brain with hard tenterhooks but she fought it back. Fought to keep her focus. Fought to keep the love she had for him in the forefront of her thoughts.

They'd both waited so long. And what they had was good. And strong.

And it would last.

They'd make it in time. They had to.

"Turn right here." Pryce pointed.

She followed his directions, taking the winding roads as fast as she dared.

"Slow down or you'll miss it. It's up ahead on the left. There."

She saw the sign he pointed to, an old wooden plaque faded from the sun. She turned, then flew down the driveway, dirt flying from the tread of her tires at all angles.

A sedan sat at the far end of the lane, a large car parked behind it. Pryce's sharp intake of breath at the sight of the car had her identifying it even before the man spoke. "That's Holden's car."

"Then let's go find him."

She was out of the car, the door hanging open in her wake, when a gunshot rang out over the still winter air.

* * *

Jack kept his arms motionless as he stared at Holden Keene across the empty barn. A gun dangled from his fingers but Jack barely paid it any attention.

He focused on the insidious expression on Keene's face. Twisted in rage, he stared at the two remaining guards still standing. The third—the one who'd ultimately captured him at Palazzo Altemps—was lying on the ground, a pool of blood surrounding his head.

"What the hell do you mean it hasn't left Tuscany yet?"

"Sir. Let us explain. There was a problem. A mix-up."

The conversation went on in a mix of Italian and English, with enough English dominating that Jack got the situation. The local inspectors had paid the vineyard a visit at the request of the contessa who'd spent the weekend at Pryce's house party.

The two men manning the shipment from the vineyard felt it best to hide the wine until the dust settled. Then they'd move it out.

Holden waved his gun once more, sending them off in a scurry toward the main house. "Get out of here!"

Keene paced the length of the barn, shaking his head as he stalked the length of the room. "Nosy busybody. Just like you."

The ropes around his wrists were loose and Jack held his hands still, unwilling to give up the one weapon he had left in his arsenal.

Surprise.

His shoulders had nearly gone numb with the effort to loosen his bonds but all he needed was one shot—one moment with Holden close to him—and he'd make his move. The morons who'd tied him up had duct-taped his ankles to each other, not to the chair, and it gave him far more range of motion than he'd have had if they'd done the opposite.

Keene continued to pace, his rage palpable in the small space.

"Did you really think you could come into my territory and take me down?"

"Until this weekend, suspicions were pointed clearly toward your father."

"Just as I'd planned."

"So what went wrong?" As questions went Jack knew it was risky, but it was also his only chance to personalize the discussion.

And making it personal might get Holden close enough to physically attack.

"Nothing went wrong except the fact that I hired imbeciles!" He waved his gun toward the dead man lying in the corner. "People who have no ability to think through a problem or act with decisiveness."

"Surely you knew that from the get-go. Fear and intimidation only get you so far. After that it's all about loyalty."

The rage that had twisted Keene's features morphed into something else as a dark sneer lit up his face. "There is no loyalty anymore, Mr. Andrews. None. My father proved that to my mother and to me and I've made a point to live my life not expecting it."

Like the skies opening up after a rain, Jack saw the picture Holden painted. Knew his own experiences had resulted in a fairly similar outlook on life.

Yet he hadn't become a psychopath.

Nor had he chosen a life simply out for his own gains.

He'd been dealt a crappy hand, too. Hell, his own father had abandoned them shortly after he was born, then his mother years later, but he'd survived. He'd played that hand and it wasn't until this trip that he realized just how far he'd come out the other side.

In some odd way, Holden Keene was his emotional

twin. A mirror of what he could have been without his sisters and without his own determination to make something of himself.

Something good.

Kensington completed all that. Made the work worthwhile and the effort something he could leave behind at the end of the day just to be with her.

He'd come out the other side.

The will to live beat through his veins in the hard, pumping waves of his heartbeat. He toyed with simply loosening the bonds and making his leap, taking his chances. He calculated the distance between himself and Holden.

As he watched Holden pace the space once more he saw a small flicker of something near the windows. He didn't need to see the person on the other side to know who it was.

Kensington was here.

And two thugs were now licking their wounds outside the barn and likely to do anything to get back in their boss's good graces.

Kensington kept her back against the outside wall of the barn and willed herself to wait for the right moment. She'd heard Holden for the past several minutes ranting at Jack, spilling his secrets and all his bottled-up anger. A wrong move and she'd put Jack in the line of fire.

And if you don't get a move on, you won't get him out of the line of fire.

The men he'd yelled at had left the barn, bitching to each other as they walked to the main farmhouse, and she sat and counted off in her mind, waiting for one of them to notice her car in the driveway behind Keene's car, but the shouts never came.

"Kensington!"

Her name echoed in a loud whisper and she turned to see the ambassador tiptoeing along the wall toward her. She'd left him in the car at the sound of the gunshot and had forgotten him.

"I moved the car."

"You what?"

"Moved it out of sight behind an old shed on the property. Too many people are here. I hid until the others were inside the house. In their anger, they paid me no attention."

Tears pricked the backs of her eyes and she leaned over and gave him a quick kiss on the cheek. "Thank you."

"The situation. Is it dire?"

"Your son has Jack."

"I will handle this."

"Hubert. No." She grabbed at his hand but he was too quick for her, shouting as he moved around the side of the house, bellowing his son's name.

Unable to reach him and remain hidden, she raced off around the opposite side of the barn. Her only hope was to come up behind Keene and take her shot.

The arrival of Hubert Pryce had Jack as shocked as he was frustrated.

Was the man involved? In league with his son? And where the hell was Kensington?

Pryce walked into the barn, his arms outstretched in greeting. "You've made me so proud. My son."

Something flickered briefly in Holden's gaze before he lowered his gun to his side. "What are you doing here?"

Jack knew that look—hell, Pryce's use of the word *son* had his own gut clenching into a tight fist—and on some level he understood Holden's need for approval. Acceptance.

"I'm aware of far more in my sphere than you give me credit for. I know what you've been doing and I'm here to congratulate you and give you my approval and support. The diamonds will be moving by nightfall."

Jack shook his head, the scene like something out of a nightmare. Pryce knew? He'd been involved all along?

Before he could question it further, Holden had his gun back up and directed at his father. "While I appreciate the reunion, drop it. You've had no idea what's been going on, despite this charade to the contrary. So I'd appreciate it if you'd go stand next to Mr. Andrews so I can keep an eye on both of you."

"Holden?"

"Move!"

The older man moved in his direction, his face out of his son's view. As he caught Jack's eye, he winked, the move so at odds with the scene that had unfolded Jack held his position a moment longer.

He needed to move. Needed to take action.

And it was only when he saw the flash of movement near the door that he took it. Lifting his hands against the bonds at his wrists, he planted both feet and leaped.

Kensington came through the door, her gun up, and Pryce used the moment of confusion to aid Jack in the attack on Keene. The sudden motion of all three of them was enough to disorient Holden, but it was the heavy smack of Kensington's gun at his wrist that had the man dropping his own gun.

Pryce leaped on his son the moment the man was down, slamming his fist into Keene's jaw. The loud echo of "No!" filled the space as Holden screamed and put his hands up, but before his father could hit him once more, Jack moved between the two men.

His bound ankles hobbled his motion, but he kept his

balance with the chair, holding onto the arms for support. He used the chair as a cage, pushing Pryce out of the way as he lowered the legs over Keene's struggling form.

"Jack!"

Kensington screamed his name, then dropped to her knees to drag at the tape around his ankles.

"Get up."

She ignored him, dragging a knife from her boot and slashing at his pants. "Hold still."

"Would you get up?" He kept one arm heavily pressed to the top of the chair and with the other he dragged at her coat. "Please come here."

He felt his legs come loose and then she stood, a satisfied smile on her face. Before he could pull her close, Dante and several of his men swarmed the room, their guns drawn as two of the officers raced toward them.

In moments they had Holden Keene in cuffs and seated against a wall with two guards for company.

Satisfied the immediate threat had passed, Jack wrapped his arms around Kensington and dragged her outside into the fresh, cool air.

"How'd you know where to find me?"

She smiled up at him, love shining in that crystal-blue gaze. "Intuition."

"While I appreciate intuition as much as the next guy, how'd you really find me?"

"I'm telling you. Intuition. In a roundabout sort of way. It was Hubert who figured out this farm was where Keene took you, but it was my intuition that told me I needed to bring Hubert with me. He wasn't behind all this."

"No, he never was. And since Tuscany, your instincts kept telling you it wasn't him."

"Yes, well, my instincts aren't infallible. I should have used them last ni—"

He crushed his mouth to hers, silencing her. He pushed everything he wanted to say into the kiss, willing her to understand how much he cared for her.

How much he loved her.

And how desperately he wanted to make a life with her.

"We'll forget about last night. And all the misunderstanding that came before. I want to share my life with you. And I want to make a life with you. And as part of that, I want to share who I am and what made me."

"I want to do the same."

"You pulled me out of the shadows, Kensington Steele. You've showed me that everything I've worked to be was time well spent. Now I'm going to enjoy all that hard work with the woman I love."

"I love you, too."

As his lips met hers once more in the cool December air, Jack knew he'd found his future.

His partner.

His forever.

Epilogue

"Grandfather, what are you about tonight? I already put out the champagne in buckets but we've still got an hour to go until midnight."

"Preparations, my girl. Preparations."

Kensington shook her head as she followed her grandfather down the hall of her apartment. His movements had a decided vigor she hadn't seen in a while and she wondered how many cookies he'd sneaked that day to put him on such a high.

Jack's smile was broad when she walked back into the living room, and she took a moment to take in her family. She and Jack had decided to spend Christmas in Seattle with his sisters and their families and the New Year in New York. And come January, they were packing his apartment in Chicago to move him here.

As she looked around at her loved ones, she knew there was nowhere else she'd rather be to ring in a brand-new year.

"Is that the edge of panic in your eyes, darling?" Jack moved up to press a kiss against her ear.

"My grandfather's very concerned about the champagne for some reason."

"It is New Year's."

"Yes, it is." She smiled up at him, pressing her lips to his.

The past few weeks had passed in a blur with wrapping up the Rome job and planning for the holidays. Keene had ultimately confessed to everything the Italian police had suspected and some additional crimes the Tierra Kimber government would be prosecuting him for.

The diamond shipment Keene had earmarked for terrorists was intercepted in Tuscany, the complaint filed by the contessa going a long way toward drawing an eye to Keene's actions. Although she'd simply had a bee in her bonnet that Castello di Carte was getting out of complying with some inspections, her complaints had ultimately been the catalyst to stopping the diamonds from making it into the wrong hands.

From the reports from Dante, the ambassador had already made inroads smoothing the contessa's ruffled feathers and rumor had it they were spending the holidays at Castello di Carte.

"You look a million miles away."

She pulled her gaze from her family, assembled around the room, and gave him her full attention. "I was just thinking about love. The funny places it finds you."

"It found us."

"It most certainly did."

"Which is why I feel the need to make it official."

Whatever she was about to say stuck in her throat as Jack dropped to a knee in the center of her living room.

The jovial conversation stopped as all eyes turned toward her and Jack. Somewhere in the back of her mind she knew what it meant, but try as she might, she couldn't seem to get a handle on anything.

Why was he on his knees?

And what was in his hands?

And what was that he was saying?

"Kensington Steele, until you came into my life, I was only half living it. I made my work my life and I now understand how much I missed out on. But you changed that. You made it brighter. More vivid. And a hell of a lot more interesting."

His hands trembled as he fumbled with the opening to the box in his hand, and then he had it open and the ring from the jewelry store winked from where it sat nestled in velvet. "Jack!"

"This was yours the moment I put it on your hand. Please tell me you'll wear it every day and you'll make a life with me. I love you. Will you marry me?"

"Yes!"

She pulled on his shoulders, dragging him up and into her arms. "Yes. I'll marry you. And make a life with you. And build all that's still to come because I love you."

The loud shouts of her family surrounded her as she leaned into Jack for a kiss that sealed their future. Then she heard the pop of a cork and her grandfather's satisfied harrumph.

"About time, Penelope. Took the boy so damn long tonight I thought it would be next year."

"Hush, Alex. He did it in his own time."

Kensington laughed as she heard her grandmother's quick and ready retort and envisioned the day she'd hush Jack when their own grandchild got engaged.

Until then, she was going to do just as Jack had said. She'd live her life. Day by day, year by year.

And she'd have Jack Andrews at her side for every moment of it.

* * * * *

There's one more single Steele—
Come back to discover Liam's match!
Don't miss
THE MANHATTAN ENCOUNTER

REQUEST YOUR FREE BOOKS!
2 FREE NOVELS PLUS 2 FREE GIFTS!

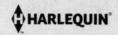

ROMANTIC suspense

Sparked by danger, fueled by passion

Trey closed his eyes and allowed the vision to play out. There
should be children in the pool, laughing and shouting as they
splashed and swam from one end to the other…*his* children.

A sense of pride, of joy, buoyed up in his chest as he thought
of the children he would have, children who would carry on
the Adair Winston legacy.

And in his vision he turned his head to smile at the woman
who'd given him those children, the woman who was his wife.
His eyes jerked open and he realized the woman he'd seen
standing beside him in the vision wasn't Cecily at all. Instead
it was Debra.

Irritated with the capriciousness of his own mind, he
poured himself a cup of coffee and went back into the great
room, where he sank into the accommodating comfort of his
favorite chair.

Lust. That was all it was, a lust he felt for Debra that refused
to go away. But he certainly wasn't willing to throw away all

his hard work, all his aspirations, by following through on that particular emotion. That would make him like his father, and that was completely unacceptable.

No matter what he felt toward Debra, she was the wrong woman for him. He had to follow his goals, his duty, to pick the best woman possible to see him to his dreams, the dreams his grandfather Walt had encouraged him to pursue.

Besides, it wasn't as if he was in love with Debra. He liked her, he admired her and he definitely desired her, but that wasn't love.

Debra inspired his lust, but Cecily inspired confidence and success and encouraged his ambition. If he used his brain, there was really no choice. The lust would die a natural death, but his relationship with Cecily would only strengthen as they worked together for his success. At least that was what he needed to believe.

It was almost eight when his cell phone rang and he saw that it was Thad.

"Hey, bro," he said.

"Trey, Debra was telling the truth," Thad said. His voice held such a serious tone that Trey's heartbeat reacted, racing just a little bit faster.

"A malfunction of the brakes?" he asked.

"I'd say more like a case of attempted murder. The brake line was sliced clean through."

**Don't miss
HER SECRET, HIS DUTY
by Carla Cassidy,
available April 2014 from
Harlequin® Romantic Suspense.**

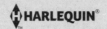

ROMANTIC suspense

DEFENDING THE EYEWITNESS
by Rachel Lee

Return to *New York Times* bestselling author Rachel Lee's *Conard County,* where a killer lies in wait

The note wasn't a threat, exactly. But for Corey Donahue, who'd witnessed her mother's murder as a child, it felt very menacing. Surprisingly, the one person she trusted to show the note to was a man merely renting a room from her—Austin Mendez. Traumatized since childhood, Corey had never trusted men...until Austin moved in.

Six years undercover had caused Austin to shut everyone out...until Corey. The vulnerability she hid from others made him yearn to break down the walls she'd erected around her heart. And with a killer closing in, two lost souls were discovering the trust they'd lost—and much more—in each other's arms.

Look for *DEFENDING THE EYEWITNESS* by Rachel Lee in April 2014.

Available wherever books and ebooks are sold.

Heart-racing romance, high-stakes suspense!